BLOOD ON
HER SHOE

BLOOD ON HER SHOE

MEDORA FIELD

COACHWHIP PUBLICATIONS

Greenville, Ohio

Blood on Her Shoe, by Medora Field Perkerson
© 2014 Coachwhip Publications
Introduction © 2014 Curtis Evans
First published 1942
No claims made on public domain material.

ISBN 1-61646-275-2
ISBN-13 978-1-61646-275-8

Cover: Great White Heron, by Audubon

CoachwhipBooks.com

CONTENTS

Blue Murder in Georgia:
The Mystery Fiction of Medora Field
Curtis Evans

MEDORA FIELD (1892-1960), or Medora Field Perkerson, to use her married name, was a prominent Atlanta journalist and the author of a once much-lauded book of Old South domestic architectural history, *White Columns in Georgia* (1952), who near the end of the Golden Age of detective fiction (roughly 1920 to the mid-1940s) wrote two tremendously successful mystery novels, *Who Killed Aunt Maggie?* (1939) and *Blood on Her Shoe* (1942). Both books were bestsellers in hardcover, both sold widely when reprinted in paperback, and both were made into films; yet until now with their republication by Coachwhip, they had remained out-of-print for nearly seventy years. Today Medora Field is best-known for having been a close friend of Margaret Mitchell (1900-1949), author of the mega-bestseller *Gone with the Wind* (1936), yet Field's own two novels merit some renewed attention, as superior examples of women's mystery suspense fiction of the 1930s and 1940s, the leading proponent of which was one of the most popular American mystery writers of all time, Mary Roberts Rinehart (1876-1958). In his 1941 book *Murder for Pleasure*, mystery genre historian Howard Haycraft justly cited Medora Field, along with Mignon Eberhart, Leslie Ford, Dorothy Cameron Disney, Mabel Seeley, Charlotte Murray Russell, Clarissa Fairchild Cushman, Margaret Armstrong, and Anita Blackmon, as one of the most able students in Rinehart's school of mystery fiction. Let us now take a closer look at Medora Field and her two mystery novels.

7

Medora Field was a daughter of the New South, having been born in 1892 to Robert Field (1868-1935) and Mary Frances Abrams (1870-1957) a few miles from the northwestern Georgia town of Rome. The great New South spokesman Henry Grady (1850-1889), managing editor of the *Atlanta Constitution*, had passed away three years before Medora Field's birth, but his impassioned advocacy of the cause of industrialization had not fallen on deaf ears in Rome, where earlier in his career he had edited the *Rome Courier* and where the Rome Land Company had been chartered in 1887, spurring a rush of commercial and industrial development that was in full stride when Medora Field was born. Between 1880 and 1890, Rome's population grew by nearly 80%. Medora's father evidently was an apostle of Henry Grady's creed, for Robert Field in 1901 was instrumental in forming the Robert Field Company, an iron and coke commission business with offices in Columbus, Ohio, and St. Louis, Missouri, that acted as a sales agent for, among other concerns, Sloss-Sheffield Steel & Iron Company of Birmingham, Alabama.[1]

Although he embraced the New South, Robert Field was a child of the Old South. He left this earth north of the Mason-Dixon Line, passing away at an Indianapolis, Indiana, hospital; yet he entered it, three years after the end of the Civil War, on a plantation outside Natchez, Mississippi, a town built on cotton that boasted, visiting tourists are told, the most millionaires per capita in the United States prior to the outbreak of hostilities between North and South. Robert Field's grandfather, also named Robert, in 1822 migrated to Natchez from Princeton, New Jersey. He came of a family of prominence, including among its luminaries his paternal grandparents, Richard Stockton (1730-1781), a Declaration of Independence signer, and Annis Boudinot Stockton (1736-1801),

[1] *Rome News-Tribune*, 17 June 1973, 8-B; Michelle Brattain, *The Politics of Whiteness: Race, Culture and Workers in the Modern South* (2001; rpnt, Athens, GA: University of Georgia Press, 2004), 30-33; *The Iron Age* 67 (17 January 1901): 31; *Atlanta Journal*, 27 November 1935; *Find a Grave*, http://www.findagrave.com/cgi-bin/fg.cgi?page=gr&GRid=53441362, accessed 21 October 2014.

a Revolutionary-era poet and intellectual, and a cousin, Robert Field Stockton (1795-1866), a United States naval commodore who helped seize California for the United States during the Mexican-American War. In Natchez, Field married Charlotte Brooks, the daughter and heiress of the owner of Anchorage Plantation, and he became a close friend of Dr. William Dunbar, Jr., a son of William Dunbar (1749-1810), the founder of The Forest plantation and a Thomas Jefferson correspondent and American Philosophical Society member. The younger Dunbar married Field's sister Mary, and Fields and Dunbars remained closely connected in the Natchez area for generations.[2]

With such a family background, it is not surprising that Medora Field wrote nostalgically of the Old South, both in her two mystery novels and in her nonfiction antiquarian study, *White Columns in Georgia*. Yet in her own life she epitomized much that was new. From an early age, Field aggressively pursued a career. She first found salaried employment at the age of fifteen when she became a stenographer to C. E. McLin, founder and president of a large Rome cotton manufactory, Anchor Duck Mills. Her first newspaper job, writing a shopping news column for the *Rome Tribune-Herald*, soon followed. Her great breakthrough came in 1919 when the *Woman's Home Companion* published a story, "The Christmas Spirit Speaks," that Field had based on her experiences masquerading as a homeless woman in Rome. Angus Perkerson (1888-1967), the editor of *The Atlanta Journal Magazine* (later *The Atlanta Journal and Constitution Magazine*), came across Field's article the next year and decided to offer her a job as his assistant. Field accepted the job offer, just as, two years later, she accepted Perkerson's proposal of marriage.[3]

Medora Field at this time has been described as "a dark-haired, square-faced, capable-looking woman with . . . an authoritarian

[2] *Atlanta Journal*, 27 November 1935; Ed Field, "Is your neighbor your relative?," *Natchez Democrat*, 6 January 2010.

[3] Harvey Dan Abrams, "Medora Field Perkerson" (undated pamphlet, reprinted from the *Atlanta Historical Bulletin*), 5-8; *The Editor* 52 (25 March 1920): 184.

manner, which some might have called bossiness, a tremendous talent for organization, a social conscience, and a quick grasp of issues. Seasoned reporters would shrink a bit when facing Medora across the desk. . . ." The same year Medora Field married Angus Perkerson, she encouraged him to hire a young lady named Margaret Mitchell as a *Journal* feature writer. During the four years that Margaret Mitchell worked at the magazine, she and Medora Field became fast friends. It was Field who, nine years after Mitchell left the staff, prompted the younger woman to submit her draft manuscript of *Gone with the Wind* to Harold S. Latham, vice-president of The Macmillan Company, who was in the South seeking novels by local authors. Macmillan would, in turn, publish Medora Field's own novel, *Who Killed Aunt Maggie?*, in 1939, followed by *Blood on Her Shoe* in 1942. Though of course neither book came close to the astonishing, once-in-a-lifetime success of *Gone with the Wind*, they both sold extremely well. In Atlanta *Who Killed Aunt Maggie?* was on the bestseller lists for months in 1939 and the next year Republic Pictures bought the rights to the book, which the studio planned to adapt under the title *The Belle Of Atlanta* (happily it was decided to retain the book's title for the film).[4]

Margaret Mitchell, though preoccupied with the filming of her own novel (and all the importunate letters she was getting from aspirants to cinematic success), kept abreast of all that was going on with her good friend's mystery. On May 19, 1939, she wrote George Platt Brett, president of Macmillan, in reference to the premiere that was to be held in Atlanta for *Gone with the Wind*, that she had gone to see Medora, who was president of the Atlanta Press Club, about having a tea in honor of the film. "Fortunately, I arrived some hours before she received the news that The Macmillan Company would bring out her mystery novel, 'Who Killed Aunt Maggie?' on September 15," she humorously noted. "There would have been no premiere discussion had I made my visit later!" On August 8, 1939, Mitchell wrote Brett, "[Medora's] book is coming

---

[4] Anne Edwards, *Road to Tara: The Life of Margaret Mitchell* (1983; rpnt, Lanham, MD: Taylor Trade, 2014), 94; Abrams, "Medora," 10-11, 17.

out on the fifteenth and every friend she has is giving her a party, so it was hard to catch her. . . . everyone who has read [*Aunt Maggie*], which includes me, thinks it's grand, and we all feel it will have a good sale." The next year, on September 1, 1940, Mitchell informed Katherine Brown, a scout for *Gone with the Wind* producer David O. Selznick, that Medora had "sold her 'Who Killed Aunt Maggie?' to Republic and she is going West, soon. . . . I thought you might be in California and run into her and think you were having nightmares about being back at the Press Club Tea at the Premiere."[5]

In a 1939 *Atlanta Journal* article Medora Field notes that she had wanted to write a novel for some time (perhaps, one is tempted to speculate, since Margaret Mitchell's success with *Gone with the Wind*), but that the "difficulty was that I couldn't think of anything to write about. I had no great message for mankind. . . ." Fortunately Field "happened to think of all the mystery novels that came to me as editor of *The Journal*'s Sunday Magazine book page. . . . Why, anybody can write a mystery! Or so I decided—until I got underway, trying to write one."[6]

Fortunately, when Field's confidence flagged, Margaret Mitchell was there to encourage her, speaking "warm and stimulating words about her friend's writing ability" and reminding her "that self-discipline and hard work are at the very core of any good writing job." With Mitchell's moral support, Field persevered and finished *Who Killed Aunt Maggie?* (it was not dedicated to Mitchell, however, but to Field's mother, an avid mystery reader). *Aunt Maggie* was received with acclaim, first from her publisher and then from newspaper reviewers around the country. "Reads as though written by Mary Roberts Rinehart in collaboration with Edgar Allan Poe," enthusiastically (if exaggeratedly) declared a Texas reviewer in the *Galveston News*.[7]

---

[5] John Wiley, Jr., ed., *The Scarlett Letters: The Making of the Film Gone with the Wind* (Lanham, MD: Taylor Trade, 2014), 231, 251-52, 352.

[6] Abrams, "Medora," 12. It is possible that Medora Field may have written the short story "Ether," published in *Black Mask* in May 1921 and credited to Angus Perkerson.

[7] Ibid., 14, 20.

When Republic Pictures was making its film version of *Aunt Maggie*, Field was emphatic about the importance of the titular murder victim. "Aunt Maggie is a familiar type in the South," she informed the film's associate producer. "Almost every family has one. She gets in your hair—true, but she also has her good points. She hasn't changed an awful lot from the Aunt Pittypat of *Gone with the Wind*. . . . everybody grieved that they couldn't have more of Aunt Pittypat in the film."[8] Sadly, not only did the script (by Stuart Palmer, the distinguished American detective novelist who created the spinster schoolteacher sleuth Hildegarde Withers, immortalized on film by Edna May Oliver) heavily alter Aunt Maggie's character, it changed nearly everything in the book, including the identity of the murderer, who is not even one of the book's characters. It is hard to imagine that Field was not at heart disappointed with a film adaptation that flattened her engaging novel into a by-the-numbers old dark house family elimination thriller. Willie Best, on hand as a comic relief butler, is given nothing to do but act terrified; however, Milton Parsons has a great role as the creepy tombstone salesman Mr. Lloyd, though his is yet another character in the film found nowhere in the novel.

In addition to being filmed, *Aunt Maggie* went through nine printings in hardback, was serialized by the Associated Press in newspapers throughout the United States, published in England and Italy, and brought out in paperback by Popular Library in the mid-1940s, eventually selling in that format alone over 125,000 copies.[9] Impressively, in a year, 1939, that saw the publication of Raymond Chandler's *The Big Sleep* and Rex Stout's *Some Buried Caesar*, not to mention novels by the British Crime Queens Ngaio Marsh and Agatha Christie, mystery debutante Medora Field had scored one of the year's greatest publishing successes in crime fiction.

Naturally such success called for a follow-up novel. Soon Harold Latham was importuning Field, "you must get down to the next

---

[8] Ibid., 17.
[9] Ibid. 19.

book." The now bestselling mystery author started work on *Blood on Her Shoe* at the beginning of 1941, but the new novel did not see publication until May 19, 1942. However, it too was a great success, hitting bestseller lists, going through five printings in hardback and actually outselling *Aunt Maggie*. "If you wish to keep your friends let us suggest that it will become necessary to purchase more than one copy of 'Blood on Her Shoe,'" advised a Maine newspaper reviewer. "For despite every protest it's going to be borrowed, passed around, thumbmarked and dogeared ere it finally comes to rest on your bookshelves." Fifteen years later Field wrote a friend and fan, champion golfer Estelle Page (1907-1983), of the scarcity of *Blood on Her Shoe*, indicating that the reviewer's contention was far from fanciful:

> I am so pleased that you liked Who Killed Aunt Maggie [Field had autographed a hardcover copy of the book for Page the previous year], and I do wish I could tell you how to get Blood on Her Shoe. After five printings by Macmillan, a printing of 175,000 pocket book size was made by Popular Library. Where they all went, I wish I knew, because I'd like a few extra copies myself. Every now and then one turns up at the second hand book stores here and I have bought several for relatives, but I haven't seen one in a long time now. . . . I have just talked to Eleanor Keeler [the wife of golf writer O. B. Keeler] and she sends you her love. She promises to send you the name of a bookstore in New York which might be a possibility—or to lend you her copy of Blood on Her Shoe.[10]

In 1944 *Blood on Her Shoe* also was adapted for film by Republic Pictures, happily much more faithfully than *Who Killed Aunt*

[10] Ibid., 19-20; *Lewiston Daily Sun*, 1 July 1942, 4; Medora F. Perkerson to Estelle Page, 2 February 1957, letter in my personal possession.

MRS. ANGUS PERKERSON
1355 PEACHTREE STREET, N. E.
APARTMENT B-8
ATLANTA 9, GEORGIA

Feb. 2 1957

Dear Mrs. Page;

I can't believe that it was
away last April that I had that nice note from
you.   I meant to answer immediately and you
will just have to forgive me.   My mother was
with me at the time, and for a long time afterward,
and was very ill.   She is now in a nursing home
and getting along fine but requires constant care.

I am so pleased that you liked
Who Killed Aunt Maggie, and I do wish I could
tell you how to get Blood On Her Shoe.   After
five printings by Macmillan, a printing of 175,000
pocket book size was made by Popular Library.
Where they all went, I wish I knew, because I'd
like a few extra copies myself.   Every now and
then one turns up at the second hand book stores
here and I have bought several for relatives, but
I haven't seen one in a long time now.   If I
should run across one, I'll be happy to send it
to you.

I have just talked to Eleanor
Keeler and she sends you her love.   She promises
to send you the name of a bookstore in New York
which might be a possibility --or to lend you
her copy of Blood on Her Shoe.

Over   Best wishes, Medora F Perkerson

Correspondence from Medora Field Perkerson
to Estelle Page. (Curtis Evans collection)

Maggie?, as *The Girl Who Dared*. The film benefits from a good tight script by John K. Butler (1908-1964), a prolific writer for pulp crime fiction magazines and B-film westerns and thrillers, such as *The Phantom Speaks* (1945) and *The Vampire's Ghost* (1945). Lorna Gray and Peter Cookson make a handsome couple and quite engaging leads, sultry Veda Ann Borg successfully depicts the twins Cynthia and Sylvia, and Willie Best returns as yet another perpetually petrified butler.

In the meantime Medora Field had begun plotting a third mystery novel, but she set this work aside in favor of the book for which she is best-known today, *White Columns in Georgia*, her history of antebellum homes that survived General Sherman's punitive wartime march though her home state. *White Columns in Georgia* was published in 1952 to much acclaim. Although she lived for another eight years, Field never published another mystery. Yet, as Howard Haycraft indicated at the beginning of Field's brief career in crime fiction, the Georgian made her mark as a notable exponent of the Mary Roberts Rinehart school of mystery, which places a high premium on suspense and atmosphere. Not surprisingly, Field was a great fan of Rinehart's books. She wrote Rinehart an admiring letter in 1940, informing the eminent author that she believed she had read everything Rinehart had ever written. Field's mystery novels also are significant as early examples of female-authored southern regional crime fiction, like the pair published by Arkansan Anita Blackmon (1892-1943) and three of the four mysteries authored by Alabaman Sara Elizabeth Mason (1911-1993).[11]

The Forties Georgia radio broadcaster Para Lee Brock hit upon an essential quality of Medora Field's mystery fiction when she

[11] Abrams, "Medora," 20. Anita Blackmon's pair of mystery novels, *Murder à la Richelieu* (1937) *and There Is No Return* (1938) were reprinted in 2014 by Coachwhip and Sara Elizabeth Mason's four titles, *Murder Rents a Room* (1943), *The House That Hate Built* (1944), *The Crimson Feather* (1945) and *The Whip* (1948), are imminently forthcoming from the same press. Together with Medora Field's two mysteries these works constitute a significant body of female-authored southern regional crime fiction from the Thirties and Forties.

discussed the author's *Blood on Her Shoe* on her program "Adventures in Literature." "*Blood on Her Shoe* has a tone of gentility," Brock perceptively observed. In the novel readers find "Chippendale furniture, Georgian silver, Wedgwood china, a bit of classical music, authentic threads of history. . . ." This "tone of gentility" in a murder novel is what many crime fiction fans today designate "cozy," or "cosy," mystery. Over the years many commentators on crime fiction (typically male) have disparaged cozy mystery. Julian Symons, for example, wrote snidely of the mystery novels of Mary Roberts Rinehart, "These are the first crime stories which have the air of being written specifically for maiden aunts." In fact, we know from contemporary reviews that the genteel mystery suspense fiction of Rinehart and her female followers actually was popular with men as well as women, and people of all ages. In this respect, I must take note not only of Field's fan letter from Estelle Page, a middle-aged golf champion, but of a fan letter Field once received from a Cadet Monsalvatge, from the context of the letter evidently a strapping young man. Cadet Monsalvatge had taken time during the Second World War to tell Field how much he had enjoyed *Who Killed Aunt Maggie?*[12] Judging from the sales of the Popular Library reprints of Medora Field's mysteries, these books had scores of thousands of readers. If Field's reading audience did against the evidence consist solely of maiden aunts, these devoted ladies must have been legion.

The comforts of the Rinehart school of cozily creepy mystery are clear enough to this middle-aged male reader, at least. Old money, a mansion, a murder (or more), a maiden and the man she loves (or thinks she loves): it all adds up to a pleasurably suspenseful story. We know that all will eventually work out for the distressed heroine, but it is a fine thing indeed to get one's withers wrung for a spell. Medora Field skillfully employs this time-tested formula in both her mystery novels, particularly *Blood on Her Shoe*.

---

[12] Abrams, "Medora,", 21; Curtis Evans, *Clues and Corpses: The Detective Fiction and Mystery Criticism of Todd Downing* (Greenville, OH: Coachwhip 2013), 193n11; Medora Field Perkerson to Cadet Montsalvatge, 15 November 1944, letter in my personal possession.

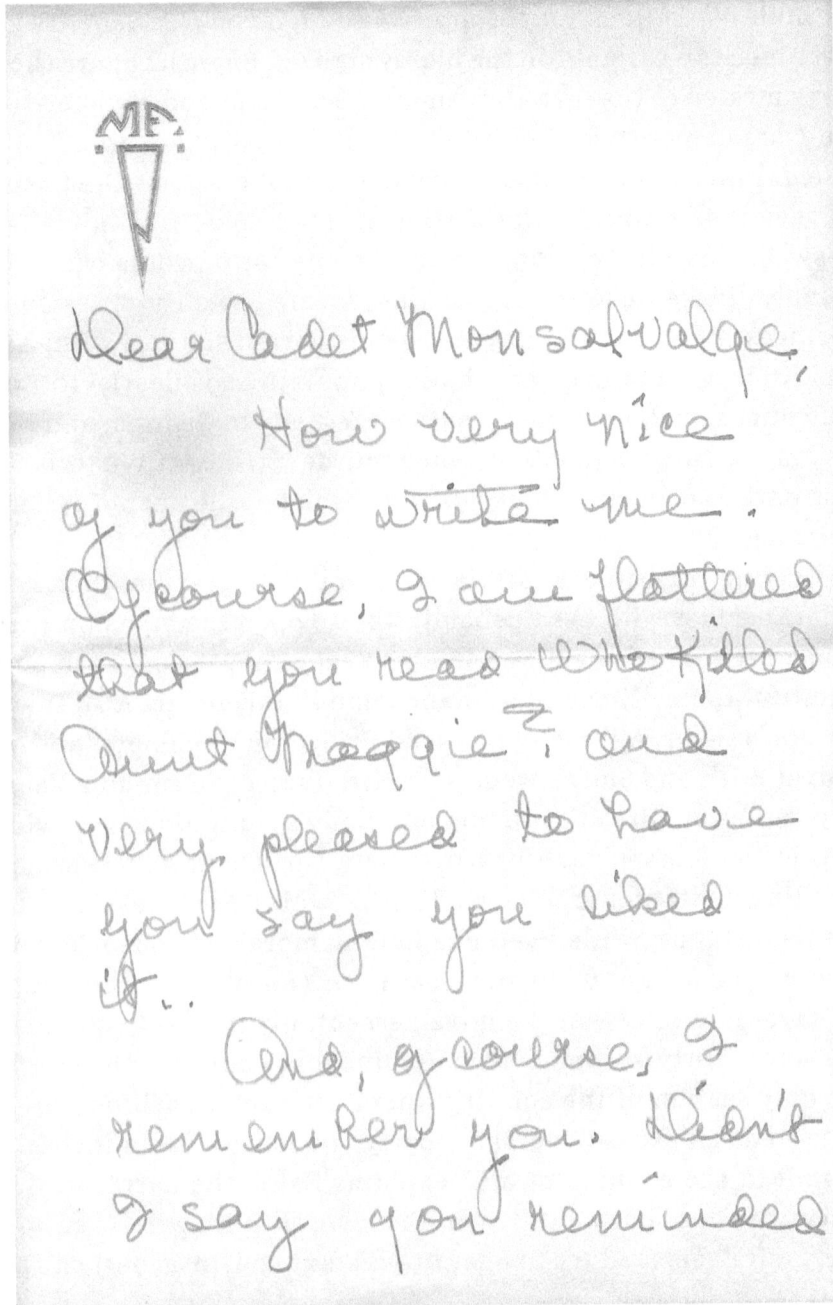

Correspondence from Medora Field Perkerson
to Cadet Monsalvatge. (Curtis Evans collection)

Both *Who Killed Aunt Maggie?* and *Blood on Her Shoe* are genteel American variants on the highly stylized English country house party mysteries that are emblematic to so many today of between-the-wars detective fiction, when it was in its Golden Age. In *Who Killed Aunt Maggie?* the country house that becomes the locus of murder is fictional Wisteria Hall, located some five miles from Roswell, Georgia, in 1939 a town of some 1600 people with some notably fine antebellum mansions, located twenty miles to the northeast of Atlanta. Today Roswell is part of the sprawling metropolitan Atlanta area and has a population of nearly 100,000 individuals, making it the seventh largest city in Georgia; and readers may be surprised to find, when murder strikes at Wisteria Hall on a dark and stormy night, just how isolated the people gathered there feel.[13]

Having inherited Wisteria Hall from her grandmother, Sally Stuart decides with her husband, Bill, to open the mansion with a house party of a few select friends to celebrate the engagement of beautiful Claire Harper and handsome Bob Dunbar. Also invited are Bob's sister, Alice, and Bill's old Princeton roommate (and best man at Bill's and Sally's wedding), Kirk Pierce, an amiable Yankee who rather admires Claire himself. Sally's Aunt Maggie, a widow who busies herself with abstruse genealogical researches, has a standing invitation to Wisteria Hall, of which she takes advantage in this instance, while Eve Benedict, memorably termed "a twice-divorced man-hunter" by the *New York Times'* Isaac Anderson in his favorable review of the novel, essentially invites herself. "Eve is a sort of forty-second cousin of mine, but I suppose the South is the only section of the country where such relationships can still be used as an excuse to crash a party you haven't been invited to, or indeed are counted at all," explains Sally, the narrator of the story, who does not want the viperish Eve slithering into her house party but decides to try to bear her distant cousin as best she can.

---

[13] Jere Wood, "Roswell creating a great community," 11 July 2014, http://www.bizjournals.com/atlanta/print-edition/2014/07/11/roswell-creating-a-great-community.html?page=all, accessed 21 October 2014.

Front cover of *Who Killed Aunt Maggie?*, paperback edition.

MEET THE AUTHOR

Medora Field

A CHRISTMAS story of Medora Field's which appeared in a woman's magazine induced Angus Perkerson, Sunday Magazine Editor of *The Atlanta Journal*, to hire her as his assistant. Two years later, the newspaper friend who first suggested Miss Field for the job served as one of the ushers when she walked to the altar with her boss.

After the publication of *Gone with the Wind* her friends kept reminding her that Margaret Mitchell once worked at a desk alongside her own. Why didn't she write a book, they asked?

Miss Field, then editing the book page, decided to take the plunge with a mystery. The result was *Who Killed Aunt Maggie?* The original edition went into nine printings and won her a trip to Hollywood as technical adviser for the film version of the book.

Back cover biography of the author

For her part, the sometimes tart-tongued Aunt Maggie makes her feelings clear to all and sundry: "It was bad manners, to say the least, for you to come here uninvited, Evelyn. Bad manners and decidedly bad taste, but I have always contended that it is too late to try to be well born at the age of thirty."[14]

At Wisteria Hall Eve seems to make it her mission to torpedo Claire's and Bob's engagement. Indeed, the reader might be forgiven for expecting that Eve will be the person Sally discovers, at the end of chapter three, choked to death in the ground floor back passageway of the antebellum mansion, but the victim turns out to be Aunt Maggie, who thus exits all too soon from the tale. As Medora Field indicated, Aunt Maggie is the novel's most memorable character, one who would have been familiar to many southerners of her day. Her speech has the authentic tang of an ancestry-obsessed southern matron of seven decades ago, as when she again puts the sinful Eve in her proper place: "Don't give yourself airs, Evelyn Pruitt. You are not a descendant. Your great-great-grandfather was only a second cousin of the Graham who built this house. You are descended from the black sheep of the family."[15]

Fortunately there is still much to hold the reader's interest after Aunt Maggie meets her doom, as the story turns for a time into a classic "old dark house" tale. Wisteria Hall is cut off from civilization, as a thunderstorm hits, the phone line is cut, and the automobile tires are slashed. The house party hosts, guests, and servants spend a frightful night indeed—especially Sally, who, in classic mystery suspense fiction tradition, inopportunely decides to look for clues by candlelight in the early morning hours. Readers will find such additional enticing elements as a rifled dead body, scraps of green paper with mysterious messages writ upon them, a peregrinating cat named Plutarch, a missing eiderdown "puff" and an old rumor of a treasure-laden secret room long-concealed somewhere within the august recesses of Wisteria Hall. Make certain to scrutinize the thoughtfully-provided house floor plan!

14 *New York Times Book Review*, 20 August 1939; Medora Field, *Who Killed Aunt Maggie?*, (New York: Macmillan, 1939), 9, 21.
15 Field, *Maggie*, 30.

When legal authority finally arrives the next day—in the form of the blustering and blundering Lieutenant Gregory and the county coroner, the blind and cryptic Mr. Dodson—Sally and Bill find that they themselves are suspected of Aunt Maggie's murder. A second slaying, committed with a dart right under the eye of law enforcement, does not absolve them of possible guilt in the eyes of Lieutenant Gregory; but providentially Sally stumbles into the solution to both murders, and all ends happily for the innocent, if not for the guilty.

To be sure, *Who Killed Aunt Maggie?* does have some deficiencies as a mystery novel, not unexpected in a debut fictional outing. Though atmospheric, the book at some 82,000 words is rather static, never straying from the confines of Wisteria Hall. As mentioned above, the colorful presence of the murdered Aunt Maggie is much missed. Sally Stuart is likeable enough, but the love interest, crucial in a mystery novel of this sort, rests with the rather bland secondary character of Claire, the object of the attentions and affections of both Bob and Kirke (as well as the animosity of Eve). Additionally, it seems at first that Coroner Dodson will function as the novel's crime solver, until Sally discovers the solution entirely *per accidens*, which is not altogether satisfactory. On the other hand, as Isaac Anderson noted, while the story's ending "may seem a bit artificial," in fact "attentive reading shows that it is foreshadowed more than once in the course of the narrative"—the essence of elegant plot construction in a mystery.[16] The reader has the chance to deduce the solution for herself and beat both Sally and Coroner Dodson to the punch.

Medora Field suffered no sophomore slump with *Blood on Her Shoe*, which is, if anything, superior to *Who Killed Aunt Maggie?* The setting of the novel is another house party at an exquisite antebellum mansion, this one Heron Point, at the other end of Georgia, on St. Simons Island. Heron Point is owned by a brother and sister, Beau (a diminutive of Mirabeau Napoleon) and Chattie (short for Chatfield) Richmond, cousins to the novel's twenty-three-

---

[16] *New York Times Book Review*, 20 August 1939.

year-old narrator and amateur sleuth, Ann Carroll. Besides Ann, the guests at the house party are Ann's older brother, Josh, a lawyer; Ann's attractive heiress friend Pat Fairchild, a Yankee; bond dealer Homer Norton, whom everyone expects Ann to marry (though Ann herself is not so very enthusiastic about this prospect); the twins Cynthia Harrison and Sylvia Scott (known, regrettably, as Sin and Silly); and Sylvia's wealthy estranged husband, David Scott ("I had an idea they were at outs, but here he comes barging in without a word of warning," says Cousin Chattie of Sylvia's spouse, adding philosophically: "He did say he planned to go to a hotel, but of course we can always use another man"). Then there is Rufus Blair, a visitor from the North whom Ann had never met before but nevertheless finds intensely interesting, and an array of black house servants: butler Woodrow, cook Pearl ("part Indian, with bronze skin, high cheekbones, and a lot of natural dignity"), maid Viola, and gardener Zack.[17]

For a lark the house party heads over to St. Simons Island's historic Christ Church cemetery to conduct a midnight ghost hunt, at the climax of which it is a member of the party who gives up the ghost, when this person is stabbed in the back with the antique Spanish dagger that had been conspicuously handled a few hours earlier by the hosts and guests at Heron Point. Two more murders follow this first killing, before Ann, more perspicacious than Sally in *Who Killed Aunt Maggie?*, solves the case (or part of the case, to be precise; there is an additional twist unforeseen by our heroine).

Blood on Her Shoe is a fine Rinehart school mystery suspense novel from the Forties. Ann makes a stronger lead character than Sally in *Aunt Maggie*, serving as more of a genuine sleuth as well as the novel's primary love interest (there is a subsidiary love interest as well with Ann's friend Pat). She also shows some commendable gumption in refusing to allow herself to be married off to a man she finds something less than enthralling and instead securing employment with an Atlanta interior decorating firm. As Ann bluntly puts it, "what with the depression and Father having

[17] Medora Field, *Blood on Her Shoe* (New York: Macmillan, 1942), 17, 101.

Front cover of *Blood on Her Shoe*, paperback edition.

left our money in a trust fund, I had to do something, or take Mother's advice and marry Homer Norton."[18] Not for nothing was the film version of the novel titled "The Girl Who Dared." There are some changes of scene as well, giving the novel a less static feel than *Aunt Maggie*. Additionally, although some of the clues on which Ann relies to reach her solution are not fairly presented to the reader, there is even greater ingenuity in the plot, which cleverly invokes the novel's title in a metaphorical sense (you will see what I mean when you read it for yourself).

Modern critics of Medora Field's mysteries are likely to point out that in the novels, as in *White Columns in Georgia*, the author writes romantically of what she sees as the glory and grandeur of the Old South. This no doubt is true. A keystone sentence in Field's nostalgic edifice is found in *Blood on Her Shoe*, when Ann and her friends visit Christ Church cemetery, leading Ann to eulogize over graves covered by weathered slabs "that mark not only the end of an earthly sojourn, but the end of an era—that long dead golden age known as the old South." It should go without saying today that not only for many southern whites but clearly for enslaved black Americans the antebellum era was no golden age. Even Medora Field seems to recognize this fact in *Blood on Her Shoe*, when she has Ann, dismissing belief in ghosts, declare: "Anyway, that ghost business was just one of the legends handed down by ante-bellum Negroes. Some of them even believed that certain members of their race rose up in the cotton fields and flew back to Africa. *It was just wishful thinking, of course* [emphasis added]."[19]

Medora Field's portrayal of pre-World War Two black house servants, like that of Leslie Ford in her better-remembered mysteries set in Maryland, will be seen as problematical by many today, it must be allowed. Her black servants "flash" smiles and "roll" eyes, are superstitious (in *Blood on Her Shoe* one chapter details a black character's naïve belief in "mojo"), and are often frightened

[18] Ibid, *Blood*, 4.
[19] Ibid., 33, 102.

by the strange events occurring around them; yet they are by no means unintelligent or lacking in character and resolve. Occasionally through her narrators Field displays flashes of insight, as when both Sally and Ann note the black characters' distrust of the police ("The law never done colored folks no good yet," observes the cook Pearl in *Blood on Her Shoe*) and when Ann notes to herself that younger black house maids like Viola now "sound exactly like the lady of the house when they answer the phone."[20]

Readers who can make allowance for the different social attitudes of a southern white woman writing moonlight and magnolia-scented mystery fiction about her section of the United States three-quarters of a century ago should be able to find great pleasure in reading the crime tales that Medora Field devised. Can you spot *who killed Aunt Maggie* at Wisteria Hall or which woman had *blood on her shoe* at Heron Point? Read on and see!

---

[20] Ibid., 101, 194. I should add that in her new book on the public memory of Sherman's March through Georgia, Anne Sarah Rubin credits Medora Field in *White Columns in Georgia* with "clear eyed understanding," seeing through sanctified southern myths of the march. See Rubin, *Through the Heart of Dixie: Sherman's March and American Memory* (Chapel Hill: University of North Carolina Press, 2014), 166.

BLOOD ON
HER SHOE

I

"WHAT'S ALL THIS ABOUT a mysterious grave in the garden down at Heron Point?" asked my tall, good-looking older brother, Josh, as he held the car door open for me. The grin I expected on his sun-tanned face was not there, and for once his blue eyes were serious.

"Let's don't overdo things," I protested. "I've already warned Pat that Heron Point is on the most isolated part of the Island, and that there's a ghost—though I must say I've never met the lady myself."

Pat Fairchild, my house guest from New York, settled herself in the car that was to take us to the Island, raised her dark eye-brows and gave a mock shiver. "I can't wait," she assured us.

"Then we'd better be getting along," Josh agreed lazily, brush-ing back his light sun-streaked hair. He ambled around to the other side of the convertible coupé, pausing to dig for his cigarette case before he climbed in beside Pat, who occupied the middle of the one seat. He finally got his long legs settled and turned on the ignition. "Tod Anderson's just back from the Island," he informed us conversationally, "and was telling me about this grave. Seems somebody found it in Cousin Chattie's wild garden, but nobody knows anything about it."

"But I thought all the old settlers of the Island were buried at Christ Church," I said.

"Of course they are," Josh acknowledged. "That's what makes it so mysterious. You see, it's a new grave and it's empty."

"An empty grave," I echoed, startled in spite of myself. "But how do they know it's a grave?" Pat asked reasonably, with a side-wise glance at Josh out of those dark-fringed Irish blue eyes which, somehow, are always a little surprising with her red-brown hair.

Josh gave the starter a leisurely jab. "Because of the size," he grinned. "Only thing I can figure is that Count Dracula is coming for a visit and has sent his bed on ahead of him. You know," he tossed at me, "how Cousin Chattie's always on the lookout for an extra man."

Mother was on the porch to wave goodbye as we swung from the driveway into Peachtree Street. The screen door opened behind her, and a black head appeared. "Wait a minute," Mother signaled. "Somebody wants you on the telephone, Ann."

"That'll be Homer," Josh yawned resignedly, as he pulled the car over to the curb. "Never saw such a guy. By the way, Homer said tell you girls he's having some trouble with his plane and may not be able to get down to the Island until tomorrow."

"Then you'd better make sure Count Dracula knows how to rumba," I flung back, "for we'll be a man short."

It was Cousin Beau, calling over long distance from Heron Point.

"That you, Ann?" he asked. And there was unmistakable excitement in his voice. "I don't think you'd better come down to the Island this weekend," he said. "I don't think—"

I missed the rest. Whether the connection between Atlanta and St. Simon's Island was bad, or whether Cousin Beau was speaking with his lips too near the transmitter, I could not tell.

"What did you say?" I asked, involuntarily raising my own voice.

"I can't exactly explain," lie hesitated, "but—but—well, I don't think you'd better come." Something about his tone, even more than his words, seemed to release an extra amount of electricity along the line. "You can send Chattie a telegram, making some excuse," he added. "Don't let her know I called. And listen, Ann, above all things keep Josh at home and don't—"

"But, Cousin Beau—" I remonstrated, as his words again became unintelligible.

A click and a crackle made it all too plain that the connection had been broken. I rattled the receiver in its cradle. How could I haul Pat and all those bags out of the car and explain that suddenly we should not be welcome at Heron Point? And what under the shining sun could Cousin Beau mean, talking in that disjointed, excited way, as though the Island was—well, unsafe or something?

I got the operator back on the line, only to have her assure me smugly that "the party hung up."

"She says he hung up," I said blankly to Mother, who had followed me into the back hall.

"Not Homer?" she asked, with a faint, indulgent smile.

"Cousin Beau."

"You must be mistaken," she objected. "Beau would be the last person in the world to do that." And it was true. Cousin Beau, big and handsome and still erect at sixty, not only looks as an ambassador should and seldom does, but has manners to match.

"It was all so jumbled and disconnected and—and funny," I told Mother. "He said not to come down to the Island."

"Not come down to the Island?" Mother echoed incredulously. "But why? You've got to go." She is one of those modern mothers with prematurely gray hair, slim and smart and spirited and inclined to be a little impatient with what she considers poor management. "I never heard of such a thing," she went on. "Beau must be drunk."

We both smiled at this, for it was impossible to think Cousin Beau could change so much in the short month since he and Cousin Chattie had left Atlanta to open Heron Point, their country house on St. Simon's Island, off the coast of Georgia.

"Sometimes, I wish I had never heard of southern hospitality," Mother said bitterly. "Every time Pat mentions going home, somebody else gives a party for her. I'd counted on this trip to the Island to wind things up, so I could get rid of that extra maid." She paused, then fixed me with a bright, probing stare, "What will you do about Mrs. King?" she demanded.

"She'll have a fit a minute," I agreed.

Mother considers my job a great joke, but two years after an otherwise successful debut season I was still—perhaps foolishly—

holding out for three little words that would sound different. And what with the depression and Father having left our money in a trust fund, I had had to do something, or take Mother's advice and marry Homer Norton.

Mrs. King (Carter & King, Interiors) had taken me on because of my "connections." And Cousin Chattie, one of the most important of these connections, had finally broken down and consented to "consider" redecorating the big rambling ante-bellum house on Heron Point plantation. One of the bags now in the luggage compartment of the car was bulging with samples of fabric, photographs, sketches, and other carefully assembled paraphernalia.

"Could it be," I asked Mother doubtfully, "that Cousin Beau objects to the idea of doing over the house? You know how sentimental he is about the old place. But if it were only that, why would he—" Stopped by Mother's reproving glance toward the dining room, where the new maid was removing breakfast dishes, I finished in a whisper, "why would he say to keep Josh at home?"

"Keep Josh at home?" Mother repeated. Evidently this floored her. But, whatever happens, she never takes the count. She stood there for a moment, just looking at me, as though I were somehow to blame. Then she motioned toward the front door and we moved out of earshot of the dining room. "Will you please tell me how you are going to keep Josh at home?" she demanded. "If he doesn't stay at Beau's, he can just as easily go to the hotel on Sea Island where—that hussy is staying. She even—" Mother's dark eyes were smoldering—"called him up from the Island last night. Just as I picked up the receiver down here, Josh answered upstairs and—"

"Oh, Mother, you mean you listened?"

"Certainly, I listened when I heard who was calling. After all, Josh is my child, even though he is twenty-seven years old and acting like a perfect fool."

"Oh, Mother!"

"You'll say, 'Oh, Mother!' when I tell you what she said. I can't make head or tail of it. Anyway, she wanted to know if he could talk without being overheard." Mother looked a little pleased at having foiled her there. "Then she told him 'under no circumstances' to let anyone know he brought a package to her when he went down to the Island last weekend. What on earth could she mean by that?"

"I can't imagine. What did Josh say?"

"Oh, you know Josh. Some wisecrack that didn't make sense. But she bit him off right in the middle of it. 'You fool,' she said, 'this is serious.' What sort of package could she be talking about?" Mother fumed. "Acting so mysterious and calling over long distance."

"It isn't like Josh," I agreed. "I've never seen him silly about anybody before." I wondered if Mother knew Josh had been drinking between those weekend visits to the Island and "that hussy." Judge Mabry would be throwing him out on his ear next thing. After all our skimping to send him to the Harvard Law School.

"Why can't Josh show a little sense and fall in love with Pat?" Mother asked of the high heavens, as well she might. With all that sparkle and charm, Pat would be the answer to any mother's prayer, even without her money. "Anybody can see she—likes Josh. Otherwise, why would she stay here five, weeks when she only came for two? I'd hoped their being thrown together on this trip to the Island—"

"Oh, goodness," I broke in, "I suppose I'd better tell them it's off. What will Pat think?"

"Wait a minute," said Mother.

Recognizing that familiar tone, I shifted uneasily from one blue-linen-shod foot to the other. "Listen," Mother said finally, her glance holding mine. "Don't tell them anything. This telephone call of Beau's is just too silly. He probably has got himself worked up about the redecorating. I'll call him back and tell him you are on the way."

"But, Mother, Cousin Beau sounded so—sort of funny," I protested. "I don't—"

"You probably just imagined it," she assured me briskly. "Now run along, baby." A gentle shove started me toward the door.

Although I am nearly twenty-three years old and pride myself on being fairly independent, there are times when Mother still can make me feel like a very small girl with long blond curls. But perhaps she was right about Cousin Beau's call and I was only imagining things, I told myself on the way back to the car. And such a lot did depend on this trip. Getting Pat started home. Redecorating Heron Point. And maybe Mother was right that the enforced intimacy of the trip might have some effect on Josh's love life.

But as Josh guided the car into traffic and Mother waved gayly from the front steps, my gaze clung as long as possible to the big, slightly shabby Georgian house built so long ago by my grandfather. Elbowed by a funeral home on one side and a boarding house on the other, its solid red brick exterior was nonetheless a symbol of safety and security that I was suddenly loath to leave.

Suppose—well, just suppose all those things did add up to something: that mysterious grave; the equally mysterious package Mrs. Scott was so concerned about; and Cousin Beau's strange telephone call.

It is nearly three hundred miles down to the Island, and the June day was pretty hot. In the face of Pat's and Josh's light banter, I found it difficult to go on being a raven perched above my own chamber door. But as we approached Brunswick, some of that earlier foreboding returned, perhaps inspired by a sudden knock in the back of the car which grew louder with each turn of the wheels.

Since we were already so near, Josh decided that it would be best to continue across the causeway to the garage at St. Simon's village, in case it might be necessary to telephone Woodrow, Cousin Chattie's colored butler, to come for us. Nobody seemed to be about the garage when we first drove into the main business street of the village, with its low buildings leading abruptly to the edge of the beach and the broad Atlantic. Then a young mechanic slithered out from under a car parked just outside the wide doorway of the garage and unfolded himself with such effortless celerity it was surprising to find him so tall.

"Had a little trouble," Josh grinned as he climbed out.

"Sounded like the differential," smiled the mechanic, whose voice was crisp and businesslike and had none of the drawl one expects in this section. His level gaze met Josh's, traveled over the car and eventually got around to the occupants. It rested there only fleetingly and, although Pat and I should not have minded, we found this cool dismissal a bit disconcerting. It was not what we were accustomed to from young men who were tall, dark, and not bad-looking, whatever their occupation.

"Well," said Josh airily, lighting a cigarette, "just look her over and tell us the worst." Turning to Pat and me, he said: "I'm out of cigarettes, thanks to traveling with a harem. Back in a couple of minutes." Pat's eyes followed as he strolled off, waving his empty cigarette case. Still calm and deliberate, Josh loses his slouch when he walks, and you would think he owned the earth instead of being down to his last penny as is so often the case.

It couldn't have been more than a few minutes later that a small colored boy materialized, apparently out of nowhere. Pat and I, deciding to stretch our legs, had paused to watch the gulls circling the lighthouse. "Uh—uh—is y'all Miss Calomel?" he mumbled uncertainly.

"Calomel," I repeated, puzzled. "Do you mean Miss Carroll?"

"Yas'm, that's hit," he agreed enthusiastically, rolling his eyes first at Pat and then at me. "The gen'leman say not to wait."

"Not to wait. What gentleman?"

"The—the young genleman. He says tell the ladies in the jirrard not to wait. He give me a dime." There it was, held out in a damp palm to clinch the matter.

"But this is foolish," I said. "Where is he?"

Starting out then and there to look for Josh, who could only be around the corner, I paused as the small messenger came panting after me. "He done gone, Miss. He done gone."

"Gone where?" I demanded.

"Don'—don' know," he stuttered.

Pat and I looked questioningly at each other, and a flush spread slowly from Pat's throat all the way up to her high cheekbones. "Gone with a lady?" I asked.

"No'm. 'Twarn't no lady. He done gone off with a mans."

Well, this was darned funny, leaving Pat and me in the lurch like this, and not a bit like Josh, whose good manners were almost as automatic as Cousin Beau's.

It was even less funny when the mechanic told us that our car would have to remain in the shop for repairs. I was completely out of patience with Josh and said so.

"Maybe he's been kidnapped," suggested Pat, smilingly.

"He'd better have a good excuse," I said.

But somehow I could not quite match the lightness of her tone. For all at once, I did not like the sound of that word—kidnapped. It tied in too well with— With what?

Well, with those two telephone calls, for instance: the one from Mrs. Scott, warning Josh not to mention a certain important package; and the one from Cousin Beau, telling me to keep Josh at home. But all I could do was to say again, "It isn't a bit like Josh."

Pat and I were surprised when the mechanic, who told us his name was Rufus Blair, offered to drive us to Heron Point. He was such a self-contained young man that it was difficult to imagine him putting himself out for anyone not actually crippled. Probably that is why we perversely did not insist upon telephoning for Woodrow to come for us.

In an incredibly short time he had shed his overalls and was back in clean tennis shirt and slacks, his sun-bronzed face and strong capable hands showing evidence of a hasty scrubbing. He was really quite nice-looking now, almost handsome, but with a faint piratic cast and an odd smile, as though he knew some humorous secret about life.

As we drove along, I gave occupants of cars we met a quick once-over, half hoping to catch a glimpse of Josh, for I could not rid myself of the feeling that there was something strange about his unexplained disappearance. We had left the paved highway and turned at last into the narrow shell road that leads to Heron Point when the peremptory blast of an automobile horn close behind made us all jump and forced Rufus Blair to cut deep into the wild shrubbery that borders the road and finally stop for the other car to pass.

"The dope!" I grumbled, as a powerful roadster came none too cautiously alongside. The youngish, rather nice-looking man at the wheel made a vague motion toward his bare head, with its dark wind-blown hair, mumbled something about a close shave, and was on his way like a bat out of bedlam. The white sand flew back from the wheels of his car, screening his disappearance, which was almost as sudden as sleight of hand.

"You might have known it," I said crossly. "A New York license plate. Nobody else would be in such a hurry."

"Are you sure there's a house at the end of this road?" Pat asked with a smile. "I never saw such a spooky-looking set-up in my life."

"Believe it or not," I told her, "all this was once cultivated land."

But only an avenue of giant live oaks survives to remind you of that once opulent plantation era. From the branches of these ancient trees, arched high overhead, hung streamers of gray moss, so long they sometimes swept the top of the car with a touch impalpable as spirit fingers. Green jungle closed in on either side—holly, myrtle, bay, scrub palmetto, fox grapes, all sorts of wild growth, with here and there a towering pine tree. It was cool after the hot concrete we had followed all the way down from Atlanta, with that suggestion of dampness in the air which means that water is not far away.

Not a sound broke the stillness as twilight deepened and the narrow shell road grew more and more tunnel-like in the gloom. I was startled out of all proportion at the peculiar cry of a marsh hen somewhere in the distance, and both Pat and I drew back with quick, indrawn breath as a gray shape materialized at the side of the road and seemed to waver toward us. Rufus Blair chuckled, turning on the headlights, and we saw then that it was only low-hanging moss which fell like a curtain in front of a slender sweet gum tree and moved gently with the almost imperceptible current of air.

But Rufus Blair himself was plainly puzzled by the sudden crashing in the bushes at the side of the road.

"Hey, who's that?" he called out, slamming on the brakes. But no one answered, and everything was quiet again.

A few moments more, and we could see the lights of Heron Point, and Rufus Blair was saying, "I suppose in the old days you would have been coming in by water."

It was true, for that was the way I had first seen the place as a child, before the causeway was built. And in spite of gracious white columns and weather-worn white paint peeling from handmade brick, it had seemed to me there was something sinister about the old house, set back on a bluff above the river and surrounded by great oaks draped with those long gray funereal streamers of moss.

This feeling came back to me now as Rufus Blair let us out at the garden entrance and drove around to the back with our bags. But as Pat and I stood for a moment, sniffing the salt marshes and the nearer perfume of gardenias, laced with the lemony pungence of magnolia blossoms, I told myself that it was silly to give way to a hangover from childhood imaginings. Just before reaching the steps, we paused again uncertainly. The screen door had opened, and a woman in a trailing flowered chiffon frock, with a white flower in her dark hair, stepped onto the porch.

"What do you mean, following me here?" she demanded. Then, lowering her voice a shade: "I could—kill you."

For a mystified moment Pat and I thought these strange remarks were addressed to us, forgetting that it was impossible for the speaker to see us as she came from the lighted hall onto the porch.

We heard a man's voice, low-pitched but tense: "I've had enough. You're not getting away with one single thing."

The woman laughed. It was not a pleasant laugh.

Clutching Pat by the arm, I dragged her around to the back of the house.

II

"HAS MR. JOSH COME?" I asked Woodrow, as soon as we had settled Pat in her room.

With that wide grin which always makes you feel he has twice the usual number of very white teeth, Woodrow assured me that he had seen neither Mr. Josh nor Mr. Homer.

"Well, who else is here? I thought Cousin Chattie wasn't having any guests but us."

"I don't think she mean to, Miss Ann," Woodrow grinned again. "But them two twin ladies just decided to stay on, and then a little while ago a gen'leman come sort of unexpected like."

"What twin ladies?" I asked with a sudden sinking sensation.

"They call 'em Miss Sin and Miss Silly is all I know," Woodrow said doubtfully, his mouth widening in spite of himself. "They wuz stayin' at the hotel on Sea Island. Then Miss Chattie invite 'em over here for a few days and they just stay on. You know how Miss Chattie loves comp'ny."

I knew only too well.

But Sin and Silly. That would just have to be Cynthia Harrison and her visiting twin sister, Sylvia Scott—or, as Mother called Mrs. Scott, "that hussy." Mrs. Harrison had spent little time in Atlanta since her husband's death, and though Mother and I had never seen her we both breathed a sigh of relief when she and her visitor joined the summer colony on the Island. We had not anticipated, of course, that Josh would go tearing down every weekend.

Josh was no doubt responsible for the twins being so cozily ensconced now as guests at Heron Point. It would not have been difficult to arrange. Cousin Chattie was always inviting people, and often forgot all about it until they showed up later with the house already full. But she did not mind doubling up and it never occurred to her that anyone else might mind. She had an idea that cocktails broke down all barriers. I could have assured her that this was one time when they would not do so. Not with Sylvia Scott among those present.

By the time I was dressed in my new white embroidered batiste dinner frock, I was a little more reconciled. Perhaps the set-up wasn't so bad after all. Pat might make it a bit difficult for Mrs. Scott. Just as I turned from the pier-glass mirror of the old Empire dressing table, smiling a little to myself, Cousin Chattie breezed in, effervescing good will as usual. "Ann, darling," she told me, "I'll make a bargain with you. I'm going to let you do over the house—"

"Oh, Cousin Chattie, you're an angel!"

"Wait, wait, my pet. I said I'd make a bargain with you." She paused and smiled at me archly, smoothing the waves of her pale brown, gray-streaked hair. "I want you to use your commission to buy a trousseau."

"But, Cousin Chattie—" I began, then bit back the words. Might as well get it over with. Then I could ask her about that mysterious grave and perhaps discover the reason for Cousin Beau's crazy telephone call. You can't get cross with Cousin Chattie, when she is so sure her way is all for the best; and argument does no good, for she never bothers to look beneath the surface of things.

Mother is always saying Cousin Chattie should reduce. But how can she worry about her weight when she never worries about anything? Tonight, a long frilled white dotted Swiss dinner dress simply added pounds to her short, dumpy figure; but as always her cheeks were a healthy pink, and her blue eyes so merry you just had to smile back.

"What's the matter with Homer?" she asked indulgently.

"Oh, Cousin Chattie, you know. He's so precise, and he wants to do everything the way he thinks people do in the great world," I said with a feeble attempt at humor. "And you know how he goes after rich people."

"Huh," sniffed Cousin Chattie. "Atlanta's just as much the great world as anywhere else. Besides," she reminded me, "Homer is in the bond business, and rich people are his stock in trade. I've often thought what a great pity it is your mother's money was left in trust. Homer could double it so easily. He's really marvelous about investments."

"Yes, it's too bad," I agreed. "Maybe then Mother wouldn't be so set on marrying me to Homer. But, Cousin Chattie, it's really more than just business. Homer is a terrible snob."

"Well," she became practical, "if not Homer, what about somebody else? Don't forget, my dear, blondes fade early, especially the fragile, pastel type." She looked me over with an appraising eye. "You're pretty enough, and you've always been popular. What do you want, anyway?"

What did I want? I found that I wanted absurdly to cry. Everybody in the family—except Josh—forever trying to marry me off. I had always thought marriage should be more than merely going through a set of motions—that there should be something that gave it meaning. But, I admitted at last, perhaps it was childish to think that life should be like the fairy stories—complete with Prince Charming. Just the same, I was a little surprised to hear my own voice saying, quite casually, "I think I'll take you up on your proposition."

Cousin Chattie looked a bit stunned, as though it had all been too easy. Then she kissed me and I made up my lips again, taking a little longer perhaps than was strictly necessary.

"Of course," I said, "Homer may have changed his mind." Belatedly, I remembered certain broad hints from Mother that Homer's attention to Pat might be more than mere politeness to a visitor.

Smiling skeptically, Cousin Chattie glanced at the tiny diamond-encrusted watch on her plump wrist. "Oh, dear, I do hope everybody is not too terribly late," she said, "Pearl is making a crab soufflé, and you know how Beau is about his food."

"Somebody was in such a hurry to get here that he practically crowded us off the road," I said.

"Oh, yes!" A shade of annoyance crossed her calm brow. "That was David Scott, Silly's husband. I had an idea they were at outs, but here he comes barging in without a word of warning. He did say he planned to go to a hotel, but of course we can always use an extra man."

It looked like a typical Heron Point house party.

"Cousin Chattie, what's all this about a mysterious grave in the garden?" I asked bluntly.

Her smile faded, and she lost a shade of her usual aplomb. "That's an odd thing," she admitted. "We've had a burglar, too. Just imagine, here on the Island. At least, I suppose it was a burglar. Nothing was taken, but a lot of things were turned upside down."

When I told her of that near encounter with someone who crashed off into the bushes just before we reached the house, she nodded with a worried frown. "Probably the same person waiting his chance to break in again. It won't be so easy this time with all the window screens and doors locked."

Finally we got back to the grave. "Oh, yes! Well, Silly found it," said Cousin Chattie. "She's making a collection of native wild flowers to take back to New York. Don't ask my why. Says she's going to find the Lost Gordonia. You know, that plant your Cousin Beau's always talking about that Bartram discovered somewhere around here back when Georgia was a colony. Seems that Bartram propagated it in Philadelphia but it's never since been found growing in a wild state. Every now and then some fool botanist pops up looking for—what do they call it?—the *Franklinia Alatamaha*—"

"But Cousin Chattie—" I interposed feebly. When I was a little girl I used to think Cousin Chattie was named for the Chattahoochee River, and Cousin Beau encouraged me in this because he said they both went on forever. But Cousin Chattie—really christened Chatfield because there were no boys in the family—always said that at least her father had not been a fanatic on French history and called her Mirabeau Napoleon.

"Well, you wanted to know how we found the grave," she reminded me now. "Silly asked if she could explore this part of the Island, because it's so wild. And then she almost fell into it—the grave, I mean—"

There was a tap on the door and Pat came in, looking like a Daiquiri frappé in her full-skirted misty white mousseline. "Pat's crazy to see the ghost," I said.

"Ellen is not very dependable," Cousin Chattie smiled, as though speaking of a flighty maid. "She's supposed to flit down the attic stairs, but I've never seen her." Then Cousin Chattie's eyes brightened with sudden inspiration. "I'll tell you what. We have a very satisfactory ghost at the cemetery. We'll stop by after the dance."

"Don't tell me the cemetery has been wired for sound and scenic effects and turned into a tourist attraction," I said.

"Certainly not," Cousin Chattie reproached. "You just wait and see."

As we descended the wide stairway, the tinkle of the old square piano came up to us from the yellow drawing room, where someone was singing in a clear, lovely voice—

"Who is Silvia? what is she,
That all our swains commend her?
Holy, fair and wise is she—"

I'm afraid I rather sniffed at the implication that any of these qualities could apply to Sylvia Scott.

Just as we reached the downstairs hall and were turning toward the drawing room, the front doorbell rang. Responding to Cousin Chattie's glance, I stepped forward to answer, while she and Pat went on into the drawing room. Light from the wide, white-columned central hallway streamed out onto the porch, but I saw no one. Thinking perhaps the caller had stepped to one side, I pushed the screen door farther open and gave a quick glance this way and that. Still I saw no one.

It was not a sound that caused me too look toward the steps of the broad porch, but rather an impression of movement and an imperceptible stirring of the air. At first I thought only that the dark figure hastily descending the steps was someone who had decided his ring was to go unanswered.

"Wait a moment," I called.

But the strange visitor did not pause. Half turning at the foot of the steps, he cast one backward glance and I had a fleeting vision of a white face.

Perhaps it was the half-light striking his eyes that gave them that queer intensity, but I had an uncomfortable feeling that even in this quick scrutiny no detail of my appearance had been overlooked. And there was something very odd about the tall, shadowy figure. Of course it was odd enough that anyone should be garbed all in black on a semi-tropic island in June. But something about his loosely hanging coat or cloak—or was it only the half-light and the encroaching shadows?—gave his shoulders a queer semblance of exaggerated width. For a moment he was there, a vague, fantastic shape on the rim of reality.

And then, like a black bat, he became a part of the deeper blackness of the night.

Josh's silly remark about Count Dracula and that grave came back to me, and I jumped, startled half out of my skin, as Woodrow spoke from the hall. "'Scuse me, Miss Ann. I thought the front doorbell rung."

"It did," I said, a little shakily. "There's somebody outside. You'd better see."

"Mighty funny," he said, when he came back, rolling his eyes. "I sho can't find hide or hair o' nobody."

Even if we could convince ourselves that the doorbell had suddenly gone cockeyed, there were Cousin Chattie's two Pomeranians, pawing at the screen door and yapping their heads off as bright button eyes peered out into the darkness.

"But you can't tell about them little dogs," said Woodrow. "Sometimes they's fit to tear up the place and it ain't nobody but me. They'd just as soon bite a friend as an enemy," he added admiringly. "Anyway, Miss Ann, can't nobody git in. I been over this whole, entire house, and everything's locked tight. Come on here now, you Bin and Jitters," he admonished the two dogs. "Git back where you belong."

Gin and Bitters, ignoring him completely, trotted into the drawing room, and I followed. The tinkle of the piano and the words of the song impinging once more upon my consciousness, I found it difficult to realize so little time had passed.

"Is she kind as she is fair?
For beauty lives with kindness—"

Kind or not, the singer was very beautiful in a long white lace dress with a red rose in her dark hair. As she turned from the yellowed keyboard to be presented by Cousin Chattie it was plain enough to see that she was one of the twins. This was Cynthia Harrison. Sylvia Scott was the twin in the red and white chiffon cut too low and wearing a gardenia in her hair. Undoubtedly it was Sylvia whom Pat and I had overheard greeting her husband, David Scott, as we arrived.

Even without the introductions, I should have been sure of this in another moment. For in the small stir created by Woodrow's arrival with a tray of drinks David Scott half whispered something to the twin in white lace which I am sure was intended for her ear alone.

"You should have been named Sylvia," he murmured. In his husky voice was that certain something that says so much more than words.

Involuntarily I glanced at the real Sylvia, hoping she had not heard. Perhaps she had not caught the actual words, but the flash in her dark eyes, like heat lightning, could mean only one thing— that a storm was brewing.

Was this why Sylvia and her husband were at odds? Was he in love with Cynthia? After all, Cynthia had not remarried after the death of her husband. But why had David Scott said to Sylvia, "You are not getting away with one single thing."

Careful to choose the side next to his good ear, I sat down by Cousin Beau on a rather worn yellow brocade sofa. Courtly and dignified as usual, his expression betrayed not the slightest indication of anything out of the ordinary.

"Cousin Beau—" I began, hesitantly.

"Never mind." He dropped his voice to a near whisper. "Seems Chattie had to keep all this crowd anyway. Just forget that call."

"I—I was afraid something was wrong," I said.

He waited so long to answer that I began to think I had made a mistake after all and was sitting on the side next to his deaf ear. He took a sip of his rum cocktail, swallowed thoughtfully, looked up at the crystal chandeliers, then around the big square room—which would have been spacious except for the clutter of Cousin Chattie's bargain antiques mixed in with nice old original pieces. Finally his glance came back to me. "Just forget that call," he said again.

"Something funny happened a moment ago," I told him. "A queer-looking man rang the doorbell and then disappeared. I saw him."

"What?" Cousin Beau asked, his tone a little sharp. But he recovered quickly. "Probably just a deliveryman who came to the front door and realized his mistake when he saw you all decked out like the queen of the May."

Which was logical, of course; but I had an entirely illogical feeling that this was not the case.

Raising his voice and looking from one to the other of the twins, Cousin Beau asked of the room in general, "Did anybody ever see two people as much alike as these charming girls? Right now, I couldn't tell you which is which to save my life."

"Well, I'm Sylvia—the one with the bracelets," announced the twin in white and red chiffon, holding up a slender sun-tanned wrist on which three flexible platinum and diamond circlets winked brightly. In the movies, I strongly suspect the censors would have felt that they had to do something about the cut of Sylvia Scott's dress. "And don't get us mixed," she went on gayly, "after all the sweet nothings you whispered in my shell-pink ear while we were gathering wild flowers."

"Wild flowers?" repeated her husband with a puzzled frown.

He glanced from Sylvia to Cousin Beau, who smiled a little inanely. In his fresh white linen suit, David Scott looked even more dark and his hair a little more wild than when he had passed us on the road.

"For my collection." Sylvia smiled patronizingly. "Cyn can tell you I won a botany prize in school. It was a big event, because she usually won all the prizes."

"Oh, Silly," deprecated Cynthia, "I never won anything of any consequence."

"I wouldn't say that," said Sylvia, smiling maliciously as she glanced at her husband. "You always had the edge, even in names. Cyn sounds so enticing. Who wouldn't rather be thought sinful than silly? That's why you can be so saintly."

Cynthia, painfully embarrassed, said nothing but turned her dark eyes toward the door as Homer appeared, looking a little too much like what the well-dressed man should wear. Lounging behind, much taller, was Josh—as debonair as though he had never thought of leaving two females in the lurch only a short while before.

David Scott glanced searchingly from one to the other of the newcomers. Obviously experience had taught him to expect a possible rival in any man of Sylvia's acquaintance. I wondered uneasily if it was Josh he had had in mind in that conversation with his wife on the porch. But there was nothing in Josh's casual smile to give away the situation. Homer appeared the more self-conscious of the two. One of those rather thick-set, determined young men with sandy hair, he is a little pop-eyed; and this feature is more noticeable when he is not quite at ease. As he moved his chair nearer Pat's and leaned toward her, raising his drink in a silent toast, I was certain, all of a sudden, that Mother was right about his interest in Pat. This would explain his self-consciousness, for of course he wouldn't be quite comfortable in the room with both of us. And here I had just told Cousin Chattie I was ready to accept him at last. I'd taken Homer for granted so long that I found this new development oddly disconcerting.

"Give an account of yourself," I demanded of Josh. "Technically, Pat and I are still waiting at the garage."

Josh looked at Pat with that slow smile of his which sort of breaks you down, and she smiled back. "Sorry," he said, "but I knew you would be all right." And that was all I could get out of him.

Sylvia was like a bright bird, black eyes darting here and there, ready to swoop down on whatever conversation offered the best pickings. "Dave is so impulsive," she murmured at her husband's rather confused apology to Pat and me for having passed us on the road. It was easy to see from his quick frown that rubbing him the wrong way was one of the things she did best.

But any reply he might have made was lost in Sylvia's next maneuver. "Oh, Dave," she called out brightly, as though she had just remembered something important, "I want you to see my sun tan."

As her husband's and all other eyes in the room turned in her direction, Sylvia stretched long slim legs out before her. Slowly, provocatively, she pulled back over those slim bare legs the diaphanous skirts of her evening frock until they were well above her knees, displaying a very good sun tan indeed.

I think David Scott was struggling hard not to make a scene. Anyway, before he could say a word Sylvia restored her skirts with a quick little flip, and her laugh rang out mockingly. "You old stick-in-the-mud!" she chided him. "What's the difference between an evening dress and a bathing suit? You'd think I was doing a strip tease." Just a shade too absent-mindedly she adjusted the shoulder straps of her dress so that perhaps a fraction less of full rounded bosom was exposed.

Cousin Chattie, who prides herself on being as modern as anyone half her forty-five years, looked as though she were going to choke. Cousin Beau cleared his throat.

"Er-rhump," he gargled. "Who'll have a drink?"

I was a little shocked to see him wink at Sylvia as he bent down to hand her another cocktail. Didn't men ever get to the age where a woman could not make a fool of them?

Sylvia downed the drink in short, impatient swallows and rose to her feet. "Homer," she said, "have you seen the etchings in the library?"

Her glance, cool and disdainful, swept the room, and then she was gone. Derisive laughter and a whiff of perfume from the gardenia in her hair floated back as Homer scrambled self-consciously to his feet and followed her across the wide hall.

For, of course, there are no etchings in the library. Only that beautiful Audubon print above the mantel, *A Great White Heron*, from which the point takes its name. And those bad steel engravings of General Lee and Stonewall Jackson draped with Confederate flags.

More drinks were passed when Sylvia and Homer came back, and Homer gulped his quickly as though afraid he might have kept us waiting. I was glad to see Josh shake his head and set his empty glass on the ugly teak table beside him. Getting rid of Cousin Chattie's bargain antiques would be my biggest job, for she is as gregarious about possessions as she is about people.

"Who brought this to the party?" Josh asked facetiously, picking up an antique dagger of dull gold that lay on the crowded table.

"It's Spanish—dug up on the place during the lifetime of Beau's grandfather," Cousin Chattie told us with conscious pride.

"Yes," said Cousin Beau, "the Spanish built missions on these coastal islands long before Oglethorpe founded the colony of Georgia at Savannah. Fact is," he went on, disregarding Cousin Chattie's impatient signal, "this Island has played a very important part in history. We speak English instead of Spanish because the British won the Battle of Bloody Marsh on St. Simon's and ended Spain's aggression in the New World. Fanny Kemble's journal of a year on a Georgia plantation, written here in the eighteen-thirties, is credited with having prevented the English from lending money to the Confederacy and—"

Sylvia could take it no longer.

"Were you contemplating something with that weapon, Josh?" she cut in.

Josh drew the dagger from its dull gold sheath and touched the point of the shining blade. "Looks pretty businesslike," he said, with his slow, lazy smile. "Ancestor of the ice pick, probably."

"Damascene steel," said Cousin Beau, a little stiffly. "Had it polished up when I ran across it the other day."

"May I see it?" asked David Scott unexpectedly.

As though there was a conspiracy to choke off Cousin Beau's historical monologue, everybody displayed a sudden interest in the dagger.

"Ugh!" shuddered Pat as she passed it to me. "What a face!"

Gingerly inspecting the delicately chased gold hilt, I could understand her distaste. Its trefoil floral design culminated curiously at the apex in a man's head—a face wearing the most saturnine expression I have ever seen.

"Here, put it back on the table," I told Josh hastily, and amid general laughter we all went in to dinner.

III

EVEN COUSIN CHATTIE must have realized finally that there was something wrong with that dinner. Not with the food, for Cousin Beau not only insists that the stately old dining room with its Chippendale furniture, Georgian silver, and Wedgwood china remain intact, but also makes a ritual of the lavish menus of plantation days. Tonight I could not decide whether his worried frown was due to whatever prompted that unexplained telephone call or to the general neglect of roast squab on rice pilau. At any rate, Cousin Chattie's favorite recipe had failed. Cocktails had not broken down all barriers.

Aside from this I could not quite shake off an uncomfortable little chill which had hung on ever since I answered the doorbell before dinner. Every time the curtains blew inward and the candles flickered in their silver holders, I could imagine a tall dark figure hovering just outside the open windows, staring in at me with that queer intensity. Irresistibly drawn toward those windows, I shivered slightly just as my eyes met Homer's. Flushing a little, for he had been stealing a glimpse at the set of his tie in the beautiful old Chinese Chippendale mirror above the sideboard, he asked, "Cold?"

"Rabbit ran across my grave," I smiled lightly, thankful that dessert plates and gold-flecked Venetian glass finger bowls were being brought in.

It was over at last, and I was upstairs powdering my nose. Standing there before the dressing table, I was startled to see Sylvia's beautiful dark head materialize in the pier-glass mirror, for there had been no knock on my partly open door. As I turned to face her, she said without preamble, "Sorry you disapprove of me."

But she was not sorry. It was like a glove thrown in one's face. I wanted to say that she flattered herself to assume that I knew her well enough to approve or disapprove, but she rushed on maliciously: "Of course, that's why you brought her along. Trying to marry her to your brother because of her money. Really, it is too amusing."

Something in my glance must have stopped her, and she turned. Pat was in the door, with a wrap over her arm, waiting for me to join her and go downstairs. She had probably heard it all.

"Really too amusing," Sylvia Scott repeated, her unpleasant laugh ringing out. She looked at Pat with calculated insolence and said, "Or perhaps it was your idea, Miss Fairchild?"

Pat's blue eyes were blazing. "You—you tramp!" she said in a throaty whisper, drawing back her long skirts as Sylvia swept from the room.

Pat and I just stood and stared at each other for a moment, and then there was Cousin Chattie caroling, "Hurry up, girls—we want to get in some dancing, you know."

But Cousin Chattie's hurrying got us nowhere, for we sat for ages on the cool dark porch, waiting for everybody to assemble. Homer was being very southern for Pat's benefit. "I must give a barbecue for you at the plantation," I heard him say. Homer always manages to give the impression that the plantation is practically a King's grant to his ancestors rather than the mortgaged farm he picked up for unpaid taxes.

"Couldn't throw in a lynching, too, could you?" wisecracked Josh. "After all, Pat's never seen one."

"It might be managed," Homer agreed, bent on being a good sport at all costs. "Anybody you would like to have—er—polished off?"

"What's that?" asked David Scott, and Homer had to explain a little impatiently that it was all a joke.

The twins were the last to appear. I thought perhaps Sylvia had changed her mind about going, after that outburst in my room.

But finally she and Cynthia could be heard coming down the stairs, laughing at some private joke of their own.

Cousin Beau snapped on the porch light, and Sylvia's smiling glance sought her husband. "How about thumbing a ride with you?" she asked unexpectedly.

David Scott gave her a quick suspicious look, his dark brows lifted, but he dutifully extended his hand for her summer wrap. Obviously he had followed Sylvia south because something needed talking over; and apparently she had decided to get through with a disagreeable job.

But David Scott could have been no more surprised than I at this quick right-about face. Sylvia had been ready to have him thrown out when he first arrived and had deliberately humiliated him before dinner. She had been in a vile mood when she came into my room. Now here she was, dripping sweetness and light. It was too much to expect that she could keep it up, and I hoped to be somewhere else when the explosion came. The words of the song, "Is she kind as she is fair?" returned mockingly, and I was ready to agree with David Scott that somebody fumbled when the twins were christened. Cynthia should have been named Sylvia.

Whether or not Sylvia's conference with her husband was completed on the way to the Cloister, I do not know. But it was Cynthia whom he asked to dance as soon as we were all seated at a table in the palm patio, with its lush shrubbery and the dew-drenched fragrance of summer flowers. As Homer and I followed them in the quick lilting of a Viennese waltz, I noticed that they went only once around the dance floor, then disappeared through an entrance into the gardens.

"Let's finish this dance," I said, when Homer suggested that we also stroll toward the beach.

I knew Cousin Chattie expected me to come to an immediate understanding with Homer, and I suspected Homer himself was leading up to an entirely different sort of understanding, one that would give him his freedom. But I knew also that I could hold him to his oft-repeated proposal, for he prided himself on being the little gentleman. I wouldn't do that, of course, and the sensible thing would be to get it all over with as soon as possible.

But the music, the counterpoint tinkle of ice in tall glasses, the women in light filmy summer frocks, all added up to a picture of gay serenity, whatever might be seething beneath the surface. For the first time in hours I felt fairly relaxed and inclined to agree with Cousin Beau that hot weather is no time for serious thinking. Anyway, the night was young. I could talk to Homer later.

"May I?" asked a vaguely familiar voice. Someone tapped Homer on the shoulder to cut in, and there incredibly was Rufus Blair, the obliging young garage mechanic. Tall and dark in crisp white linen, with that smile which came so near to being a laugh in his sleeve at life in general, he might have been any nice young man. Which made it all the more strange that the dance floor should suddenly become the deck of a pirate ship and that I should have the queer feeling as we danced away that Homer had just been forced to walk the plank.

It was all crazy, and I felt a little giddy and unexpectedly gay as I looked up into Rufus Blair's sardonic dark eyes. "Who are you, anyway?" I asked, not caring at all.

"Just a damn Yankee," he grinned.

"But that war's over. Hadn't you heard?"

"That's what I thought until I came down here," he grinned again. "Anyway, don't be too hard on me for taking advantage of your brother's perfectly natural mistake. I had—a purpose."

That smile of his took out all the sappiness, really made me wonder whether he was laughing at Josh or me or both.

Then all at once he was candid and simple. "I'm a bird who likes to fool with his own car," he explained engagingly. "Besides, it's less expensive. At the garage they very kindly lent me an over-all. Seems there's no limit to southern hospitality."

The music stopped, and I took him over to the table to introduce him to Cousin Chattie. Where the rest of the evening went, I don't know, but as I told Rufus Blair good night I thought the day which had begun so badly was ending very well—except that Cousin Chattie was now rounding everybody up for a trip to the cemetery: "We must get there before twelve o'clock," she kept insisting.

Pat and I smiled at each other ruefully, for we had forgotten entirely Cousin Chattie's ghost-hunting program. And nobody wanted to leave the dance.

"All a pack of foolishness," Cousin Beau grumbled, and I think the rest of us agreed. That ghost couldn't be anything but a trick, of course.

But there is something eerie about the way the dark closes in on the Island when you have just left the bright lights behind. Tonight it seemed to creep in like a mist from the marshes, dimming the car's headlights as we skimmed along the causeway connecting the two islands, and as we took the turn into the road to the cemetery that same darkness became a black curtain dropping from an encroaching jungle of trees, muffling sound, shutting off the rest of the world.

Cousin Chattie certainly picked the right approach, I thought, as we turned the last curve and came finally to the small historic church which even in daylight has an isolated air. Cloistered by surrounding live oaks, their branches arched high overhead to form a vaulted ceiling, the church itself might be the inner shrine of a cathedral. But the pendulous gray moss contributes most to the effect, as though the trees were draped in perpetual mourning for those who sleep beneath the weathered slabs. Slabs that mark not only the end of an earthly sojourn, but the end of an era—that long dead golden age known as the Old South.

We parked the cars across the road, and Cousin Chattie herded us through the gate along the holly- and myrtle-bordered flagstone path leading to the church. As our eyes gradually adjusted themselves to the intense darkness, we could discern the dim white of tombstones off to our right.

I must confess a certain relief when Cousin Chattie led us in the opposite direction, though I still had an uncomfortable feeling that my back was unduly exposed. For something seems to happen to a cemetery at night. Darkness shrouds those vaguely white stones with an awesome mystery. I felt an urge to look over my shoulder just to make sure there was nothing to see.

Panting a little, Cousin Chattie paused finally, and we all stumbled to a halt. "Yes, this is the spot," intoned Cousin Beau. "We are standing under the Wesley Oak. John and Charles Wesley preached in its shade when they came to the Colony of Georgia with General Oglethorpe. We—"

"Oh, Beau," Cousin Chattie protested, "this is not a sightseeing tour."

"Damn!" exclaimed David Scott. "If I could just see anything!" Then he apologized and explained that he had stepped on a dead branch or something which had risen up and socked him on the shin.

Cousin Chattie took charge again. "Now, listen, everybody. Face back toward the gate, and stand apart. No one must hold on to anyone else." This meant that we were facing the graves at the right of the entrance, perhaps some two hundred feet distant. "What time is it?" she asked in a stage whisper.

"One minute of twelve," said Josh, evidently consulting the illuminated dial of his wrist watch. "Almost the zero hour."

"Sh-h-h!" hissed Cousin Chattie.

But we stood there much longer than a minute, nobody daring to say a word. The night and the dark hung heavy and breathless about us, as though a summer storm might be brewing. And it was very quiet. I had left my wrap in the car, and suddenly the air seemed unexpectedly chill, perhaps because the drive had cooled me off too quickly after dancing. I was surprised to find myself shivering. And it seemed that not even a cemetery should be so quiet. Unless—unless it was waiting for something to happen.

But that was absurd. What could happen? I thought of the man who said he didn't believe in ghosts but that he was afraid of them. Darn Josh, anyway, putting ideas in my head about Dracula and the undead foraging around to gorge themselves on human blood and vanishing neatly into convenient graves.

If there was only a wall or something back of us, I thought. Standing like this, one felt so exposed. And then behind me somebody or something moved—moved so stealthily that there was only the sound of a twig breaking underfoot, followed by a quick indrawn breath; neither would have been audible except for the deathly silence.

"Who's that?" I breathed, half turning. I was jerked back to attention by Cousin Chattie's sibilant "Sh-h-h!" and her long drawn, dramatic, "Loo-ook!"

I looked, and there is no use trying to appear sophisticated and casual when every hair on your head suddenly has been shot with electricity.

An unearthly light was moving among the tombstones beyond the gate. Now there were two lights, like huge fiery mismatched eyes. The lights moved again as though seeking some particular spot. Then there was only a single light again—hesitating above one of the graves.

As suddenly as it had appeared, the light was gone. It was gone, but not before we all had seen a white figure rise up from that grave and start slowly toward us: a vague white figure in flowing robes, edged with a sort of luminous radiance. As we gazed, a shrill scream broke on the heavy night air, paralyzing the senses so that for a moment I did not realize it had come from one of our group. Then I almost screamed myself, for in that split second while the echo still hung in the air, horrible things began to happen.

I was too startled to do anything but hold my breath. Somebody was shoving against me in the dark. No, not shoving, leaning heavily, then slumping downward, slowly slipping to the ground at my feet. I heard a faint sound, like a little moan or a sigh. I knew what had happened then, and sanity returned. "Somebody's fainted," I cried, my voice not yet under control.

The next few minutes will always be a blur in my mind. Suddenly everyone was milling around, forgetful of the white figure at the far end of the cemetery. There was a babble of voices, and everybody seemed to be trying to strike matches. In the dark, I knelt down to see who had fallen against me. I reached out my hand and drew it back quickly, for it had touched something cold and hard.

There was a flicker of light, and I began to shake and my teeth to chatter. Cousin Beau pulled me to my feet, and I leaned back against him, feeling very ill. For the wavering flames of the matches picked out the blood-red poppies on the white chiffon of Sylvia Scott's dress as she lay face down on the ground. They picked out the poppies darkly, but lent a malignant gleam to the saturnine face on the dull gold handle of Cousin Chattie's antique dagger, plunged to the hilt in Sylvia's sun-tanned back. Blood welled up and spread around the dagger hilt—red like one of the poppies.

There was a fantastic moment when I thought perhaps it was an act of some kind—a part of Cousin Chattie's ghost parade. Then I realized that my right hand was sticky with blood from having touched that dagger in the dark.

IV

MATCHES HELD UNSTEADILY by Josh and Homer made a small ring of light revealing a weird picture—Cousin Beau's hand holding Sylvia's limp wrist feeling for the pulse that could mean life or death.

As fresh matches flared, their flicker struck the faces of the three men, bringing out deep lines of strain. Even Cousin Chattie was quiet. And when Cousin Beau finally released that wrist, his slow carefulness left no need for words. But it did not seem possible, Sylvia Scott had been so alive, so full of venom. How could she be dead so suddenly, so completely?

"Where is Dave?" Cynthia Harrison cried out, her voice rising shrill.

"I'm here, Cynthia," he told her, gently, close at her side.

"What?" she asked dazedly.

"Right here," he repeated. "This is Dave."

"You killed her," Cynthia accused, in that same shrill voice. "Have him arrested, somebody. Don't let him escape." Then she fainted, and David Scott caught her as she fell.

"She doesn't know what she's saying," he told the rest of us hoarsely. "It's shock. For God's sake, get a doctor."

"Yes, yes," Cousin Chattie quavered. "Why doesn't somebody do something?"

But the question was what and how. There we were in an isolated cemetery in the middle of the night, the dark so heavy you could almost reach out and touch it. And there at our feet where

59

we might stumble over her unless we moved with caution, was Sylvia Scott, with a dagger in her back. That dagger from the yellow drawing room at Heron Point, recognized with horrified exclamations by each of us.

"We must get Cynthia to the house at once," Cousin Beau told us in a voice that he tried hard to keep steady. "All of you girls must go. Ann, do you feel like driving? I think the men will have to stay here until—"

"But," Josh protested, "I'm afraid the police will expect every-one to stay. This—this—is murder, you know. I—"

What else he was going to say I don't know, for Cousin Chattie went into a mild case of hysterics.

"Just forget your legal training," Cousin Beau told Josh grimly. "This is no place for women. Homer, you'd better go somewhere in a hurry and telephone for a doctor and—" He seemed to be trying to swallow something that would not go down.

"Yes, sir," agreed Homer soberly, "and the police?"

"Yes," Cousin Beau admitted.

Murder. At the thought, I began to tremble all over again. For I had been standing next to Sylvia. I had even heard the murderer's stealthy approach. It would have been so easy to strike the wrong person there in the dark. Suddenly, I realized how the killer had been able to pick his target. That gardenia, a white patch in Sylvia's black hair, would have been faintly visible. All the women except Sylvia, I now recalled, were wearing white frocks. Sylvia's was white and—red.

As we made our slow way toward the gate, David Scott bearing Cynthia in his arms, the rest of us stumbling along in the dark, I ventured an uneasy glance toward the tombstones among which the ghost had materialized. What was that fantastic apparition which had held all eyes while the murderer struck? Because of the perfect timing of the blow, the ghost had an alibi, whatever might be said of anyone else.

The graves were shrouded in darkness now. But as I looked—I grabbed Josh with a strangle hold. "There it is again," I shrieked.

That strange light was moving above the graves. For a moment there were two lights, like huge eyes. Then that white figure loomed up. I held my breath as the lights disappeared and the figure which had seemed to move toward us, faded slowly into nothingness.

Everybody was talking, but I heard only Josh, who was giving me a little shake. "Get hold of yourself, baby. It's just a car going past. Those funny lights are a reflection of the headlights on the tombstones. It only happens when a car swings too far over on the left-hand side of the road."

"Oh," I gulped, still holding onto him, "but I saw more than lights. That—that—white figure—"

Josh managed a hollow laugh for my benefit. "The lady's a tombstone, too," he explained. "It's the way the light strikes behind it, or something that gives an optical illusion of movement. Now don't ask me why. I don't know."

The car responsible for this strange phenomenon had pulled over to the side of the road and stopped. As we came through the gate we recognized Rufus Blair blinking in the headlights.

At the moment, it did not seem strange that he should materialize out of nowhere like that. Perhaps I had lost my capacity for surprise, but I was conscious only of a feeling that here was help. There was something about Rufus Blair that inspired confidence.

Listening gravely, he kept his expression under perfect control, which somehow made our excited account of what had happened sound all the more fantastic. Cousin Beau accepted his offer of assistance with obvious relief and suggested that he drive us to Heron Point and remain until the men of the party were able to return.

"Better be getting along," Cousin Beau cautioned as he helped Cousin Chattie onto the front seat beside Rufus. "Feels like rain." A quick flash of lightning streaked across the sky, followed by a roll of thunder.

"But what about Sylvia?" Cousin Chattie inquired tremulously. "We can't just leave her there on the ground to be soaked by the rain."

Cousin Beau cast an uneasy glance toward the back seat where Pat and I were supporting Cynthia between us. But she did not stir or give any indication of having heard. Since that outburst against David Scott, she had seemed to be in a complete coma. "Won't take long for an ambulance to get here," Cousin Beau told us, giving Cousin Chattie an affectionate pat on the arm as Rufus touched the starter.

"Do come home as soon as you can," she implored, clinging to his linen coat sleeve.

"How did you happen along, just at the right moment?" I asked Rufus.

"I suppose it does call for a little explaining," he admitted soberly. "But, you see, I was the ghost."

"I asked him at the dance," Cousin Chattie explained, her voice still a little uncertain. "I'd meant to tell Woodrow to drive by the cemetery at twelve o'clock, but I forgot. Oh, how could I know—"

"Nobody could," we assured her.

"After I drove by the cemetery," Rufus went on, "I turned around at Frederica. It's a dead-end road, you know. As I came back past that big tree at the cemetery, it struck me that things didn't sound quite right. I drove on, but I kept wondering. So—I turned around again."

Certainly, nothing in the world ever seemed as welcome as the lights at Heron Point. White dotted Swiss frills trailing limply, Cousin Chattie went from room to room, turning on all the lights, marshaling reserves to hold that dreadful dark at bay. "It creeps up so," she shivered. "I feel as though hands were reaching out. Hands holding daggers."

With the crystal chandeliers agleam behind her in the yellow drawing room, she stepped through the wide doorway into the little-used blue drawing room. Then we heard her scream. She was pasty-faced when we reached her and could hardly speak.

"Something—" she gasped, one hand over her heart, the other pointing toward the half-open door into the hall. "Something went running out—on four feet."

"Probably just a dog," Rufus told us, gently piloting her back into the yellow drawing room, and motioning Pat and me to follow.

"Oh, no," Cousin Chattie shuddered, "it was much too big!" She sank into a chair, her usually merry blue eyes wide with horror. "I only had a glimpse of something—like the shadow of a huge animal."

"Stay here, all of you," Rufus admonished. "I'll take a look around."

Cynthia Harrison lying on a sofa, the long skirt of her lace dinner dress cascading like white foam onto the dark green Aubusson rug, roused for a moment to stare dazedly out of her great dark eyes. Then the long black lashes fluttered against cheeks pale beneath their tan. Snow White, in her seeming death, was not more still.

"I think a little brandy or sherry for both of them," Pat whispered to me, starting toward the door.

"No, no, stay here. It isn't safe," Cousin Chattie cried hysterically. "I'll ring for Woodrow." Clutching the petit-point bellpull as though it might be her last hold on life, she looked over her shoulder uneasily. "I don't know what it was," she shuddered again.

I tried not to think of werewolves and of that strange figure I had seen melting like a shadow into the darkness when I answered the doorbell just before dinner. Or of something or somebody who had crashed off into the bushes as we approached Heron Point a little earlier. I tried only to remember that this night would end some time and day would break. It would all look different then.

Rufus came back in a few minutes to report that he had seen nothing. "Are you sure it couldn't have been one of those Poms?" he asked Cousin Chattie, smiling. Gin and Bitters could be heard protesting loudly from the back porch where Woodrow had tucked them in for the night.

Cousin Chattie obviously would have liked nothing better than to think so, but she shook her head. "There's no way for them to get out, and they're too tiny. Anyway, do you think one of my own pets would run from me?"

Woodrow, just roused from bed and too sleepy to see anything unless it knocked him down, came in and was dispatched for sherry.

"It was probably just the shadow of a swaying curtain," Rufus told Cousin Chattie, as she repeated her story between sips.

To reassure her, we all went into the blue drawing room, turned out the lights and turned them on again. It was not a very convincing demonstration, for the night was unusually still and no curtain moved or cast a shadow on the wall next to the hall door.

Cousin Chattie, warmed by the wine and wanting pathetically to agree, said, "Well, maybe so." But her frightened blue eyes could not believe.

Rufus carried Cynthia upstairs, and Pat and I put her to bed. All the life appeared to have been drained out of her. Her body was there in the big, wide bed, but all that was Cynthia seemed to have gone away—with her twin sister perhaps. I did not like leaving her alone; but she refused to have anyone stay, and when the doctor arrived he prescribed complete quiet. So, turning out all but the night light, we left her. As we waited for the men we tried not to talk about the murder, rather taking for granted that David Scott would be arrested: aside from his quarrel with Sylvia which Pat and I had overheard, there was Cynthia's accusation in the cemetery. So it was a shock when he stalked in with Cousin Beau and Josh, his dark hair on end, his eyes feverish.

To cover the awkwardness of the moment I asked, "Where's Homer?"

Josh and David Scott waited for Cousin Beau to reply. He moistened his lips and fumbled in his pocket for a cigar.

"You don't mean," Cousin Chattie burst out excitedly, "that they've arrested Homer?"

"My dear," Cousin Beau reproved, "you should have been in bed long ago. Anyway, don't upset yourself by jumping to conclusions. You're just like the police. Homer went to telephone, you remember? Well, simply because he hadn't got back to the cemetery when the police arrived, they decided he was trying to escape in his plane. He's probably just having car trouble somewhere."

"How perfectly absurd!" said Cousin Chattie. And it was, of course. Homer barely knew Sylvia Scott. Anyway, he was not the type. Murder is one of those things that just isn't done, and Homer never veered from the correct thing.

As Rufus was saying good night for the second time in one evening the doorbell rang. It sounded strangely loud and ominous at that hour of the night in the big quiet house where, until lately, doors were never locked. A moment later Homer, sandy head thrust forward, eyes popping as they do when something puts him out, was ushered in by Woodrow.

"Yes, sir," he answered Cousin Beau's question, "it was a flat tire. How could that dumb cop think I would telephone him first if I wanted to escape?" Homer looked around the room truculently, as he dropped into a chair. "And to think," he added, "I almost didn't come down to the Island this weekend."

He downed the drink Josh handed him, strangling a little. "Had a hell of a time," he went on. "Spare was in the luggage compartment, and the lock rusted. On top of that, the jack wouldn't stand up."

"I must speak to Woodrow," Cousin Beau interjected.

Homer flushed with embarrassment at having seemed to criticize Heron Point hospitality. "But I wasn't driving one of your cars," he explained a little awkwardly. "It was getting late when I arrived at the airport this afternoon, so I had a car sent over from the village to use this weekend."

He poured himself another drink and gulped it at one swallow.

The police, it seems, had tried to put handcuffs on him, but had finally stowed these away and got out a tire pump. They would be calling early in the morning, Homer said. "Safe enough to leave us until then," he pointed out. "Nobody but a fool would try to make a getaway from the Island."

And it was true. Although St. Simon's is fairly large, twelve miles long by three miles wide—not including smaller Sea island, which is connected by a short causeway—we could be isolated completely by a few well directed words from the police. The toll keeper would stop any car attempting to leave by way of the five-mile causeway to the mainland. The Coast Guard station would be on the alert for boats, and the airport could hold Homer's plane as well as refuse passage to the rest of us.

Pat dropped into my room for a chat before saying good night, as she used to do when we were at boarding school. "I might," she said oddly, "be accused of this murder myself." The wide skirts of her white mousseline frock spreading around the low slipper chair, not a hair out of place on her red brown head, she looked immaculate as usual though minus a bit of her sparkle.

"Are you crazy?" I asked.

"I only meant if someone happened to overhear my little run-in with Mrs. Scott."

"I had a lot more cause to be angry with her than you did," I said.

"Because she went after Homer—dragging him off to the library before dinner?"

"Oh!" I said a little blankly, for I had been thinking about Josh. "Well, anybody who wants Homer is welcome to him."

"Do you mean that?" asked Pat curiously.

"Why not?" I answered, determined to maintain the light touch and to leave Pat a free hand if by chance she was interested in Homer. (To do him justice, he could make himself quite charming to rich people.)

"Poor Homer," I said, "it must have been a terrible shock, having the police think he was trying to escape. Homer, of all people!"

"Yes," agreed Pat, "but do you realize what it means—the fact that no arrest has been made?" She stood up and moved toward the door, stretching her shapely arms above her head. "It means the murderer is still in our midst. I'm going to lock my door, and I'd advise you to do the same thing."

But I discovered that the key to my door was missing and there was no bolt. Of course, Cousin Chattie would never bother about such details, though the key might have been lost a couple of generations earlier. I placed a straight chair under the knob and climbed into the big, high four-poster bed. That chair might not keep anybody out, but it would certainly make enough noise to wake me.

I dropped off immediately; but it could not have been very sound slumber, for only a little later I awoke thinking somebody was trying to open my door. Listening closely, I realized that the sound actually came from overhead: rats on a rampage in the attic.

But could rats make that muffled, bumping noise? What could it be?

Lying there, it was impossible not to remember that old story about the young wife whose dead body was kept in a sealed metal casket at Heron Point until the bereaved husband could carry it back to Virginia. He had been compelled to have the casket moved temporarily to the attic because the servants refused to go near the room in which it stood. That had given rise to rumors of strange noises in the attic, as though the imprisoned corpse was struggling to escape. There were rumors, too, of a ghost on the stair.

But that was all a long time ago. I had slept in this room often with never a hint of anything to suggest ghostly meanderings. Anyway, this very evening had furnished practical demonstration that there is always a scientific explanation of such things. Dropping back on the pillow, I resolutely closed my eyes.

Then I sat up in bed with a jerk. What could have caused that heavy thud—as though somebody had fallen on the floor directly above me? For a moment I half expected whoever it was to come crashing through.

Complete silence followed. Then, as though the crash in the attic had found its echo outside, there was a rumble of thunder. The storm which had threatened so long broke with a heavy downpour of rain.

V

THE NOISE OF THE RAIN made it impossible to hear anything else, even though I sat up in bed to listen. No use trying to fool myself. That dull thud on the attic floor could not have been made by rats. It was strange that no one else seemed to have heard, but I realized the disturbance had been concentrated directly above my own room.

I turned on the bedside light and looked at my wristwatch lying on the table. Nearly three o'clock. Good heavens, what could anyone be doing in the attic at this hour? A burglar had visited the house on Friday. Could he have returned and forced an entrance in spite of locked window screens and doors? Or—here I really sat up straight—could it be the murderer, prowling around on some business of his own? Hiding some clue, perhaps? The more I thought of it, the more certain I became that this was the answer. Certainly nobody had any legitimate business in the attic at three o'clock in the morning. Yes, it must be the murderer.

I sat there, muddled and scared, trying to think what to do. The only bell in my room rang in the butler's pantry and there would be no one to answer it at this hour. I must rouse one of the men. Cousin Beau would probably be sleeping on his good ear, but Josh would wake easily, even though his door might be locked.

Slipping out of bed and into my green silk jersey housecoat, I groped my way to the door. I had no candle or flashlight and dared not turn on an electric light for fear the overhead prowler might come down the stair unexpectedly.

Josh would be in his old room in the east wing, formerly the nursery, so that I should have to cross the wide upstairs hall and turn left down a narrow passage. I didn't like venturing out into that yawning darkness; but something had to be done, and if I started yelling the murderer might escape.

With hands held in front of me I inched my way, finally gripping the rail of the stairwell thankfully. The rain had settled to a gentle patter, and the house seemed full of a sort of listening silence. Then my heart climbed into my throat. Off to the right, near the top of the attic stairs, I heard a slight creaking sound.

For a breathless moment I stood there unable to move, nerves keyed for some further sound. Around me again was that dreadful, listening silence—silence that chilled me through and through. Too late the fact came home that who ever was abroad in the old house might not deal gently with anyone who got in his way.

Hurrying, I stepped on the hem of my long, slithery silk house coat and almost fell. Panic seized me, as I tried to untangle myself, and in that brief moment of uncertainty I lost my bearings. I was not sure which way to turn and I was not sure whether the noise I now heard came from the attic stairway or was only the beating of my own heart.

I suppose I stood there only a fraction of a minute, frozen by fright and indecision. And in that instant the entire upstairs hall was illuminated as though a floodlight had been turned on. It was only a flash of lightning, but that flash showed a head peering cautiously around the wall of the enclosed attic stairway.

The head was jerked back so quickly I could not tell whether it belonged to a man or a woman. But one thing was certain: I myself had stood revealed as if by a spotlight.

That flash of lightning had also given me my bearings. It was only a few steps back to my own open door, while Josh's was relatively far away and might be locked. Pure reflex action did the rest. Perhaps it was instinct that kept me from slamming the door, once I was in my room. Perhaps I thought, if I closed it softly, the murderer would not know which room sheltered me.

I stood there, panting behind that closed door—that door that I could not lock. I should have yelled and raised the household, but I was too scared to reason. It seemed to me that safety lay in silence, and at the moment I was much more interested in my own safety than in tracking down the murderer.

Straining my ears against the door, I listened. Not a sound. Then I heard the telltale creak of a floorboard. And then I bit my fist hard to keep from screaming. For someone had stopped just outside my door. Through thick wooden panels I could hear the quick breathing of the person who stood there.

Was he listening for my next move? Or was he considering entry, with the idea of silencing me forever? He could not be sure, of course, that I had failed to recognize him. Not once while I stood with my ear pressed against that door, paralyzed with fright, did I think of the person on the other side as David Scott; and certainly not as Homer or Cousin Beau or Josh. Conceivably I could have opened the door to face someone I knew. I thought of that person only as the murderer—someone strange and terrible.

How long I stood there, I do not know, but gradually I began to realize that there was only silence on the other side of the door— silence so complete that I began to doubt my own ears. Surely no one could have moved away so quietly.

I couldn't just have imagined it all, I told myself. Even now the murderer might be lurking in that dark hall, waiting for me to take some foolish step. But I was still too frightened to risk venturing out again. Stealthily, I replaced the chair under my doorknob, bringing up the slipper chair as an added barricade. Dragging the chaise longue to a position well behind the door and arming myself with the brass poker from the fireplace, I sat down, weak with reaction.

I couldn't just have imagined it all, I told myself again. But I had to admit that it was cut to a pattern and that, nerves already shaken, my mind would have been a perfect receiving set. Pat's admonition to lock the door. That legend of a ghost on the stair. The noise overhead.

But things were carelessly piled in the attic. Something might have worked loose. As to the rest of it—well, old houses were full of sounds. Trying to reason it all out and to reassure myself at the same time, I was brought to my feet, every nerve suddenly taut, by a hideous scream. It was so much like Sylvia's fateful last scream that for a moment I thought I might have dropped off to sleep and in a dream was reliving that horror of the cemetery.

But this time the screams continued, and I could hear running footsteps in the hall and exclamations. In my haste to learn what was happening, I forgot all about the elaborate defense system in front of the door, until I ran afoul of the slipper chair.

Still groggy after extricating myself, I bumped into Pat's familiar fragrance in the hall. The lights were on, and the excitement centered in Cynthia's room. We found the men already there, clustered about the bed and looking befuddled as well as disheveled.

Cynthia was sitting up against the pillows, the white lace of her silk nightgown slipping from one shoulder. In the dim light of the bedside lamp she was wild-eyed and pale. David Scott at the head of the bed was making futile efforts to soothe her; her screams had stopped, but she kept up an unintelligible moaning. Then I realized what she was saying: "Catch him! Don't let him get away."

Pat, inclining her head toward Cynthia, framed the words with her lips, "Just a recurring nightmare." Anyway, if Cynthia meant David Scott, couldn't she see him standing there? Looking at Pat in her pale rose satin housecoat, hair smoothly tied back with a rose-colored ribbon, I wondered what my own appearance was and discovered with some surprise that I was still gripping the poker.

Cousin Chattie came in, pulling about her plump figure a rumpled white silk kimono embroidered in huge blue peacocks. Babbling of smelling salts and aromatic ammonia, she was almost as incoherent as Cynthia; but Josh got the idea and dashed out, returning a little later with brandy. Some of it spilled on the sheet as Cynthia gulped a small swallow. Looking from one to another, she made a visible effort for calmness.

"There was somebody in there," she declared. "I heard him."

"In where?" squeaked Cousin Chattie, glancing apprehensively over her shoulder.

Cynthia pointed to the bathroom door connecting her room with Sylvia's, and Cousin Chattie shrank back against the bed as the men made a dive. Pat and I followed, and what we saw brought us up short just inside the door.

Wild disorder was everywhere. Bureau drawers were open, and their contents churned upside down. Hatboxes and bags had been dragged from the closet. The covers had been torn from the bed and left in a heap on the floor.

I tried to tell about the noise I had heard in the attic, but nobody would listen because the men, now as excited as Cynthia, were all over the place. Nobody stopped to think that there had been ample time for a getaway. "I'll take the lower floor," Homer yelled as he flung himself down the stairs.

"Where's Beau?" Cousin Chattie shrieked. And then we realized Cousin Beau had been absent during the entire hullabaloo. "I can't bear it," she sobbed as Josh and I followed her to Cousin Beau's room. "I know he's been killed."

Josh turned on the light, and there was Cousin Beau, lying peacefully in bed. His eyes blinked open as the light shone on them.

"What's the matter?" he asked, sleep apparently having wiped out all memory of the murder. Although polite, he still managed to convey the idea that he expected an explanation of this invasion of his privacy.

Cousin Chattie gulped with relief, but this did not prevent her demanding, "Beau Richmond, do you mean to say you've slept through all this?" She collapsed in the nearest chair. "Of course you would be sleeping on your good ear. I declare, we could all be murdered in our beds and you would know nothing about it."

Josh and I faded. I for one was not certain which ear Cousin Beau had been sleeping on.

The search continued with more noise than direction. Cousin Chattie came out again in time to protest like any housewife when David Scott turned the linen room upside down, as though anything more dangerous than lavender sachet might be lurking between the sheets and pillowcases. Josh, at the head of the attic stairs, called down that the door was locked from the inside, which automatically made it unnecessary to investigate the third floor.

As I was opening my mouth again to tell about the noise in the attic, something stopped me cold. Could Josh have some reason for avoiding any search of the attic? If there had been fingerprints, they were now obliterated by his own. As he came down the steep stairs, looking unusually tall in his old towel robe, light hair mussed and shoulders minus some of their customary assurance, I thought again of Sylvia Scott's anxiety about that mysterious package.

Could Josh have been hiding this package in the attic when I heard all that racket overhead? Not because he was implicated in Sylvia's murder, but because the package might in some way make it appear so? If that attic prowler was only Josh—exercising legal caution—certainly I should not be the one to give him away. I must have a word with him privately.

While I was thinking all this, and thinking too that nobody showed the least self-consciousness or guilt Cousin Beau appeared. Pajama coat tucked into daytime trousers, bathrobe over all, even his white hair neatly brushed, his dignity seemed impregnable. As we followed him into the wild confusion of Sylvia's room, I caught a glimpse of his face in the mirror of the old Sheraton bureau. For, a moment his guard dropped and there was something that might have been panic in his eyes. Then he turned and, facing us, was himself again. "We'll lock this room until the police come in the morning," he said.

"Maybe Josh or I should spend the rest of the night in there," Homer suggested when we were outside, "just in case—anyone— should come back."

The room, I thought inconsequently, was a perfect picture—a bit on the surrealistic side, perhaps—of what my mind must look like. "Better lock it until morning," Cousin Beau said, dropping the key into his bathrobe pocket.

Josh looked at his wristwatch. "It's nearly four o'clock," he said. "Suppose I sit up for the rest of the night."

"I'll keep you company," offered Homer.

Cousin Beau looked doubtful for a moment. "All right," he agreed finally. "Better have Woodrow give you some coffee."

Pat and I each offered to spend the rest of the night on the chaise longue in Cynthia's room, but she said this would only make her nervous. And, anyway, if the men were doing sentry duty, what would be the use?

Which seemed to apply to my own case as well. Suddenly feeling all in, I went back to my room and almost fell into bed. In a few hours at most, I would have a talk with Josh. If he had not been in the attic, I would go straight to the police about that misadventure in the dark hallway.

The rain had stopped, and light was seeping in through the blinds. The house was quiet as though nothing had ever happened to break its peaceful serenity. Outside there was the early morning chatter of birds. It would be a hot day, but this big, high-ceilinged room was cool and sweet with the fragrance of magnolias blossoming below the windows. Drowsiness crept over me even as I told myself I would not sleep.

I did not hear the opening of my door.

VI

My room was shadowy with half-light, for it was morning outside when I went back to bed, even though the house appeared to be wrapped in the dark silence which is only sleep. And like that half-light, I myself lay suspended between sleeping and waking, in a vague, shadowy land where fact and phantasy meet and merge in dream.

At least, I thought it was a dream—for I could not rouse myself or seem to break the lethargy that bound me. I could only watch with fascinated horror. The white panels of the door seemed to be moving inward. It was very strange, because I had not seen the doorknob turn. But slowly and silently that door was opening a little way, as though whoever or whatever stood outside was waiting to make sure I was asleep.

"But I am asleep," I told myself. "Tomorrow you will see. Tomorrow—"

Was it shadow or substance, that dark blob moving against the white wall just beyond the crack of the partly opened door? What could it be? It looked like a huge spider, but no spider was as large as that.

Then I realized that it was a hand. A gloved hand, holding something long and pointed like a blade. For a moment the blade was suspended there and then the hand was empty.

The dark blob that had become a gloved hand became a blob again and was no longer a pattern against the white wall, but only a shadow. And then the shadow was gone. The shadow was gone,

because everything was dark—dark like falling into a pit. Only there
was no bottom to the pit and no light anywhere.

Slowly the outlines of my room began to take form as the black-
out faded and the profound relief of returning consciousness swept
over me. I could hear Gin and Bitters yapping downstairs and a
car door closing, followed by strange, masculine voices. Who could
be about at this unholy hour? I looked at my watch and saw that a
long time must have elapsed since that vision of a hand moving
along the wall just inside my door, for it was now nine o'clock.

Dreams are strange things. Although I had been sure I saw my
door opening, I had not seen it close. But it was closed now. Just
beyond the door and directly below the spot where I thought I had
seen that hand against the wall was the chair which I had failed to
replace under the doorknob. On the chair lay my green house coat,
dropped there carelessly when I came back after helping to turn
the house upside down in search of that visitor to Sylvia's room. I
remembered now, I hadn't replaced the chair because both Homer
and Josh were on patrol duty.

Opening the blinds, I saw that it was a wonderful day for lounging on the beach and getting a real swim before lunch. But all that
was out, of course. What did one wear when facing the police, I
wondered. This white linen play suit would have to do, with skirt
over the shorts, of course. But no stockings—not even for the police—not with such a good tan.

I picked up my house coat and something clattered to the floor.

At first I was not sure what it was. It looked like a long blade
without a handle. Then I realized that it was the sheath of a dagger. Of the dagger. The dagger that had killed Sylvia. That delicate
trefoil design was unmistakable. My heart pounded under the lace
of my thin silk nightgown.

The dagger sheath lay on the floor like a live thing, threatening
me. How had it got into my room? Why had the murderer put it
there? Because he thought I recognized him on the stairs? Was this
a warning? Or could it be an attempt to divert suspicion my way?
Of course, it might be only that he had thrust the dagger sheath

into the first convenient unlocked door in order to get rid of it—
but I was too upset to find much relief in that supposition.

And I had not the faintest notion who had planted this incriminating evidence in my room. There would be no fingerprints, of
course, for the murderer had worn a glove.

Gloves. Where was that glove that had looked so much like a
huge spider against the wall? I picked up my housecoat and shook
it. There was no glove. Then I moved the chair and drew back involuntarily. There on the polished floor, just beyond the edge of
the old Persian rug, lay a glove. Not just an ordinary glove, but a
worn, discolored old cotton glove, such as Cousin Chattie wore
when gardening.

Cousin Chattie? But that was impossible.

Somebody tapped on my door and turned the knob. Before I
could do more than replace the chair, the door opened and Pat came
in, almost too fresh and bright in a rose dust chambray tennis dress.

"Why, Ann, what's the matter?" she asked.

"Why—" I began.

"Isn't that tub about to run over?" she interrupted, with a glance
toward the bathroom.

"Gosh!" I said, and made a dash for it.

"Well, hurry up," she called after me. "I'll be downstairs, waiting to have breakfast with you. The police are already here, I think."
And the door closed behind her. Evidently she had not seen the
gold sheath lying on the floor.

Carefully picking up glove and sheath with a handkerchief, I
wrapped them in a piece of tissue paper and laid them on the bedside table. I must take them to the police immediately, I told myself, nervously spilling twice enough of my pet bath salts into the
tub. And I must lose no time in broadcasting the fact that I had
not recognized the person who stood on the attic stairs—that I was
still completely in the dark as to his or her identity. Her? But I
could not suspect Cousin Chattie or Pat. Cynthia, of course, was out.
That was the whole trouble. I could not really suspect anyone. David
Scott might have killed Sylvia, but why would he be prowling in the

attic? Aside from Josh, the rest of us had not even known Sylvia very well.

Ready at last to go downstairs, I resolutely picked up the tissue-wrapped package from the table. But with my hand on the doorknob I hesitated. The police had been pretty stupid about Homer. Suppose they tried to make something out of my possession of the dagger sheath and glove. Suppose they decided I was an accessory, shielding someone. It was too much to hope that they would not find out about Josh's—interest in Sylvia. Suppose they tried to break me down—made me tell about that package she discussed with him over long distance. What would they make of it all?

For a long moment I stood there, trying to reason things out. Fear and doubt can conjure up so many possibilities. I knew Josh could not be guilty of murder, but his affair with Sylvia might implicate him in some way. People went to the electric chair because of circumstantial evidence. I must talk to him. Afterward I could see my way more clearly. Meantime, I would put this incriminating evidence out of sight.

Standing on a chair, I shoved the sheath and glove far back on the top shelf of the clothes closet. As I opened the door into the hall I felt as though eyes were watching me from that closet.

Yes, the police were in the library, Woodrow told me when I joined Pat at the long refectory table on the porch outside the dining room. They had already talked to David Scott, who could be seen nervously pacing up and down near the boat landing, lighting one cigarette after another, taking a puff or two, then flipping it into the water. Cousin Beau was with the police at the moment.

The dining room adjoins the library, and now and then we caught snatches of conversation. The words sounded strange in that peaceful setting, with the green marshes in the distance and the river glinting in the sun off the point: "Dagger. How'd anybody get hold of such a weapon?" demanded a belligerent masculine voice.

Woodrow was at my elbow. "Mama say she's fixin' y'all's waffles right now. She say you got to eat to keep your stren'th up."

It was a surprise to find that I could really swallow food, for I had not needed the police to remind me of the dagger. Not with its sheath lying on my closet shelf.

Cousin Beau came out, looking harassed but still very aloof and dignified. Absently greeting Pat and me, he sent Woodrow up to wake Josh and Homer. "Can't help it if they haven't had much sleep," he said. "Police want everybody in the library as soon as possible."

He stood gazing out at the river, which I had a feeling he did not see at all. Then he turned to me. "Ann, I've got a job for you. Chief—er—Lindsey wishes to talk to Mrs. Harrison—Cynthia. See if she can come down, won't you?"

"I'll take up her coffee," I said.

Cynthia did not answer my knock, nor was she in the bathroom. I found her finally in Sylvia's room, still in her silk and lace nightgown, with a pair of white linen play shoes in her hand. She stood there, brooding over them, with an odd expression on her face.

She looked startled at my entrance. "I—I was trying to see if anything had been taken," she said, brushing the dark hair back from her forehead and glancing around the disordered room with eyes which this morning had a haunted look.

"But what could have been taken?"

Cynthia gave her head a quick, impatient jerk and opened her mouth as though to say something, then smiled wanly and made a hopeless little gesture with her free hand.

She could not possibly see the police, she told me. "When I think about last night—" Her voice broke and her dark eyes filled with tears.

She still had the play shoes in her hand as I guided her back to bed. I took them from her and put them in the closet.

Cynthia drank her coffee black, forcing it down as one would medicine, and refused fruit or toast.

"About the police," I said, removing the tray. "I'm afraid—"

"All right," she agreed reluctantly, "I suppose it will have to be done some time. Tell them they can come up a little later. After all, there are a good many things I should tell them."

"Then you still think—" I began, remembering her accusation of David Scott.

She looked at me as though trying to bring her mind back from some far-off place. "Dave? Oh, yes! But there are other things that might—" Her voice trailed off.

"Other things?" I repeated.

"Things I did not think of last night," she said vaguely. "Things that might throw light, you know."

I managed not to drop the tray. "You mean—somebody else?"

"Who knows?" she said listlessly, closing her eyes and lying back on the pillows, as still as—as Sylvia would always be. Shock, David Scott had said. Well, twins are supposed to be very close. And if, as seemed to be the case, Cynthia had tried to give moral support to a twin undoubtedly weaker in character, this would naturally make the shock all the more severe.

As I closed Cynthia's door behind me, Viola, the upstairs maid, was just coming out of Pat's room. "Tell Mr. Beau he can see Miss Cynthia as soon as you've put her room to rights," I said.

Dashing around to Josh's room, I found it empty. Obviously he had just gone down to breakfast. Homer would be there too, of course, with Woodrow in the background. No chance at the moment for any private conversation. Back in the main hall, I paused at the attic stairway, my mind pulling me first one way and then another.

If I could only be sure it wasn't Josh who had made that trip to the attic in an effort to conceal Sylvia's mysterious package! Of course, if it was the murderer— I glanced around uneasily. Anyway, something had happened in the attic last night. For Josh's protection I should try to find out whatever I could before the police went tramping over everything. With a final glance around the hall, I hurried up the steep stairs.

Because of the tall trees outside, little light finds its way through the low windows; but I had played in the attic as a child and knew my way about among the broken-down furniture, old trunks and bandboxes and the accumulated cast-offs of several generations.

On the attic floor, just above my room, stood a huge porcelain vase. Although the outside was very dusty, there was no dust inside. Then I noticed the cover of the vase lying on top of an old mahogany chest of drawers. The cover was dusty too, but smudged from handling. Obviously someone had removed it recently from the vase. But that was as far as I could get with my deductions.

The vase was empty. So were the drawers of the chest. With no idea of the size or kind of package I sought, it was difficult to know where to look. Everything was thickly coated with dust. Last night's visitor had probably bumped into that walnut whatnot, now tilted drunkenly amid a clutter of small bric-a-brac upset from the shelves. It would be like Cousin Chattie to have the whole thing transported upstairs "as is."

I had almost given up my search when I heard cautious footsteps ascending the stair.

I looked around for some means of escape though I knew there was none. But with the police in the house, I told myself, there was no real reason why I should not boldly meet anyone who might be on those steps. This thought reassured me somewhat, gave me courage for what I did next. Behind me was an old walnut armoire. I stepped inside, leaving the door open a mere crack to enable me to see with out being seen.

The footsteps came on.

Slowly the attic door was pushed open. Then Pat stuck her head inside. She took a further step and stood blinking. "Yoohoo!" she called. "Ann, where are you?"

Opening the armoire door, I stepped down with as much nonchalance as I could muster and suddenly found myself sprawling.

"What on earth are you doing?" Pat asked, helping me to my feet and trying hard not to laugh.

"Just practicing my dancing," I told her bitterly, surveying a long, rusty scratch on my leg.

"But what is that device of the devil you are all tangled up in?"

"Oh, that!" I said and began to laugh helplessly. "That's a hoop skirt."

"The maid said you were here," Pat told me as we examined the odd, graduated coils of wire.

"I've always thought she had eyes in the back of her head. Listen, Pat. Somebody was up here last night and tripped over this thing, just as I did. Whoever it was, also removed the cover from that vase."

Before she could do more than look incredulous, we heard someone else mounting the stairs.

It was almost comic, really. All of Pat's motions were repeated by the new arrival. Head peering in. Eyes blinking in the half-light. Only it was not comic, for this time the visitor was Josh.

"Hey, Ann!" he called, and I breathed again. Then he saw us and his face lit up with a smile, half humorous, half questioning. "Whew!" he whistled. "What a time to go antiquing! Cousin Beau wants to know if Cynthia is ready to—talk. Come on and find out, won't you? I felt some delicacy about breaking into a lady's bedroom, and Cousin Beau's in a tearing hurry."

Josh sauntered nearer, whistling again. "Say, what's the matter with you? Have you and Pat had a fight?" If he had been in the attic last night, he certainly gave no sign of it now.

I was dusty from head to foot and disgusted into the bargain. "You see about Cynthia," I told Pat, as we went downstairs. "I'll have to take another bath and change."

Even with all my hurrying, Woodrow was at the door before I had time to do anything about that package on my closet shelf. "Mr. Beau say they waitin' for you in the lib'ry, Miss Ann."

Of course, there was no key to the closet door. Nothing to do but say a prayer and follow Woodrow.

VII

ALTHOUGH THE LIBRARY is a large room and there was a breeze from the ocean side of the Island, everybody had that sort of restive look that people get at funerals when they wish they could smoke. A short and squarish officer in a too tightly fitted khaki uniform was introduced by Cousin Beau as Chief Lindsey. The Chief gave me a quick appraising look out of narrowed hazel eyes. His perfunctory nod, as he reluctantly followed the other men in rising, said plainly that he saw no sense in all this getting up and sitting down because of a young chit who should have been on hand at the start.

While deferring to Cousin Beau as a member of a family long respected in that section, Glynn County's Chief of Police managed to let us understand that he was not impressed by the background of the crime. Heron Point or Alabaster Alley, Major Richmond's house-party guests or a deep swamp moonshiner were all the same to him. Which is as it should be, perhaps, but a bit of a dose, nonetheless.

I could not help thinking that it was all like something in a badly cast play with the wrong stage setting. There we sat, straight and stiff and still, in the big room with its book-lined walls, its engravings of Confederate heroes, its tattered battle flags. You could not spot the villain, anywhere. You could not even say that this one or that had peered around the wall of the attic stairs last night as the lightning flashed. I felt baffled and queerly exposed.

It could not be true and yet it was true. For here was the Chief of Police, and he expected to convict one of us of murder.

The breeze that stirred the faded maroon damask draperies seemed to stop short just inside the windows as Chief Lindsey swung around in his chair and scowled at David Scott. "Let's be getting on," he snapped. "What about this watch business?" Definitely on the hard-boiled side, he flung the question like a hand grenade.

But David Scott, completely sunk in gloom, did not seem to realize that he was being addressed. While Chief Lindsey waited for him to come out of his coma, Cousin Chattie, regarding the scratch on my leg, asked in a stage whisper, "How did you get that?"

Chief Lindsey swung to attention immediately, transferring his scowl to Cousin Chattie, who remained happily unconscious of the fact. "In the attic"—I tried to frame the words silently.

"Has all this got anything to do with the case?" the Chief asked with elaborate sarcasm, while Cousin Beau shifted in his chair, his hands gripping the sides.

Everybody was looking at me now. "Yes," I said, taking the plunge. "There's something I think I should tell you. Last night—" I paused and glanced around the room.

"Perhaps," Cousin Beau suggested, as though speaking to a child, "it might be just as well to let the Chief conduct the investigation in his own way."

"Let's have no suppression of evidence," barked Chief Lindsey, running a hand over his thin light brown hair. "What did you have to say, Miss—er—"

"Carroll," said Cousin Beau quietly. Far back in his gray eyes a little flame seemed to flicker for a moment.

No room was ever so quiet, and never have I felt myself so uncomfortably the center of attention. "It's about last night," I said again, my voice suddenly weak. I told them about the noise overhead and about going out into the hall.

"But, Ann," Josh broke in, "what a fool thing to do! Suppose—"

"Go on, Miss—er—Carroll," prompted the Chief, shutting him off.

"The storm came up," I said, "and there was a flash of lightning just as somebody poked his head around the wall of the attic stairs—"

The words died in my throat as the breathless quiet was shattered by a sudden crash and the tinkle of broken glass. "Oh, my heavens!" gasped Cousin Chattie.

David Scott, pouring water from the silver pitcher on the heavy Empire table at his side, had dropped a glass which struck the edge of the table. Otherwise it might not have broken on the thick pile of the gray Aubusson carpet, where the water now spread darkly. One look was enough to tell why Cousin Chattie had cried out as though in pain. For instead of the usual silver goblets, someone—probably Viola—had brought out those priceless old Stiegel flip glasses used by Cousin Beau's grandfather when he felt the need of a toddy. Everyone had forgotten me entirely, and all eyes were now focused on David Scott. "So sorry," he muttered, his face flushed.

"It's nothing," Cousin Chattie assured him, recovering quickly. "I—I was startled. It's just that I'm not accustomed to murders. They make me jumpy."

Under Chief Lindsey's disapproving stare, David Scott smiled at her a little grimly.

"All right, Miss Carroll," the Chief came back impatiently.

"But—" I said.

"Don't try to shield anybody," he ordered.

"But I don't know who it was. You see," I insisted, goaded by his incredulous smile, "whoever it was, jerked his head back too quickly."

There was a visible lessening of tension. But was it relief or disappointment I read on the faces around me? Quite patently it was disappointment and something like disgust on Chief Lindsey's face. "But you do know it was a man?" he insisted, squinting at me.

"I—I'm not sure."

The Chief sprawled back in his chair, making no effort to conceal his displeasure. Then he sat up abruptly, took a look around the room, and shot a question. "How many of you men are wearing wristwatches that show the time in the dark?" he asked, evidently reverting to some subject under discussion before I arrived on the scene.

Josh straightened in his chair. "My watch has an illuminated dial," he said.

"Only you and Scott." Chief Lindsey looked from one to the other. "All right, Mrs. Richmond, would you mind comparing them?"

"Why," Cousin Chattie said blankly, "I don't understand."

"Just look at Mr. Scott's and Mr. Carroll's watches and tell me which one was—er—offered you to tell the time by there in the cemetery," he explained, carefully polite.

"Oh," she said, "you mean when we were waiting for— for the ghost?"

He nodded, trying not to seem impatient.

"What's all this?" Josh asked, as he rose and standing by David Scott, pushed back his sleeve and held a sun-tanned wrist for Cousin Chattie's inspection.

Cousin Chattie looked helplessly at Cousin Beau, then forced her distracted gaze to rest on one, then the other of the two watches. "Well," she said, "well, of course, I can't be sure, but I think—"

She leaned back abruptly and closed her eyes. "Oh," she wailed, "it isn't fair to make me do this."

"Mrs. Richmond," Chief Lindsey reminded her shortly, "we're trying to investigate a murder."

"That's what makes it so horrible," she said, glancing appealingly at Cousin Beau, who nodded his head encouragingly. "And I didn't notice especially," she went on. "How was I to know it would be important? And I could be mistaken, you know. But I think—" she pointed to the watch on David Scott's wrist with the dark, silky hair tangled in the leather strap—"yes, I think this is the one."

"Well," Homer broke the waiting silence, "it would certainly be a relief to know what this is all about."

Chief Lindsey gave him a look of frank distaste. "You are sure you are right?" he asked Cousin Chattie, who simply leaned back in her chair, eyes closed, and paid no attention to him.

"Have you got all this?" Chief Lindsey asked his assistant, an overgrown young patrolman, who was busy with notebook and fountain pen. "Last night in the cemetery just before the murder,

Mrs. Richmond asked the time. Mr. Scott says he held out his wrist-watch for her to see, but at the moment she thought it was Mr. Carroll's watch, because Mr. Carroll answered her question by saying it was one minute to twelve."

Apparently the idea back of all this elaborate drama was to establish the relative position of each person in the group at the time of the murder. But thanks to Cousin Chattie's insistence that no one hold on to anyone else, this involved unexpected difficulties. We had stood there in the cemetery, conscious of one another's nearness, just as we should have been now if the room were dark.

But every time anybody came out with the statement that he thought he had been near one person or another, that person always had different ideas about the identity of his neighbors.

It was pretty generally agreed that Cousin Chattie was standing at the head of the group and I near the foot, next to Sylvia. Cousin Chattie's voice, when she asked the time, seemed to have established this idea in everybody's mind. If David Scott was near enough to hold out his watch for Cousin Chattie's inspection, he was accordingly, about as far as possible from Sylvia.

It was almost an alibi.

"It don't stand to reason," Chief Lindsey argued, "that not a single one of you should know anything about what anybody else was doing. You were all right there together when it happened."

"But I've already told you," said Cousin Beau patiently, "it was so dark you couldn't see your hand before your face. And besides, we were all trying to look in the opposite direction. Mrs. Scott was stabbed in the back, you know."

Chief Lindsey's expression plainly said it was too much to believe that any place could be that dark.

Then he tried a new tack. "Of course, you understand," he said, almost persuading us that he could be affable, "we'll have to hold an inquest. The coroner tells me this can be arranged for tomorrow afternoon, but if we can get things cleared up today, it might be possible to excuse anybody who has to get back to his business Monday morning." He looked from one of the men to another, but nobody spoke.

"You probably are not familiar with such things," he went on, "but an inquest is not considered necessary when there is an eye-witness to a murder—aside from the killer, of course." Chief Lindsey paused expectantly, but still nobody said anything.

"All right," he snapped finally, "we'll have to do it the hard way, I guess. Now, Miss Carroll," he swung around at me in that disconcerting manner he had, "you say you were standing next to Mrs. Scott. Were you on her right or her left?"

"Oh—let me see. She fell against me—on my right side."

"That would mean she was standing on your right?" His question was casual, too casual.

"Why, yes! At least, I know she was on my right when she fell." I shivered a little, for it all came back so vividly Sylvia's limp form slumping against me there in the dark.

Chief Lindsey cleared his throat, and some subtle change in the atmosphere told me that I had not been standing in a very good place.

"Oh," I gasped, "you mean you think that I—that the person on her left—oh, but—"

"I would like to remind you, Officer," Josh broke in, and I was surprised at the cold hardness of his voice and eyes, "that there is a small technicality you are forgetting. My sister had nothing to do with this, but you are putting her in the position of a witness required to testify against himself."

"How do you know she had nothing to do with it?" Chief Lindsey pounced.

Josh smiled, but there was no humor in the smile. "Your question comes within the same category," he said coldly. Any other time it would have seemed funny to hear Josh using such language.

"Okay," agreed the Chief grudgingly. "Anyway, we don't expect the murderer to testify against himself. But it's not going to hurt anybody else to tell what they know about this."

His narrowed eyes swept the room; then he said abruptly, "All right, everybody, we'll take a little recess."

David Scott looked up in surprise at the general movement, then absently got to his own feet. "Do you suppose I could see Cynthia?" he asked me guardedly.

Before I could reply, Chief Lindsey interrupted. "Miss Carroll, will you kindly remain for a moment?"

Not greatly surprised, I sat down again, thinking he wished to question me about the person I had seen on the stairway.

Josh and Cousin Beau exchanged glances. "I'll stay," said Josh a little grimly.

"Not so fast," Chief Lindsey snapped. "You can't find any technicality against the separate questioning of witnesses."

"All right," Josh agreed calmly, "I'll act as her counsel."

There was a little argument then as to the legality of one suspect defending another. "Where do you get that suspect business, anyway?" Josh demanded, blond head thrust forward, blue eyes like steel. He did not look at all like the gay young man about town who could put debutantes and dowagers alike into a flutter by smiling down at them in that special way he has.

"All right," the Chief yielded. "You say, Miss Carroll," he swung at me, "that you don't know who was on your left. What about making a guess at it? Or is there some reason why you prefer to keep quiet?"

This is part of the technique, I told myself. They try to make you angry, so you'll talk without thinking. I felt my face flushing, but my voice was fairly steady. "I only know that I heard somebody move," I told him. "It startled me. Everything was so quiet. I asked who it was, just in a whisper. But Cousin Chattie shushed me—"

"Which direction did the sound come from?"

"It must have come—from the left. Mrs. Scott and I seem to have been at the end of the line. But somebody could have been on her right, of course. All I heard was a sort of stealthy movement and a crackle like a twig or a leaf breaking underfoot. Then something like a breath drawn in quickly. It seemed to come from behind me, but. that is all I really know. It was just afterward that we saw the ghost, and then Sylvia—Mrs. Scott—screamed. And then everybody was moving around, and if anybody was behind me he could have stepped aside easily enough."

"Do you remember who was nearest to you afterward?"

"I've thought a lot about that," I admitted, "but everybody was moving about, trying to get a light. It was all—very confusing. I just don't know." The Chief leaned back in his chair and, turning his head, muttered something to his assistant. The young patrol-man self-consciously flipped the pages of his notebook, scanned a line, and nodded.

Chief Lindsey sat up again. "I understand," he shot at me, "that you quarreled with Mrs. Scott before her death."

"What?" exclaimed Josh and I together, and I suppose I turned red, white, and blue. So far as I knew, Pat was the only witness to that embarrassing encounter in my room; and surely she would not have told. Even if she had, it was absurd to connect Sylvia's tirade with her death.

"But I didn't quarrel with her," I protested.

"Miss Carroll, you don't deny that you had—words?"

"She—had words," I admitted slowly.

"What do you mean?" Chief Lindsey glowered.

"Mrs. Scott came to my room just after dinner, and—well, I suppose you would say she tried to pick a quarrel. That is she said some very—insulting things."

"I suppose you didn't say anything back?"

"No, I didn't."

Even Josh looked a little incredulous.

"Well," I protested, "there wasn't time really. While she was still talking, someone else came in."

"But it is true that Mrs. Scott accused you of trying to break up—er—a friendship between herself and your brother?"

Josh and I looked at each other, both struggling to present an impassive front. "You might as well tell what happened," he said finally. "Somebody seems to have been spilling more than he knew."

"Yes," I told Chief Lindsey faintly.

"You disapproved of this—friendship?"

"Wait a minute, Lindsey," Josh broke in angrily. "She doesn't have to answer that question."

But the Chief paid no attention. "Miss Carroll," he hammered, "you disapproved of Mrs. Scott's interest in your brother. You

wanted him to marry your rich friend, Miss—Fairchild. On top of
this, Mrs. Scott insulted you by telling you she knew all this." He
paused for his words to sink in, regarding me with half-closed eyes.
"All right, you knew she was at outs with her husband and that his
presence would make him a likely suspect. You knew that everyone had handled the dagger—fingerprints would not matter. You
wanted Mrs. Scott out of the way, and you were standing next to
her when she was killed." He paused again, his eyes boring into
mine. "How do you think all this will add up before a jury?"

Too stunned really to believe I was hearing the things he said,
I just sat there, my cheeks burning, my throat dry.

"Don't be a fool, Lindsey," Josh told him, voice deadly calm.
"You know you have no evidence to support any such charge."

Chief Lindsey swung around in his chair and glared at Josh.
"Evidence," he snarled. "I'll have plenty of evidence before this
investigation is over. Mrs. Scott was killed, wasn't she?"

"Evidence?" I repeated. "Why—" and stopped, realizing Chief
Lindsey would never believe that sheath and glove had been planted
inside my door.

"What were you about to say?" he demanded.

"N-nothing," I stammered. "I just don't see how there could be
evidence of something I didn't do."

Under the barrage of repeated questions, my thoughts raced
backward and forward in a torment of conjecture, from David Scott
to Homer to Cousin Beau to Josh. David Scott was certainly the
logical suspect, in spite of any near alibi. Homer? That business of
the etchings had obviously been staged by Sylvia for ulterior reasons, either to embarrass me or to confuse her husband, in case he
suspected an interest in Josh. No, it could not be Homer. Cousin
Beau? Josh? Oh, no!

Finally Josh rose to his feet. "Even you," he told Chief Lindsey
with a cold blue stare, "should realize you aren't getting anywhere
with this."

Surprisingly, he let us go.

VIII

THE QUESTIONS I WAS SO ANXIOUS TO ASK Josh had to wait. Chief Lindsey's assistant followed us out of the library to summon Pat, and Josh insisted upon sitting in with her as he had with me. Whipped down by that grueling third degree, I still could take in the way Pat looked up at Josh out of those surprisingly blue eyes and the little gesture of appeal as she put out her hand to touch his sleeve when he held the library door open for her.

Apparently Chief Lindsey could think up no valid objection to Josh's plan of acting as counsel for more than one client. Anyway, Josh remained inside. But I had a pretty fair picture of the Chief's expression and the argument that ensued before he gave up. With his threat of "evidence" still ringing unpleasantly in my ears, I started up the stairs, determined now to dispose of that tissue-wrapped sheath and glove on my closet shelf.

"Wait a minute, Ann," Cousin Beau stopped me, probably thinking I was headed for a good cry—and not so far wrong at that. "Don't get upset. They've got to question everybody." He patted me on the shoulder and, though his glance shifted, his eyes were full of kindly concern.

"But—but that policeman practically accused me of the murder," I choked. "Why can't he see that it must have been Mr. Scott? I told you about that fuss he had with his wife."

"Scott admits all that," said Cousin Beau. "It seems that Sylvia refused him a divorce except for a cash settlement that would bankrupt him—"

92

"Then why?" I broke in.

"Lindsey says Scott claims to have evidence that gave him reason to believe Sylvia might accept a more—equitable settlement.
Says Scott was giving her a chance to talk things over. He'd had a
detective watching her."

"You mean on account of another man?" I looked up at him
dumbly. "Was—that why you wanted Josh to stay away?"

"How did I know Scott would come barging down here?" Instant regret at having admitted the fact shone in Cousin Beau's
eyes, for his telephone call was still unexplained. Taking refuge in
a quick change of subject, he frowned at me. "Look here, Ann, I
don't want you running around in dark halls at night. Don't you
realize what a chance you took?" He continued to gaze at me sternly
for a moment, then his expression softened. "Come along, we must
phone your mother. She'll be hearing about all this on the radio."

It was a pretty long conversation. Cousin Beau talked first, and
when I finally got away from Mother's various injunctions, he was
nowhere in sight. But Homer was.

"You need a little air," he told me solicitously.

"Wait until I get a fresh handkerchief," I said, using the first
excuse that came to mind.

But Viola was in my bedroom, flinging sheets and pillowcases
about. Impossible for me to go rummaging on closet shelves until
she finished. Anyway, the police would be busy with their questioning for some time yet. Nonetheless, I went back downstairs with
reluctant feet.

Homer and I strolled toward the pier, where for a moment we
joined in the watching silence of a great blue heron that stood
motionless in the shallow water, waiting for some unfortunate fish
to swim his way. Just so the murderer had waited in the cemetery,
I thought, as the heron's long neck shot out and downward in the
swoop that spelled success. The great bird, turning, gave us a wary
glance, flapped its wings, rose upward, and sailed gracefully away.

"Too bad we can't fly out of this as easily," I said.

"It's a God-awful mess," Homer agreed. "I hope they don't try
to hold us after the inquest. I've got a lot of things to do at the

office. And Wednesday night I'm supposed to dine with the Wiltons."

"Oh, Homer! Those awful Wiltons?"

"What you never seem to understand," he told me a little impatiently, "is that some things have to be done for business reasons. Besides, there's the Grahams' cocktail party Wednesday afternoon for Lord and Lady Heyward, who are over here on this good-will tour."

Homer rolled the titles around on his tongue lovingly, apparently forgetting all about the murder. I remembered his excitement the first time he saw inside the huge Graham estate at a football breakfast given for me just after my debut. He would never get over it if the murder caused him to miss Wednesday's party. And the irony of it all was that he had come near calling off his trip to the Island this weekend because of trouble with his plane.

Feeling pretty sorry for myself, I said, just to jar him a little, "Did you know the police are trying to—pin this murder on me?"

Homer took his hands out of the pockets of his blue slacks and gazed down at me incredulously. "Y-you?" he stuttered. "But, Ann, that's crazy. They—they can't— We'll do something," he assured me, giving my arm a little squeeze. "And listen, Ann, I want you to promise me something—" He paused and looked down at me anxiously.

"What?" I asked uncertainly.

"This business of trying to track down the—murderer last night. Promise you won't do anything foolish like that again. Call on me if you need help, won't you?"

"But that's what I was doing—trying to call Josh, I mean."

"Well, don't take any more chances. Better for the murderer to get away than for anything to happen to you."

First Josh, then Cousin Beau, and now Homer—all warning me to be careful. If only one person had shown some concern, it might have meant something—might have meant that he wanted to make sure he had not been recognized in that lightning flash—and that his concern was really for his own safety.

"You're sweet, Homer," I said.

"I just want to take care of you," he smiled, as I led the way back toward the house.

Sounds of an argument made us pause. Cousin Beau, trying to cope with the press and still maintain his dignity, was not making much progress in either direction.

"Now, what's this house got to do with it?" he inquired with wasted sarcasm. "You can get all the pictures you want at the cemetery. The Wesley Oak is very historic—"

"Oh, Lord," Homer groaned, "the newspapers! What will everybody say?"

Since I was wondering the same thing, I should not have held Homer's remark against him. But he did manage some how to convey the impression that such things do not happen in the better house parties, and that Sylvia's murder was less important than his own convenience.

"Let's get away from here," he said as he grabbed me by the arm. Diving behind the tall clumps of box and skirting the oleander trees, we hurried toward Cousin Chattie's wild garden, the most isolated spot on the Point. As we rounded the oleander hedge, we both stopped short just in time to avoid tumbling into a chasm at our feet.

"Great Gosh!" gasped Homer. "What's this?"

It was an excavation more than six feet long, about four feet wide and several feet deep. Obviously this was the so-called grave we had heard about. As Homer and I surveyed it from this angle and that, we noticed that it was a little wider at one end than at the other. "But," Homer asked, "if it isn't a grave, what is it? And if it is a grave, why?"

The queer pit was so near the oleander hedge that roots of the trees were exposed. Rain the night before had left the earth a little soft, although today was dry and warm. The spot was shaded, but here and there the sun sifted through. One slanting ray fell across the grave, and as we gazed downward something caught my eye and I drew back with a little exclamation of surprise.

What I saw appeared to be a very large drop of blood, glistening at the bottom of that mysterious grave.

"Homer," I gasped, pointing, "do you see—"

Homer looked and then looked back at me. "Can't be blood," he argued, his eyes bulging.

"Looks like Josh was right," I said, managing a shaky laugh.

"How do you mean, right?"

"Oh, you know how Cousin Chattie is always so sure she's going to have an extra man at her house parties and always ends up short as she did this time. Well, when Josh heard about this—grave, he said maybe Dracula was coming and had sent his bed ahead of him, so he'd have a place to disappear into when daylight came. Of course," I babbled, Homer's blank stare reminding me that he always took everything literally, "I know nobody believes in vampires. But last night just before dinner—"

Some slight impression of movement caused me to look up, and I stopped, petrified, all my strained flippancy gone, my spine prickling. There on the other side of the grave, staring at me through a gap in the oleander hedge, was a face—the face of that strange visitor who had rung the doorbell last night and then disappeared into the darkness. His eyes held mine with that same odd, penetrating stare, and though I could see little more than his head and shoulders he still seemed to be garbed in loose, funereal black.

"Ouch!" Homer protested, as I dug the fingers of both hands into his arm and struggled to speak.

"Hold it," commented a gay voice from the opposite direction, and Homer and I snapped to attention just in time to have a photographer's flash bulb plop in our faces.

"Just the proper expression of fright," grinned the young man who followed his camera into the open, hat on the back on his red head.

Dazed and blinking, I wheeled again toward the gap in the oleander hedge. It was empty. But the person who had stood there only a minute before could not be far away. "Homer, hurry," I cried, grabbing his arm, frantically trying to drag him after me.

Mistaking my appeal as a protest against the picture just snapped, Homer lunged for the camera. "You can't do that," he growled.

But the red-headed young man was too quick. Leaping to one side, he teetered on the edge of the grave, lost his balance, and went overboard, landing on his feet like a cat, camera still in hand. Sheer surprise at this unexpected turn held me in my tracks as he stooped to reclaim his hat which had fallen to the ground.

"Great jumping polecats!" He whistled. "What's this?"

Then he laughed aloud and climbed out of the grave on the farther side, holding something in his free hand. "The mystery of the missing red fingernail," he announced derisively.

Across the chasm he extended it for us to see. A woman's fingernail, nearly half an inch of it, lacquered with blood-red polish.

"Suppose I'll have to turn it in as evidence," our visitor remarked cheerfully. "Might be a clue, you know. Trouble is, the police never do appreciate intelligent cooperation." He took another look at the pit yawning below him. "What's all this, anyway? A grave for the corpse?"

Only half hearing, I dragged Homer around the oleander hedge. "There was a man here," I whispered. "I saw him. Come on let's catch him."

"Well, for Pete's sake," Homer protested, "I thought you wanted to get away from photographers. The woods are probably full of them."

"But it wasn't a photographer," I told him desperately. "It was that—that man who rang the bell last night. That man in black. Hurry—hurry."

"Now, Ann," Homer began. Then, realizing that I was in no state to be reasoned with, he gave up. "All right, let's find him." But we didn't. For one thing, he had a head start on us. For another, the wild garden beyond the oleander hedge is a jungle.

Out of breath and with nothing but a few scratches to show for our trouble, we turned back. Homer tried to be a good sport, though I knew he hated getting hot and mussed. "Seems to me you're seeing an awful lot lately," he grinned. "Sure you haven't had a touch of sun?" Then he stopped dead still and his eyes grew speculative. "Say, you don't suppose that—whoever you saw on the attic stairs could be the same person you saw just now?"

I shook my head. "The man at the door last night and the man I saw just now were the same. I'm sure of that. I don't know about the other."

As we trudged along, I had a queer feeling that the face I had seen through the gap in the oleander hedge was still peering at me from some safe hiding place in the all-encompassing green. We came to the grave again, and I glanced at the opening in the hedge. It was empty, of course.

"I don't suppose that fingernail could be a clue," I said. "Even if it was Sylvia's, what could it prove? Besides, she struck me as the sort of gardener who would let somebody else do the digging."

Homer kicked a clod of loose dirt into the excavation, frowning at his discolored white shoe. "I wonder. Didn't Blackbeard bury a lot of loot on one of these islands? You don't suppose Sylvia was after treasure, do you?"

"Maybe that would account for her interest in wild flowers," I agreed. "She'd heard Cousin Beau talking about the Lost Gordonia—a plant, you know. He's got a lot of old papers and maps and things. But wouldn't Blackbeard have buried his stuff on Blackbeard's Island?"

"Seems more likely," Homer agreed morosely. "But, look, Ann, have you thought about this?" His brown eyes were popping. "Sylvia found this grave and, the next thing anybody knows, she's dead."

I hadn't thought of it, and I didn't like to think of it now.

The moment we were in the house, I went on a still hunt for Josh. "He's in the library," Cousin Beau told me, gravely pushing forward a chair. "You see—"

He hesitated, and something about his manner unnerved me suddenly.

"What is it?" I cried.

"The police," Cousin Beau's voice was a little thick, "have a letter Josh wrote Sylvia."

"But what does it say?" I tried to keep my own voice steady.

Cousin Beau shook his handsome white head. "They won't let anybody see it. But—Lindsey says it's incriminating evidence."

IX

INCRIMINATING EVIDENCE. Lindsey had made good his threat.

"Now, now," Cousin Beau put out a hand as I started for the library. "They won't let you in. Anyway, there's nothing you can do. I've just talked to Reuben Allen on the telephone, and he's ready to fly down from Atlanta the moment we think it's necessary."

I didn't know much about such things, but I had heard Josh say Mr. Allen is the best criminal lawyer in the South. Cousin Beau would never have called him unless— I couldn't bear to think of it. And I couldn't bear to think of Josh on the other side of the library door, his sun-tanned face a mask—Chief Lindsey hurling the same questions over and over. Could it have been Josh in Sylvia's room last night, searching for this letter when Cynthia sounded the alarm? He would realize, of course, that what he had written would look different after Sylvia's death.

How had the police found the letter? Had they searched the place while Homer and I were on that wild-goose chase in the garden? Surely they had not known of any such letter when they questioned me. If the police were ranging over the house, they might have visited my room.

Weak-kneed, I climbed the stairs.

But the package containing the dagger sheath and glove was still on my closet shelf. Something to burn your hand if you thought about it, but quite innocuous-looking in its tissue-paper wrapping.

Where to hide it? That did not matter much, of course. All along, the problem had been to get rid of it without being seen. Safely out of my hands, nobody could prove the dagger sheath and glove had ever been in my possession.

Taking a bright scarf that I sometimes used to tie over my hair, I draped it across my arm, neatly concealing the package. But all the way downstairs, I felt as self-conscious as though I were smuggling a body. Pausing until the wide, central hallway was comparatively clear, I made for the powder room, holding myself down to a normal walk. As I passed the telephone closet, Homer was saying in just the proper voice to some interested or curious caller: "Yes, the police seem to be as much in the dark as the rest of us. . . . Yes, I'll tell Major and Mrs. Richmond you phoned."

Then I was safely in the powder room, and the door shut. With a sigh of relief I opened the drawer of the dressing table and dumped sheath and glove inside, using my handkerchief to shove them back as far as they would go. The tissue wrapping I dropped into the waste basket.

Josh was a little haggard-looking when he came out after that long inquisition, but he straightened his shoulders and tried hard for a grin when he saw my scared face.

"I want to speak to you a minute," I told him.

"Let's skip it," he said, as I followed him to the far end of the hall.

Father's faint arrogance and Mother's gayety, their individual armor against a too-prying world, were combined in Josh's casual charm to mask a deep, sensitive pride. I found it difficult to rush in where even Mother feared to tread.

"That letter?" I faltered. "It—it isn't anything—is it?"

His fingers shook slightly as he lit a cigarette. "It's not anything for you to bother about," he said firmly.

"The police seem to be bothering about it."

"All right." Josh bit the words out. "Say I was in love with her. Say I was jealous of her husband. Say I killed her because she would not divorce him and marry me. That's what that dumb policeman is saying, if you must know. The fact that Sylvia would not marry anybody who wasn't lousy with money would never get through his thick head."

"But is David Scott rich?"

"Not rich enough to fork over a hundred thousand in cold cash in times like these. That's what she wanted."

"What was in the letter, Josh?" I forced myself to ask.

He looked down at me as though goaded almost beyond endurance. "The hell of it is," he said, "whether you believe it or not, I was trying to sign off with Sylvia."

"W-what?" I could only gasp my relief.

"Oh, God," he groaned, "it all sounds so silly now. Just because I wanted to get loose, she tried to hold me. Honestly, Ann"—his blue eyes were tortured—"that's the way it was. You—you wouldn't understand. But I'd told her I was through—that I wouldn't see her this weekend. To clinch things I said you and Pat would be here and that Homer and I were expected to—be with you. So she wangled this invitation from Cousin Chat and dropped me a note when she got here, just to show how clever she was. It burned me up, and I wrote her and—"

Josh turned on his heel and gazed at one of the old maps on the wall. "Let's—skip it," he said.

"Listen," I told him desperately, "I'm going crazy with all the wild things that are happening and nobody telling me anything. Cousin Beau won't talk. You won't talk. What's the matter with you? I'm your sister. Remember?"

"Swell brother, I am, getting you into all this!" Josh's smile was not on quite straight, and in his deep blue eyes was the same look they'd had when I broke my arm at the age of five and he felt so badly because there was nothing he could do to help. "What do you mean, Cousin Beau won't talk?" he asked.

Josh was apparently just as mystified as I when I told him about Cousin Beau's telephone call. "I suppose he didn't want us to come because Syl was here. Old busybody had already had me on the carpet about her." He pulled out a crumpled pack of cigarettes and extended it toward me. "Haven't seen anything of my cigarette case, have you?"

"You probably left it at home. No," I remembered, "you had it there at the garage. It was empty. That's why you went to buy cigarettes."

"Then I must have left it—" He broke off and did some elaborate fumbling for matches.

"Well, anyway, even if it's lost, somebody will return it," I said. "It has your name on it."

"Yes." His smile was still a little askew. "Joshua Richmond Carroll, III. No mistaking that."

"Josh," I plunged, "where did you go yesterday? There must have been some reason for leaving Pat and me at the garage to get here the best way we could."

"Well, for heaven's sake," he asked irritably, "how did I know the car would have to be left? And, anyway, what was to keep you from phoning Woodrow to come for you?" The words made sense, but his tone was evasive. Besides, as I had said before, it wasn't like Josh.

The lunch gong sounded, and there was no fooling myself, Josh looked genuinely relieved. But, I noticed when we were all at the table, he ate little.

A fingerprint man came out in the afternoon and put us all, even Cynthia, through his inky routine. He and Chief Lindsey prowled in the attic and in Sylvia's room and scared Cousin Chattie out of both her nap and her wits when they got into her room by mistake. At her insistence, the fingerprint man also spent some time in the blue drawing room, making elaborate tests, though what she expected these to reveal was not clear. An animal might have left tracks on the ground, but not on a heavy Aubusson carpet. Supposing, of course, Cousin Chattie had really seen anything of the kind. Any moment I expected Chief Lindsey to invade the powder room and come out waving the dagger sheath and glove and bellowing at the top of his voice.

Finally both the Chief's assistant and the fingerprint expert went back to town; but he himself remained, stubbornly determined to wear us down. Pat and I figured Cynthia must have told him about that scene with Sylvia in my room, for he had also questioned Pat on the subject. There was no doubt that Cynthia discovered Josh's letter among Sylvia's things and sent it to Chief Lindsey. After all, we reminded ourselves, the dead woman was Cynthia's twin sister.

Rufus Blair was among Sunday afternoon's many callers, who in spite of battle, murder, and sudden death, were served the same rum punch that has been a tradition at Heron Point for more than a hundred years. "Ask him to stay on to supper," Cousin Chattie told me. Both Cousin Chattie and her white linen frock looked a little wilted, but she was naturally of a cheerful disposition and obviously determined not to give in to nerves. "I like that young man," she added, "but I never saw anybody who could be so polite and so noncommittal. What's he doing down here in summer?"

I had wondered the same thing. In winter the Island takes on a crisper accent, as northern visitors fly south with the birds, but in summer it is full of southern drawl and anything else sticks out like a sore thumb. Well, we should probably never see Rufus Blair again, so it couldn't matter. But as I looked at him across the candle-lit sheen of old mahogany, sitting there so bronzed and broad-shouldered with that something about him that might have been handed down by a pirate great-grandfather, I felt a curious little pang. Cousin Chattie says girls always trust the wrong men, and I suppose it is true. For I felt perfectly certain that we would muddle through this nightmare much more quickly if Rufus would just stick around.

"Like to ask you a question, Blair," Chief Lindsey shot at him unexpectedly, and not only Rufus but the entire table came to attention. "I was just thinking," the Chief went on. "Last night, as you approached the cemetery"—he paused, looked up and down the table, then brought his narrowed hazel eyes back to meet Rufus Blair's dark ones—"before your headlights picked up the tombstones, they must have grazed that big tree where everybody was standing. Did you—happen to catch a glimpse of—anybody?"

Rufus Blair's eyes were thoughtful as he turned the question over in his mind and Chief Lindsey fiddled with his salad fork. The silence around the table was electric. For just at that moment when Rufus Blair's car was approaching the Wesley Oak, somebody had stood ready to plunge a dagger into Sylvia's back—perhaps with arm upraised.

You could feel the loosening of tension as Rufus slowly shook his head. "I wasn't thinking about anything but focusing the head-lights on the tombstones," he said. "It was so dark I was afraid I might miss. If I saw anything else—I wasn't conscious of it."

Much to everybody's relief, Chief Lindsey left soon after sup-per. I had just come out of the telephone closet, having answered the millionth call that day, or so it seemed, when he stopped me there in the back hall and muttered in my ear, "Better lock your door tonight."

"What?" I asked uncertainly.

"Somebody might not have believed what you said—about not recognizing that party on the stairs."

"Oh, well, thank you, but—"

"I suppose you were telling the truth?"

"Of course, but I thought you thought—"

"Maybe you did." He looked down at me shrewdly. "But I'm just telling you in case—" He broke off as Homer, passing through the hall, stopped with a questioning look.

"Thought he might be heckling you," Homer explained as Lindsey stamped out.

Pat had the bright idea that a bridge game might raise general morale, but it could hardly be called a success. Josh got out the cards and Cousin Chattie, usually the most enthusiastic player, half-heartedly took her place at the table. Rufus offered the ex-cuse that he would have to be leaving shortly, and David Scott merely looked blank and shook his head on general principles. Homer was commandeered finally but reneged twice in succession on the first hand. Every now and then we could hear Cousin Chattie inquire plaintively, "What's trumps?" And she jumped like a scared rabbit when Rufus stepped up behind her chair to say good night.

"I think," he told me a few minutes later, "that I'll drive by the cemetery before going to the hotel. I'm certain I didn't see any-thing, but—well, it might bring something back. I'll phone you in the morning."

"I won't sleep a wink, waiting." Yielding to a sudden impulse, I added, "Why can't I come along? Woodrow can follow in the sta-tion wagon and bring me back."

Horrified at the thought of visiting any cemetery after dark and this one in particular, Woodrow rolled his eyes but dutifully prepared to follow. As the headlights cut a thin path before Rufus' car, I myself was not quite so enthusiastic, for the night and the junglelike growth of the Island closed in darkly, weaving a spell that made conversation seem a little forced and voices sound unnatural. I was definitely relieved when we turned into Couper Road and finally reached the concrete highway.

As we approached Christ Church, driving close to the fence along the left-hand side of the road, the trunk of the great tree was outlined for a split second in the headlights' sweep. Surely last night Sylvia must have been visible, too, I thought.

"Look," Rufus said, and I saw again that eerie light moving between the graves beyond the church. Even when you knew beforehand what to expect, it was startling and weird and crazy. One light. Two. Like huge terrible eyes in the dark. Then only one. Then that white figure rising up.

But there was another figure, now. I dug my fingernails into the palms of my hands. I would not believe it.

There was Sylvia. Back from the dead—standing motionless, looking straight at us with wide, staring eyes, her red lips drawn back from her white teeth. There was something animal-like about that fixed stare.

It was incredible and horrible, but there she was. And then she vanished.

I did not know that I had grabbed Rufus' arm until he stopped the car and was climbing out, quite naturally trying to take his arm along with him. "Did you see her?" I whispered, my throat dry.

"I saw something," he agreed grimly, "and I'm going to find out what it was."

"It was Sylvia," I shivered.

"Let's don't go botherin' the dead," Woodrow chattered as he climbed out of the station wagon. Whether he also had seen Sylvia or was simply objecting on general principles did not seem important.

Rufus was rummaging in the glove compartment for his flashlight, swearing under his breath when he failed to find it. "I'm coming with you," I said doggedly. After all, there was no choice. I did not want to go, but I wanted less to remain with Woodrow, already scared half out of his senses.

"All right." Rufus took me reluctantly by the arm. Woodrow stuck so close behind that he stepped on my heels as we made our way into the cemetery, and over to the new graves where the light had appeared.

We could see enough to find our way about, but not enough to distinguish objects more than a foot distant. There was only cold stone where the apparition had appeared and no sign of any figure which once might have been flesh and blood.

But Rufus was bent on being thorough. We stumbled about, falling over graves, getting scratched by briars and stopping breathlessly as a lizard scuttled off in the underbrush.

We tried the door of the church, but it was locked. With Woodrow protesting but still sticking close, we went behind the church to the old graves in their enclosed lots, mosquitoes singing in our ears like the vampires they are.

"I don't like this," I shuddered. "Suppose you find a ghost. What are you going to do about it?"

"I'm not looking for a ghost," said Rufus quietly.

"You mean you think it was the other twin? But she's ill in bed."

"It may not have been the other twin."

"But—"

"Probably just association of ideas," he said a little shortly. "We were thinking about the twin who was killed. But even if it was only somebody hanging around the cemetery, why should she disappear like that? And why should she be here alone at night?"

"I'd rather figure it all out at a distance," I said.

And then Woodrow, just behind me, let out a long shrill shriek. "They got me, Mr. Rufus, they done got me." Scared speechless I could have followed my hair straight upward, but Rufus' voice was calm. "Wait a minute," he told Woodrow, "you might be able to run a little faster when I get your coat loose from this broken spike in the fence."

"All I want," Woodrow told us with chattering teeth, "is to get out o' here alive."

But Rufus had thought of another place to investigate. "That broken-down old vault. Gosh, I wish I had a light of some kind!" he said as we moved forward uncertainly.

Suddenly, in the dark the ruins of the vault loomed before us. If it was Sylvia's ghost we had seen, surely here was its perfect lair. Rufus struck a match and peered in. The pinpoint of light only made the interior darker by contrast. Cautiously he stooped and edged his way inside. Woodrow and I stood tense, waiting.

"I don't see anything," said Rufus, his voice oddly muffled.

Then my blood ran cold. As clearly as I had heard it that first evening at Heron Point, when Sylvia came out on the porch to greet her husband, I now heard her unpleasant mocking laugh.

"'Fo' God, Miss Ann," Woodrow whimpered, "you hear that?"

"Hurry," I told Rufus shakily. "Let's get away from here."

"I thought I heard someone laugh," he said.

X

COMMON SENSE TOLD ME that if I had seen anyone there in the cemetery, it had to be Cynthia.

Her twin was dead, stabbed through the heart. And I did not believe the dead came back to cemeteries or anywhere else. I did not believe in vampires. Well, at least, I did not believe in them now that I was safely back at Heron Point.

But if it was unlikely that Sylvia would revisit the cemetery it was equally unlikely that Cynthia would be haunting the place where only the night before her sister had met such a gruesome death.

Still, I had to know, so I went directly to Cynthia's room. Of course, she would have had a head start on us, leaving the cemetery, for we had stumbled about in the dark as Rufus tried to decide exactly from which direction the sound of that blood curdling laugh had come. And once we were in the car Woodrow had fumbled with the starter, choking and flooding the motor before we were finally on our way back to Heron Point.

When there was no answer to my tap on Cynthia's door, I turned the knob. The door was locked.

"Yes," came a listless voice, as I knocked more loudly, "who is it?"

"It's Ann—Ann Carroll. May I come in?"

"Just a moment."

Cynthia opened the door a mere crack. "What is it?" she asked.

"May I come in?"

She hesitated a moment. "Of course," she smiled, opening the door wide. Cynthia was in nightgown, negligee, and slippers. "I've been trying to get to sleep," she said, as she climbed into the high bed, "but every time I'm about to drop off, somebody knocks on the door."

"Oh, I'm sorry," I told her. "I just—wanted to know how you were feeling."

"Awful." She pulled up the sheet and gave the bellpull a jerk.

"Can I get you something?" I asked, my eyes following her gesture.

"Oh"—smiling wanly—"I don't want anything, really. That was for protection."

"Protection?" I repeated, startled.

Cynthia raised her head from the pillow and looked at me out of great dark eyes, their expression fathomless. "I don't feel very safe in the room with—with anyone."

"But why not, for heaven's sake?"

"After what happened to my sister?" she asked.

"I still don't understand."

"Well"—her smile was ironical—"for one thing, someone might not wish me to appear as a witness. After all, I naturally would be expected to know more about—about who might have a motive."

Viola knocked at the door and came in, and I was not sorry. It seemed to me that Cynthia had been completely unbalanced by her sister's death. "Bring me a glass of lemonade, please," she told Viola.

"Well," I said when the door was closed again, "I'll be on my way. I just wanted to ask how you are and whether there's anything I can do. Oh, I'm sorry," I apologized, "how dumb of me." I had purposely opened the closet door, pretending to mistake it for the door into the hall. A look into the bathroom would have been welcome also, but I could not use the same trick twice. Anyway, everything in the closet was in perfect order—dresses on hangers, shoes in a neat row. As I opened the door into the hall, I almost collided with David Scott. "I want to see Cynthia," he said in some confusion.

"No, no," she called out peremptorily. "Go away. Ann, don't let him in."

"But, Cynthia, I just want to talk to you."

"I've told you there's nothing for us to talk about."

"But, Cynthia, please—"

"If you don't stop annoying me, I'll ask Major Richmond to call the police."

"But, Cynthia, be reasonable. I—"

"Ann Carroll, will you please close my door? Go away, both of you. I'm ill. I can't—"

What else she said, I do not know, for I realized that if I did not close the door David Scott would force his way inside.

As I stood there, facing him, we heard the key turn in the lock. "I'm sorry. She's really ill," I said.

"I know she is," he acknowledged, one nervous hand pulling so hard at his dark hair that I expected to see big tufts come out by the roots. "There isn't anything I wouldn't do for her. Why should she treat me this way? I haven't been able to see her since—" He left the sentence unfinished, shrugging his shoulders helplessly. It seemed reasonable enough that Cynthia should not wish to see the man she believed to be her sister's murderer. The fact that he was in love with Cynthia herself would not make him any more welcome. But naturally I could not say this to David Scott. "Maybe she will feel better tomorrow," I consoled him, starting toward my own door.

"Miss Carroll," he said, close behind me. As I turned, something in his eyes startled me, something so quickly veiled I could not be sure it had been there at all. He shot a quick, darting glance toward the one dim light burning at the farther end of the big hall and moving nearer, lowered his voice almost to a whisper. "That person you saw on the stairs last night? Who was it?"

The tinkle of ice in a glass is always a pleasant sound. This time it was doubly so, for it meant that Viola was coming up the back stairs with that pitcher of lemonade for Cynthia.

"I don't know," I told David Scott, backing away.

"You are sure?" His eyes were fastened on mine as though he would probe through to the truth.

"Quite sure," I said, trying to make my voice sound casual as I motioned Viola toward my own room.

"I kin bring her another," she said, depositing the tray on the bedside table.

"That isn't what I want," I told her. "You must wait until Mr. Scott goes away before you knock on Miss Cynthia's door."

"Yes'm, I know that," said Viola, at once conspiratorial. "She say not to let him git in her room nohow. He done wrote her a note, and she won't even read it. She make me take it right back to him. She say she never want to see him again. She—"

"All right," I cut in. "Listen, Viola, has Miss Cynthia been out of her room this evening?"

Viola's black hand rolled and unrolled the hem of her crisp white apron. "I sho ain't seen her out, Miss Ann."

"You are sure?"

"Yes'm, Miss Ann."

Viola took a cautious peep at the hall. "He done gone," she nodded vigorously, returning for the tray. "You sure you don't want no lemonade, Miss Ann?"

To make a further check on Cynthia's possible activities, I visited both the caretaker's house and the servants' quarters. Apparently no one had seen her leave the place or return.

But Pearl, the cook, had questions of her own.

"What they doin' all that diggin' for?" she demanded. Pearl is part Indian, with bronze skin, high cheekbones, and a lot of natural dignity, but there was an unnatural glitter in her eye as she waited for my answer.

"What digging?" I asked.

"Out in the garden. That there grave. 'Tain't the right place."

No use to ask what she meant. Just be casual. "Where is the right place?"

She gave me a sly smile. "How come you askin' me?"

"Pearl, if you know something, you'd better tell. The police will find out, anyway."

"Let 'em find out," she said, adding darkly, "The law never done colored folks no good yet."

"But you could tell me."

Pearl shook her head. "'Tain't nothin' you need to know, baby."

I used to be a little afraid of Pearl when Josh and I were growing up next door to the old Richmond house before Cousin Beau and Cousin Chattie moved out to what the newspapers call fashionable Pace's Ferry Road. Most of the time she pampered us with gingerbread men and let us scrape the bowls when she made icing for cakes. But she could be stern and forbidding too, and I knew I should get nothing further from her tonight.

Pat was waiting in my room when I got back. She was all ready for bed, her pale rose housecoat over her nightgown.

"Listen, Ann," she said, the words tumbling over one another, her blue eyes almost as dark as their long curling lashes, "I've got the big jitters or I'm going crazy or something. We all thought it was just hysterics when Mrs. Richmond said she saw that big, creeping thing last night, but—"

She paused, looked at me uncertainly, and tried to smile.

"Well," she went on hesitantly, "has anyone ever really seen that ghost in the upstairs hall?"

"Don't tell me you've started seeing things, too," I said. "Anyway, that ghost business was just one of the legends handed down by ante-bellum Negroes. Some of them even believed that certain members of their race rose up in the cotton fields and flew back to Africa. It was just wishful thinking, of course."

"Look," said Pat, pushing back her sleek red-brown hair. "You don't have to do that way. Not with me. I'm twenty-three years old, the same as you are. And I saw her—or it—or whatever it was. Out there in the back hall, where there isn't much light."

Ordinarily Pat is a calm person. That trustee of the Fairchild estate saw to it that she grew up not only with a strong body, but with a mind that could take a fairly literal view of life. If she thought she saw something, she had good reason for it.

"Oh-h!" I inhaled a long deep breath. "So it really was Cynthia at the cemetery. I didn't think she could get in and out without someone seeing her."

It was Pat's turn to ask questions, but she only looked doubtful when I told her about that upsetting vision in the cemetery. "I could have sworn it was one of the twins," I said.

"Well, I was sure it must be Cynthia I saw in the hall," Pat admitted, "because there wasn't anyone else it could be. But Cynthia was in her room."

"You saw her? What time was it?"

"Around ten o'clock. When did you go to the cemetery?"

"About nine. I know, because Rufus said I should be getting some sleep after being awake most of the night before, and I looked at the clock. He's such a self-contained person I wondered if he was really concerned about my welfare or only wanted an excuse to leave. You remember how Cousin Chattie jumped when he came up to the bridge table to say good night?"

"It was like that all evening," Pat agreed wryly. "Nobody could remember what cards had been played. About ten o'clock Mrs. Richmond said she couldn't stand it any longer and asked Major Richmond to go upstairs with her to turn on the light and take a look around the room. I came up with them, but the boys and Mr. Scott decided to stay downstairs and have a highball. Major Richmond told them they'd have to mix it themselves because Woodrow had gone with you."

"The time would be about right," I decided. "Cynthia could have got back from the cemetery by then."

"But she was in her room," Pat insisted. "Major and Mrs. Richmond had just said good night to me, and I was on the way to my room. It's darker toward this end of the hall, you know, and— Well, that's when I saw it."

"Did this—did it look like Cynthia?"

"It was just a figure," Pat shivered, "in some sort of light robe or something. I said, 'Is that you, Cynthia?' But nobody answered— and then—it just melted away—in the opposite direction from Cynthia's door."

"There are the back stairs and the stairs to the attic and that passage to the nursery," I reminded her.

"Yes, I know," Pat nodded her head. "Josh and Homer and I searched them all. But before any of that, I went directly to Cynthia's door and knocked. I—wanted to think it was Cynthia I'd seen. But she answered from the inside. I turned the knob but the door wouldn't open."

"You are sure she was inside the room?"

"Do you think I'm crazy?" Pat demanded. "Of course, I'm sure. She said 'Yes' and 'Who is it?' and sounded cross. Josh says there's only one entrance to Cynthia's room, aside from the one through the bath from Sylvia's room. Nobody could have got to either room without my seeing her."

"No, of course not," I agreed. I remembered that when I had knocked at Cynthia's door just a little while ago she had said "Yes" and "Who is it?" Doubtless she would have admitted Pat also, if Pat had insisted.

"I asked her if she was all right or something of the sort," Pat went on, "and she said 'Yes,' and I told her I was sorry to have disturbed her. Then I flew down the front stairs to the library. No," she repeated stubbornly, "I couldn't be mistaken about that. Cynthia was in her room, all right."

"Pat," I said, "I'm terribly sorry, but just before we came down here, Cousin Beau telephoned and told me to call off the trip. You remember I went back in the house after we were in the car? Well, Mother insisted that he couldn't have any real reason and told me to run along since we had already started and she would call him and say we were on the way. We both had an idea that maybe he just didn't want to be bothered with the redecorating. There couldn't be any real reason, we thought, because Cousin Beau and Cousin Chattie are the most hospitable people in the world. The house is always running over with guests. How on earth could any-body think anything like a murder would happen? And now—all this other— Do you think it could be something staged, just to get rid of us?"

"But what would be the sense in that? The police won't let us leave. And, anyway, nobody knew you were going to the cemetery tonight."

"Look!" I said. "There isn't any key for the lock on my door. How about taking on a roommate?"

"Nothing would suit me better," Pat agreed, and we both laughed a little weakly. We gathered up my night things, and should have been glad of a police escort, complete with sirens, for the few steps from my room to Pat's. Even though you don't believe in ghosts, there are times when a dim hall can look pretty uninviting.

Something had happened to Heron Point. Last night, because of a remark of Rufus Blair's, I had remembered my first glimpse of the place from a boat years before. White columns on a bluff above the river, the broad porches of the house shaded by great oaks hung with those funereal streamers of gray moss. I had never seen Spanish moss, and to my childish eyes it gave Heron Point a slightly sinister look, like something on an island of evil enchantment in a fairy story. But Heron Point had long since become a friendly, familiar place, full of happy memories.

Tonight—it was as though time had turned backward.

XI

"SYLVIA TRICKED DAVID into marrying her," Sylvia's grandmother told me on the way home from the airport.

When it was time to meet the plane Monday morning, David Scott was being put through another third degree by Chief Lindsey and Cousin Beau asked me to take over.

"Mrs. Markham seems to be the only relative Scott thought it necessary to notify," he explained. "Well, I hope she can decide on plans for—moving the body. Can't do anything until after the inquest, of course, and Scott seems uncertain about whether the funeral should be in New York or New Orleans where Mrs. Markham lives. Cynthia's in no shape to decide anything. She's just lying there as though she didn't care whether she ever got up or not. Well," he added heavily, "maybe Mrs. Markham can decide something, but I doubt it. Probably go into hysterics."

But that's just where he was wrong, I thought, as soon as I had a glimpse of Mrs. Markham. She was a cute old lady, plump and pretty, tripping away from the plane in high heels, cool gray silk crepe, and pearls, a small gray hat adorned with moss-pink roses set coquettishly on her neatly coifed white head. "So sad," she murmured, "so sad," and then dismissed it all and devoted the next few minutes to research on the subject of my ancestors. But I didn't mind. It was exactly what my own grandmother would have done. When it was over, we were acquainted and Mrs. Markham approved of me.

Probing as skillfully as any surgeon, she soon had all the details of the crime, at least as far as I could tell her. "Sylvia was my own grandchild," she said at last, shaking her head, "and it's terrible—the murder, I mean. But I wasn't exactly surprised. Sylvia always did say it was a mistake when they let David out of the insane asylum."

"W-what?" I gulped, narrowly missing a stray chicken.

"Naturally"—Mrs. Markham gave me a sidelong glance—"I wouldn't say anything about it, except for the peculiar circumstances. But really it is something of a relief to know David can plead insanity, for I'm sure she drove him to it."

It was fantastic, I thought. Chief Lindsey back at Heron Point, cross-questioning David Scott, who of course, would have all the cunning of the insane. And here, as we drove along this peaceful road, everything green around us, a cardinal flashing off to the right, sun shining hot overhead, the solution of the murder was being dropped into my lap by a prattling old lady.

"Sylvia was her mother all over again," Mrs. Markham told me. "Yes, she was her mother all over again. My son's wife was an actress," she explained, "but a member of a very fine old family—one of the Tennessee Barretts; and I could only hope it would work out. When she and Charles were married, I'd been a widow a good many years. Colonel Markham was so much older." Leaning down, she slipped off one, then the other, of her gray suede pumps. "It's the hot weather," she smiled impishly, sitting back and wriggling her toes.

"Charles was my only child." Mrs. Markham picked up the thread of the conversation as she would her knitting. "He was the sweetest baby and so bright in college. It nearly killed me when he eloped just before he was to graduate." All of the smile and most of the softness were suddenly wiped off as she looked back across the years. "Wilma Barrett was a terrible person, my dear, terrible. Very beautiful and fascinating, of course, but— Well, there's a word people don't seem to mind using nowadays that describes her perfectly." For a moment Mrs. Markham appeared regretful that she was too much of a lady to use that word. "A terrible person," she repeated.

"We set a lot of store by heredity here in the South," she went on, "but with Sylvia it was both heredity and psychological environment. The twins were only four when Charles and Wilma were divorced, and there in the courtroom the children themselves took sides. Even the judge was impressed, and that is why he allowed them to be separated. Sylvia stayed with her mother, and Charles brought Cynthia home to me. Charles had almost drunk himself to death by then, and a little later—he was killed in an automobile accident." A faint fragrance of attar of roses floated on the hot summer air as Mrs. Markham touched her eyes with a tiny scrap of lace.

"Maybe it would be better not to talk about it," I suggested. "Aren't you tired after the trip from New Orleans?"

"Oh, no, indeed!" She straightened up and managed a small smile. "I was quite comfortable on the plane. Just like a picnic, really. Box lunches and orange juice every other minute."

And I was thinking that I must find out all I could and hurry on to Heron Point. Suppose David Scott ran amuck and killed somebody else? Maybe that was what happened Saturday night. I remembered the way he tore past us Saturday afternoon; his fits of gloom before and after the murder; that glitter in his eye as he stopped me in the hall last night to ask if I had recognized the prowler on the attic stairs. Did Mrs. Markham know he was in love with Cynthia? Trying to steer the conversation back, I said, "The twins seemed very different in temperament."

She nodded her head. "Given a normal childhood, I don't suppose the difference would have been so marked. But even when they were quite small and Sylvia came for vacation visits with Cynthia, they weren't as much alike as twins are supposed to be. Our family doctor was very much interested. He read up on it and lent me a book of case histories about twins who had been separated for one reason or another. It seems they do vary more than you'd expect. It's all very scientific," she added impressively, "very scientific."

"Where is their mother now?"

"She died when the twins were twelve," Mrs. Markham told me, adding in a dramatic whisper, "Drugs."

After hearing this it seemed remarkable to me that either of the twins was normal. And as though she had read my mind, Mrs. Markham said with a sigh: "It was quite a problem. I tried never to make the slightest difference—you see, I had them both after their mother's death. I tried so hard to do my duty by them."

"I'm sure you did," I assured her.

"Of course they were fond of each other," she conceded, "but in different ways. Cynthia always seemed to feel that she must protect Sylvia, and Sylvia was extremely jealous of Cynthia. Whatever Cynthia had, Sylvia wanted. It might be just a crooked stick, but the fact that Cynthia valued it was all that was necessary. Sylvia envied Cynthia because Cynthia had the Markham charm. Outwardly, of course, Sylvia was just as attractive, but she was really the soul of selfishness. She would go along for a while and everything would be smooth; then her bad disposition would crop out. Naturally, she could not keep friends. And when it came to beaux"—Mrs. Markham shook her head—"she could never hold them. Fascination is all very well, but men do hate scenes. I was afraid Sylvia would never get a husband." She lifted her eyes as though contemplating the ultimate calamity.

"But she did," I reminded her thankful we were getting on toward David Scott at last.

"Ah, yes, but she tricked him into it. Tricked him. Wouldn't let him go, even when he asked for his freedom. But"—Mrs. Markham shook her head again—"I couldn't help feeling sorry for Sylvia that time. You see, Cynthia was engaged to be married to Bob Harrison of Atlanta. You know the family, of course. And as usual, whatever Cynthia had, Sylvia wanted. I don't think Sylvia was so much in love with Bob—she just couldn't bear the idea of Cynthia getting married and leaving her an old maid—at twenty-one." She smiled. "Well, anyway, when Sylvia took Cynthia's engagement so hard, I gave her a trip to New York to visit a school friend. She met David Scott and made a dead set at him, and when she came South he followed. He was really quite mad about her."

"Mad?" I questioned.

"Oh, just in love. Though I often think that is the worst insanity there is. Especially when you consider the marriages that result from it. Well, the usual thing happened. Sylvia blew up over something. David is high-strung himself, and they quarreled bitterly. Things went from bad to worse. David turned to Cynthia for sympathy. She was in love with Bob, of course, and engaged to marry him. Oh, dear, what a time we had!"

"What did you do?"

"David wanted to break the engagement, but Sylvia held him to it."

"How could she?"

"How could she? Well, David, of course, is an honorable young man, a gentleman. After all, he had proposed to her. Besides I think there were times when he felt that being married to Sylvia was next best to being married to Cynthia. They were so alike in appearance, and it is uncanny how they have the same little mannerisms and tricks of expression. That is," she amended, "did have. So difficult to realize Sylvia is dead. So difficult."

"I suppose they had a double wedding," I prompted as we turned into the avenue of live oaks leading to Heron Point.

She smiled brightly. "Yes, and you never saw two lovelier brides. I couldn't tell myself which was which as they stood at the altar in their misty white veils, both looking like angels. At the reception afterward, there was a lot of joking among the guests as to whether the new husbands could be sure they were starting out on the honeymoon with the right bride. That was because the twins sometimes played tricks on their young men friends by exchanging identities. But of course, if you knew them very well, there was never any great difficulty about which was which." Mrs. Markham paused and looked about her, taking note of the moss-hung live oaks and recognizing a plantation road. "I'm afraid you'll have to help me with my shoes," she said. "I just know my feet have swollen and I'll never get them back on again."

I stopped the car and lent a hand. "Thank you, my dear, thank you." She smiled a little breathlessly as she sat back finally and surveyed her small feet, now correctly shod. "Colonel Markham always said I had the highest arches he ever saw."

Making a last desperate effort to get to the point about David Scott, I said, "Sylvia's marriage seems to have lasted quite a while."

Mrs. Markham did a little mental calculation. "Eight years," she said, looking rather surprised. "But she was always crazy about money, of course, and David was generous. He tried to make the best of things, but I'm afraid she wasn't very—faithful to him. I'm sure she'd have divorced him long ago if she could have got enough money out of him. I always thought that was why—well, that it explained her behavior that time—" Mrs. Markham paused and regarded me a little doubtfully.

"It must have been a terrible ordeal for you," I said.

"Well, no, I wasn't there," she admitted reluctantly. "You see, David had been drinking a lot; but that was not surprising, what with Sylvia's demands and the struggle he had for a while with his business. He—well, I'm sure it was just a nervous breakdown from all the strain he'd been under. Later"—she lowered her voice as the white columns of Heron Point became visible through the green of the trees—"he accused her of trying to keep him in the—the hospital.

"I hate to admit it," she finished in a rush, "but I think Sylvia would have been quite capable of doing so—provided it means she would have full control of his property. David always wanted a child, but Sylvia put him off with one excuse or another and after that episode about the—the hospital, well, she always gave the impression she wasn't quite convinced David might not go off the deep end any time. Of course," she admitted, "David is very high-strung and gets upset easily; but if you know him he's really very sweet."

Woodrow took the bags up to Sylvia's room, which had been put in order for her. Mrs. Markham had to knock on the door of the connecting bath and explain who she was before Cynthia opened her own door.

"Oh, Cynthia, darling!" crooned her grandmother, finally admitted into the darkened room. "Just suppose it had been you."

Naturally I lost no time in confiding to Cousin Beau what Mrs. Markham had told me about David Scott, and he himself passed the information on to Chief Lindsey. The Chief had an interview with Mrs. Markham, who looked a little serious afterward. But this did not prevent her from engaging in a lively discussion of family connections with Cousin Beau at lunch. "And this jambalaya," Mrs. Markham remarked appreciatively, "I've never eaten anything more delicious, even in New Orleans. I must have the recipe."

Cousin Beau smiled spontaneously for the first time since we had arrived at Heron Point, and the whole atmosphere of the room was lightened and relaxed. Nobody told Mrs. Markham that Pearl always made jambalaya out of leftovers, whatever they happened to be. The marvel was Pearl hadn't added a little poison this time—there had been so many leftovers, due to a general lack of interest in food.

Instead of making a nuisance of herself as Cousin Beau antici-pated, Mrs. Markham restored some degree of balance to our de-moralized household, and we were all glad she was there. Which made it even more difficult for me to believe my eyes when she sent for me to come to her room shortly before time to leave for the inquest.

Gone was all the gay coquettishness; her eyes were rimmed with red, and she had that look which Cousin Beau calls "pale around the gills." It seemed rather late to be registering shock and grief. In fact, I had had a sneaking suspicion that Mrs. Markham rather enjoyed the drama of the situation.

She sat up on the chaise longue and clasped her small, blue-veined hands tightly in her lap in an effort to control their trem-bling. "My dear," she asked, in a voice that was high and thin and brittle, "who will be with Cy-Cynthia and me while the rest of you are at the inquest?"

"Why," I said uncertainly, "Woodrow will have to drive, of course. But Pearl will be here and Viola and probably some of her relatives and Zack."

"Zack? Who is Zack?"

"Zack's everything," I smiled, "Officially, the caretaker and gardener."

"Ask him to come up and sit in the hall, won't you?" She made a valiant attempt at a smile.

As I stood up to go, Mrs. Markham glanced around the room uneasily, looking over my shoulder in a way that made me decidedly uncomfortable. What could have happened, I wondered. Had Mrs. Markham started seeing things too? None of the men had appeared to take it seriously when Pat and I told of our experiences of the night before. And nobody had mentioned anything of the sort to Mrs. Markham—which made it all the stranger that she should be acting in this peculiar manner.

The key turned in the lock as I closed her door behind me.

XII

"WELL," SAID JOSH GRIMLY, "so they are going to put us under the rule."

We had just arrived at the funeral home where the inquest was to be held. From the hot glare of the sun and the equally uncomfortable glare of publicity and flash bulbs, we were conducted into a small reception room, crowded with overstuffed wine-red furniture which seemed to hold in its capacious cushions all the distilled essence of the heat sizzling upward from the pavement outside.

It was considerate of the authorities, I thought, to allow us a little privacy and to station a policeman at the door to see that we were not molested. Consideration, however, seems not to have been the main idea.

"Under the rule?" Cousin Chattie repeated suspiciously. "What's that?"

Josh looked at me and flashed a wry smile. "It means we are to be kept in this hot box and taken before the coroner and his jury one at a time, so none of us will be able to hear what the others say."

"Oh, dear!" wailed Cousin Chattie, very much the lady in distress in a cool white and black print dress and a black cartwheel hat. I remembered how she often said men look at you twice when you wear a big hat—once because of the hat and again to make sure what is under it. Today I was certain she had thought only that the hat would offer an effective screen.

124

"It's just a formality, dear," Cousin Beau hastened to assure her. Composed and dignified as usual, his manner gave no indication of what thoughts might be chasing their tails in his mind.

David Scott was called first. He seemed to have a good grip on himself, and for once had finished a cigarette before throwing it away.

"Now, Ann," Josh cautioned me, "don't get scared just because you have to swear that you are telling the truth. The thing to remember is—if they had enough evidence against any one person, he would be under arrest. In that case, he would not be sworn, because he could not be compelled to testify against himself. That's why," Josh glanced around at the others, who were all listening, "so many confessions are later repudiated."

"All right," I said, trying to sound casual, in spite of the fact that I felt pretty wilted inside and out. Automatically, I opened my bag and took out the mirror to see what had happened to my hair on the long drive across the causeway.

"Don't start worrying about the impression you are going to make on the jury," Cousin Chattie told me fretfully. "That blue linen was just the thing to wear. But"—she fanned herself futilely with a handkerchief—"we are all going to suffocate in here with the door shut. Beau, ask that policeman why we can't have it open."

"Won't do any good, Cousin Chat," Josh told her. "They don't want to take any chances that we will hear what's going on."

"Try to relax, dear," Cousin Beau suggested.

"Relax," she sniffed. "In here?" She looked around the small hot room, and it seemed to me that people never reflect their background quite so much as when they are away from it. For Cousin Chattie couldn't have felt any more out of place than we all looked.

Lot of good it would do Josh now, I told myself, to let his gaze linger on Pat in her tailored brown linen sports frock, her hair held back by a red ribbon that brought out all its red-brown lights. None of this might have happened if Josh had not been so blind, I reflected bitterly. Homer—well, Homer never would have become involved in an affair with Sylvia. As his eyes met mine and smiled encouragingly, I was willing to agree that Homer's unswerving devotion to the correct thing had its points.

The door opened again. This time Josh was called.

He stood up, tall in his crisp white linen, smoothed back his sun-streaked hair, and winked at me as he made his way out of the crowded room. I could only smile vacantly as he passed, for it struck me suddenly that they were calling the main suspects first.

"Just a formality," Cousin Beau murmured, reaching out to pat my hand.

I strained my ears to hear what was going on in the chapel beyond the narrow corridor. "What time is it?" I asked a little later, thinking my watch had stopped.

Finally I could bear it no longer, and stood up restlessly.

"Anything you want, Ann?" asked Homer. "Can I get you a drink or something?"

"No, thank you. I just—" Leaving the sentence to die on its feet, I walked over to the door and stood there, listening. Everything seemed unusually quiet. My hand was on the doorknob, and I turned it soundlessly, opening the door a crack.

"Better come back," cautioned Cousin Beau.

The policeman had his back to the door and had moved a little way along the corridor to listen. Somebody in the chapel cleared his throat, then began to speak.

"'Dear Sylvia.'" It was Chief Lindsey's familiar voice. He was reading Josh's note. You could have heard a pin drop. You could have heard my heart beat.

"'You'll regret it,'" the Chief went on. "'Anyway, I've warned you—'"

Perhaps I made some inarticulate sound, for the policeman turned, the curiosity in his eyes giving way to surprise and something not unlike sympathy. He shook his head at me as he moved nearer.

"You'll have to go back, Miss—Miss—" he whispered. "I have to keep the door shut."

"But it's so hot in there," I whispered back, desperately. "Don't you see—it's my brother?"

He was a rather young policeman, and his face flushed and he stammered a bit as he said uncertainly: "Well, it's against the rules. I don't know—"

Josh was saying something now, and we both listened. He was trying to explain that note as he had tried to explain it to me the day before. He had not meant to threaten Sylvia's life—he had only meant that, if she insisted upon remaining at Heron Point, she did so against his wishes—that his time would be taken up otherwise and so on. He was trying not to mention that he was expected to be Pat's date—trying not to mention Pat's name at all. Even to me it sounded like floundering.

"Better go back," cautioned the young policeman. "They'll be coming out in a moment."

The door was scarcely shut behind me when it opened again and my name was called. Cousin Chattie smiled encouragingly as I rose and Cousin Beau said yet another time, "Just a formality—"

"The testimony you shall give in this inquest to be the truth, the whole truth and nothing but the truth—"

The words were a blur, just as the room was. Then slowly, perspiring contours began to emerge. I found myself seated in a chair beside a table, and across this sat a short, stout man, wearing a limp gray seersucker suit which had shrunk in the seams, a damp white shirt, and an off-center bow tie. Obviously he was the coroner.

At one side was a smaller table at which a woman stenographer sat, pen poised above notebook. She regarded me with thinly veiled curiosity, and that stenographer, waiting to write down every word, was somehow more frightening than the coroner himself. But where was the jury? Weren't they supposed to sit in a box or something?

Then the coroner, fat hands clasped in front of an impressive bay window, asked the first question. "Speak so the jury can hear you," he added, motioning toward the men in the front pews, three on either side of the narrow aisle, almost close enough for me to touch them.

We had to go through it all: that scene at the cemetery—everything. If I could only have a glass of water! "Speak so the jury can hear you," the coroner told me again.

I raised my voice, and then—it was very strange, but all at once I knew that the crowd was friendly. I was experiencing something with which actors are all familiar, that fusing of spirit on the part of an audience which tells unerringly whether that audience is for or against them. This assurance of approval was unexpected and heartening. I began to feel that Cousin Beau had been right after all, and that it was just a formality.

Then the coroner picked up from the table a rather soiled envelope and with his stubby fingers extracted a small sheer square of linen—a not very fresh handkerchief.

"Miss Carroll," he asked, "will you examine this?"

It was my handkerchief, one of a dozen given me by Pat, my monogram in exquisite embroidery in one corner. But what made my hands cold and my face hot was the brownish discoloration on that small square of linen. I could feel again the sticky substance on my fingers after touching that dagger buried in Sylvia's back.

"You—recognize it?" asked the coroner.

I nodded, unable to find my voice.

"It is the handkerchief with which you held the dagger?" Suddenly the coroner was gimlet-eyed.

"No," I cried. "Oh, no!"

A sigh and a murmur swept the chapel. The coroner rapped on the table. "Order," called Chief Lindsey. He took the handkerchief and held it up for the jurors to see.

"Blood," he said succinctly.

My glance followed his. That juror, who looked as though he might have played football not so many years ago he was not sleepy any longer. He looked uncomfortable. The older one next to him, who kept fingering his cheek and his nose, now held his chin cupped in his hand, regarding the handkerchief with unblinking scrutiny. The one with his lips closed in a tight line—there was a gleam in his eyes now. I could guess what he was thinking. But the others—

"Where was the handkerchief found?" This was the juror who looked like a bookkeeper.

The coroner nodded to Chief Lindsey. "With the body when it was brought in," the Chief said, his gaze resting briefly on each juror.

"Is there anything you would like to say?" the coroner asked me.

"Yes," I swallowed hard. "I've already told you how I touched the dagger by accident, there in the dark, after Mrs. Scott was—stabbed. I remember the blood on my hand. I suppose I must have used this handkerchief to wipe it off. I—don't remember."

I could see how it must have been. That handkerchief had fallen on Sylvia, who was later covered over by her evening wrap. They had found the handkerchief in the morgue or wherever the body was taken. Apparently, the police had not known about it until today.

The juror with the tight thin lips was opening them. "Fingerprints," he asked, "the handkerchief was used to conceal fingerprints?"

"Oh, no!" I told him quickly. "Everyone had handled the dagger before dinner. Why would fingerprints matter?"

The coroner looked questioningly at Chief Lindsey.

"There was only one print on the dagger when we tested it this morning," said Lindsey. "Only Miss Carroll's—the print she made when she says she touched the dagger in the dark."

But this was amazing. The room began to blur again. Perhaps I only imagined it, but the crowd did not seem so friendly now.

The coroner said abruptly, "Witness dismissed."

I was led blindly from the room to join Josh and David Scott, interned in the office of the establishment.

"I can't understand about the fingerprints," I told Josh. "Everybody handled the dagger. It seems to me that this would make it perfect, from a standpoint of concealing identity. Why would the murderer wipe off all the fingerprints before using it?"

"Perhaps," Josh answered, "he was afraid his own prints might show up too well. The others might be smudged over by his or something of the sort. Or," Josh was thoughtful, "it could be that he didn't handle the dagger at all beforehand and was afraid somebody would remember."

I tried to recall that scene in the yellow drawing room Saturday evening. As nearly as I could remember, the dagger had been passed from one hand to another, making a complete circuit of the group. Even Sylvia had stretched out her slim fingers and held it for a moment, smiling a little maliciously. I couldn't be sure about Cousin Beau and Cousin Chattie—only that both had discussed the dagger while the rest of us passed it around.

The inquest was over finally.

"We find that the deceased met her death at the hand of a person unknown—"

Until then I did not realize how very tense I had been. Although I had tried to keep the thought out of my mind, I had been dreadfully afraid they would arrest Josh. Now I could only squeeze his hand hard and turn my head away so no one would see I was suddenly blinking tears.

XIII

CHIEF LINDSEY TRIED A NEW APPROACH when, one by one, he put us through our paces in the library, Monday evening. Hot and tired-looking, his thin light brown hair damp with perspiration, he picked up an envelope from the desk as I sat down to take my turn.

"Miss Carroll," he waved the envelope at me a little wearily, "I'm taking for granted you told the truth about this handkerchief there at the inquest this afternoon. Well," he went on as I nodded my head, "why not look at all this sensibly? You seem to think I'm your enemy. As a matter of fact, I'm only trying to track down the person who is guilty of murder, and to protect the innocent. I've got a hard job, and in helping shield the murderer you are making that job ever harder.

"Wait a minute." He held up his hand as I opened my mouth to protest. "I know you are honest in what you think. But look at it this way. You are trying to shield somebody you believe to be innocently involved. Has it occurred to you that in doing this, you are helping the murderer to cover his tracks while that other person remains under suspicion?" Leaning forward in his chair and narrowing his eyes, he gazed at me severely.

"What makes you think I'm shielding anybody?" I asked, realizing too late that such a question was practically an admission.

But the Chief chose to ignore my slip for the moment, proceeding with his own line of reasoning. "Have you thought about it this way, Miss Carroll? The murderer not only stabbed a helpless victim in the back. He deliberately took advantage of a group of people with whom he had only a short time before sat down to dinner as a friend among friends. While protecting himself, he cast suspicion upon all the rest of you. He picked a time and a place—on impulse, no doubt—but nonetheless a time and a place when everyone was least likely to be on guard. You think he ran great risk when he stabbed Mrs. Scott there in the cemetery with the rest of you standing by?" Chief Lindsey shook his head. "There was no reason why any of you should suspect one of your group of such intention. The murderer was, as I have said, among friends. Nothing is easier to take advantage of than friendship—to use as a cloak for treachery."

"That's all very well," I said, "but I still can't see why you haven't arrested Mr. Scott. Mrs. Markham says—"

"Yes, I know. I talked to Scott's doctor over long distance. He thinks Scott has recovered."

"Oh!" I said flatly.

"Of course, you can't always tell about such people. He might crack under strain. Yes, I know he had motive and opportunity, but none of the evidence points his way. And why would he take the risk of killing his wife if he were able to get the divorce he wanted without an unreasonable settlement?"

"I still think he's the only person who could be guilty. But what about the man who rang the doorbell Saturday evening just before dinner and disappeared? He could have hidden in the cemetery. He could have been listening outside when Cousin Chattie announced at dinner that she expected to take us all on this crazy ghost hunt?"

Lindsey smiled ironically as he poured water from a silver pitcher into two goblets and handed one to me. "The house," he reminded me as he raised his glass, "was securely locked. How would he have got the dagger?"

We always came back to that.

"But Cousin Chattie thought she saw someone in the blue room after—after the murder."

"Someone?" Lindsey raised sandy brows, leaning back in his chair as he set the empty glass on the silver tray.

"Something," I admitted. "And last night Pat and I—"

"Be sensible, Miss Carroll," he broke in, frowning. "You don't really believe in this ghost business. It's all mass hysteria, brought on by shock. You went to the cemetery to see a ghost, and you've been seeing ghosts ever since."

I shook my head. No, I didn't believe in ghosts. But I couldn't help thinking of Mrs. Markham's strange behavior. She had not been at the cemetery to see the first of our ghosts—that strange vision conjured up by automobile headlights. By common consent, nobody had told her anything beyond what happened at that particular time. But undoubtedly she had got the jitters soon after she reached Heron Point. I could still see her scared blue eyes as she peered over my shoulder when she asked that Zack be sent up to stand guard in the hall while the rest of us were at the inquest.

"Miss Carroll," Chief Lindsey swung at me with something of his old belligerence, "have you forgotten that the murderer very likely recognized you in that lightning flash when you stood in the upstairs hall? Have you considered that he's ready to turn on you the moment he happens to think you are a menace to his safety? Do you still want to go on protecting him?"

"I don't know who it was," I said miserably.

"But"—his voice dropped again and his eyes narrowed—"you do know other things you are not telling."

How could I say, "Cousin Beau knows something—otherwise, why did he telephone me Saturday morning?" How could I say, "Josh brought a package down to the Island for Sylvia Scott a week ago—a package that she didn't want anyone to know about?"

But I could tell him about the dagger sheath and glove. After all, the police had my bloodstained handkerchief. This could be no more incriminating. If they wanted to take me off to jail, I was too tired to protest.

Whether Chief Lindsey believed my account of how the dagger sheath and glove came into my possession, I do not know. But he did not question the point or even ask me to bring the sheath and glove to the library. "You say they're in that dressing-table drawer in that little room in the hall? O.K. I'll check on them myself. Just as well that nobody sees you with them. Let him think you are still too scared to do anything."

He sat for a moment, thinking. "Why," he asked, only half aloud, "didn't the murderer just throw away the sheath there in the cemetery? My hunch is he never took it out of the house—just hid the dagger in his coat pocket or in the glove compartment of his car. Probably used a handkerchief to hold the dagger and got rid of that afterward. Later on he decides to divert suspicion from himself by planting the sheath and glove on somebody."

"Then you think it might have been an accident they were planted in my room—maybe just because the door was unlocked."

"Could have been," he agreed. "Could have been a warning not to try too hard to decide who you saw on the stairs." He sat there, slumped in his chair, then suddenly straightened up again. "By the way," he told me, "the only fingerprints we found in the attic were yours and your brother's and Miss Fairchild's."

"But—"

"Never mind," he said, standing up and stretching his square, stocky frame. "Just remember the murderer has got his eye on you. Keep your own eyes open and your door locked. Report to me anything the least bit out of the ordinary. Most cases are not solved by detecting. Somebody makes a slip, or somebody gets a tip. Yes"—he allowed himself the faint ghost of a smile—"that's what usually turns the trick—a slip or a tip. Which doesn't mean," he added, as he held the door open for me, "that I'm not on the job twenty-four hours a day."

Thanks to Rufus Blair, I could lock my bedroom door. While I was meeting Mrs. Markham at the airport and thinking I had solved the murder, Rufus had come to Heron Point and taken a wax impression or something. The key was delivered to Pearl while we were at the inquest. I had missed him both times, but he telephoned just after dinner.

"This is Sherlock Holmes," he said, and my spirits lightened unaccountably at the sound of his voice. "Have you decided which twin you saw in the cemetery last night?"

Daylight had diluted my assurance somewhat. "It was probably just association of ideas, as you said," I told him, thanking him for the key. Grateful for his thoughtfulness, I could still remind myself that he would never take on any responsibility except as a whim—not with that smile of his. And that no one would ever know what he was thinking back of it.

"I was just thinking," he said, and I almost dropped the receiver, "that it wouldn't be a bad idea to keep that key on a yellow ribbon around your, neck, except when it is actively in use. You see," he went on humorously, and I could see the way he smiled, "it's quite a piece of craftsmanship; in fact, made by a fine Italian hand. You shouldn't leave it lying around. Somebody might take a fancy to it, and there you'd be without a key again."

For a moment after we said goodbye, I sat there absently holding the telephone in ray hand—thinking about Rufus Blair, wishing he was not quite so self-contained, wishing we knew a little more about him. A click on the line brought me rudely back to reality. On one of the four Heron Point extensions someone had been listening to our conversation.

I could not guess who it might be any more than I could guess who murdered Sylvia. But I could find Cousin Beau and demand a showdown. He had evaded me long enough. Determinedly I set out in search of him. But Cousin Beau was nowhere to be seen.

Guided by the glow of a cigarette, I found Josh a little later on the side porch. "Woodrow called him to the back a while ago," he told me when I inquired about Cousin Beau. "He's probably gone up to bed. You'd better be collecting some shut-eye, too," he added with brotherly tact. "I was thinking at dinner, you looked sort of played out."

It was the last straw. I flung myself down beside Josh and burst into tears on his white linen shoulder. "Where did you go Saturday afternoon?" I gulped.

"For Pete's sake!" Josh got out his handkerchief and proceeded to cope with the situation. "Listen, baby, I took a drunk man home. He was about to be arrested for driving while under the influence and needed looking after."

"Well," I sat up, "why on earth didn't you say so?"

"Because," Josh hesitated, "he was a friend of Sylvia's. A Dr. Dexter who followed her down here from New York. He'd rented one of those fishing shacks over at Aaron's camp, and he'd never have got there by himself. It was a messy complication, so I sent word to you at the garage not to wait. When you put on the pressure about it before dinner Saturday night, I didn't go into details because— it would have been embarrassing to Sylvia."

"You might have told me later," I sniffed.

"And let myself in for a lecture? I knew how you felt about Sylvia."

"It wasn't a very nice way to treat Pat. I'm surprised she speaks to you, anyway."

"I explained to Pat Saturday evening. She understood perfectly."

"Oh," I swallowed hard, "but you couldn't tell your own sister!"

Josh chuckled. "Come on now. Up to bed you go."

"Wait a minute." I drew a long breath. "What about this Dr. Dexter? Could he have come over here Saturday night? Could he be the man I saw looking through the oleander hedge? Could he have—killed Sylvia?"

"It's a swell idea, but it won't do. If Dexter got out of bed before Sunday afternoon, I'm no judge of binges," Josh declared. "He was all shot when I picked him up at the village, and he insisted on a couple of big swigs after I got him home. He's probably still soaked. I'm going to run over in the morning, see how he is, and pick up my cigarette case. I remember offering him a smoke. It was a fool thing to do, because he dropped the cigarette on the bed and I thought he was going to set the mattress on fire. I laid my case on the table and made a grab for the lighted cigarette—then forgot the case."

After such disarming frankness I could not bring myself to ask Josh about Sylvia's mysterious package. I could not tell him Mother had listened in on his conversation. Probably there was some simple explanation of the package also, and I had been harrowing myself for nothing.

Josh climbed the stairs with me and at the door of my bedroom gave me a peck of a kiss on the forehead. But even with Rufus Blair's key turned in the lock—even with my eyes closed tight, I could not shut out the fantastic company that trooped into the room and stood about my bed.

That tight-lipped juror. What was he doing in my room? He had looked at me just that way this afternoon. That glint in his eyes. No, this was not the juror. This was David Scott. And he was mad. I must escape somehow. But I could not escape, for there was Sylvia, standing with her lips drawn back. She was coming nearer. She was bending over me.

Those teeth—

"No," I cried, putting my hand to my throat, and the sound of my own voice roused me from that hagridden half-sleep into which overwrought nerves had unleashed all the terrors that conscious-ness held at bay. I snapped on the light. They were all gone now: the figures that had stood about my bed.

Yes, the room was quite empty, except for its familiar furnish-ings. The light struck brightly here and there: on the old Sheffield candlesticks on the Empire dressing table; on the silver doorknob. A single light, striking here and there, could play odd tricks: could make a doorknob seem to turn.

But this was no trick of light or imagination. That handle was turning. It was turning, and the door strained inward. But the lock held.

Then, as I waited, there was a faint tap on the door. A tap repeated.

Sitting up in bed, I asked as calmly as possible, "Who is it?"

"It's I. Cynthia. Let me in."

A long moment elapsed before I could force myself to move. Then I opened the door and she glided in, flowing white negligee billowing about her. She looked so much like Sylvia as I had imag-ined her a few moments before that I had to remind myself that this was Cynthia in the flesh.

But why did her lips look so full and so peculiarly red? I knew it was only imagination run wild, but after all, Rufus Blair had also seen that apparition at the cemetery and for a moment at least had shared my belief that it was one of the twins.

Cynthia smiled mockingly, and I could not repress a shudder at the sight of those white teeth. "Get back in bed if you like," she said softly.

But that was something I did not intend to do. I did not want Cynthia standing there by my bed as Sylvia had seemed to stand.

"That's all right," I forced myself to say, backing away from her. "Won't you sit down?"

She did not seem to move, but to float nearer, eyes fastened on mine, fingers clenching and unclenching. She was somehow bigger than life, like her own shadow—like some overpowering force of evil bearing down upon me. Was this Cynthia or Sylvia? I might be going crazy, but at this moment I could not tell.

Spirits cast no shadow. I'd read that somewhere. If there was no shadow— But I could not drag my eyes from hers to seek this reassurance. My back was literally against the wall, my breath no more than a flutter in my throat.

Then she spoke, still in that same soft, throaty voice. "Have you solved the murder yet?"

Her eyes were close, so close that I felt rather than saw them—animal eyes, the eyes of a cat ready to pounce on a helpless victim. Summoning all my strength I raised my hands to push her away. As I did so, my right elbow knocked against the lamp on the bedside table. It fell to the floor with a crash and the room was plunged into darkness.

XIV

WHEN I FINALLY GROPED my way to the bathroom as the nearest point
of contact and got the light turned on, Cynthia had disappeared. I
thought, as I had before, that the shock of her sister's death had
completely unbalanced her. Tomorrow Cousin Beau must insist that
she be moved to a hospital and David Scott taken into some kind of
custody before the place became a complete madhouse. A little
more of this, and I myself would be ready for a nice padded cell.

Meanwhile, making sure that my door was locked again and
resolving not to open it if the house burned down, I climbed back
into bed. Time dragged as it does when you are wakeful at night. I
was just beginning to feel a little relaxed and drowsy when it
seemed to me that I could hear sounds in the attic. Not very loud,
but, yes, footsteps. Somebody was prowling around up there again.

The sounds died away, and I sat up in bed; but I could hear
nothing further. The house was completely still. Finally I decided
I had been mistaken about it all and dropped back on my pillow.
Then bedlam broke loose on the floor above me.

What I had heard Saturday night was nothing compared to the
rolling and tumbling and crashing now going on. A couple of giants,
heaving the broken-down furniture at each other, could not have
done a better job.

Turning the light on and grabbing my housecoat, I made a dash
for the door. I could hear footsteps and loud voices just outside,
and opening the door, I found the hall brightly lighted. Pat was
just coming out of her door.

Somebody was already on the way upstairs. It was Josh, with David Scott practically riding on the coat tails of his pajamas. Neither had taken time to put on a bathrobe. Josh was banging on the attic door and shouting: "What's going on here? Open up."

"Come back," I shrieked at him. "Don't you know you may be killed?"

"Why should the door be locked?" Pat put into words the question in my mind.

Down the hall, toward the front bedrooms, Cousin Chattie was shrieking: "Where are you going, Beau Richmond? Come back here."

Strangely enough, Cousin Beau's bathrobed figure was hurriedly disappearing down the stairway to the first floor. Cousin Chattie stood gazing after him, a picture of middle-aged panic, nervous hands clutching her inadequate white silk kimono, face smeared with cold cream, gray-streaked brown hair straggling from under the silk net worn to protect her wave.

"Come back," she called again. But Cousin Beau was out of sight.

Adding to the general effect of a four-alarm fire, Mrs. Markham and Cynthia, from behind closed doors, were clamoring for enlightenment.

Abruptly the noise in the attic ceased, and Josh, banging on the door again, demanded that whoever was on the other side open up.

In the dead silence that followed, we heard the key turn in the lock and the creak of the opening door.

"Watch out there, now. Don't try any tricks." It was Homer's voice, a little thick, but grimly determined. I almost fainted with relief. Homer had caught the murderer.

There were sounds of a slight scuffle, mixed mutterings and grunts. "For God's sake," Josh ejaculated, "what's going on?"

It was impossible to make head or tail of all the babble as they came stumbling down the attic steps, sounding like an army of tanks falling over each other. First David Scott, hair tousled, eyes burning, cheeks flushed, lurched into view. Then came Josh, likewise flushed and disheveled. Then Homer, his face bloody, his white shirt stained with red, white slacks looking as though they had been used to wipe up the attic floor.

"Oh, my soul!" Cousin Chattie slumped against me, but curiosity kept her conscious.

Last of all appeared Chief Lindsey, angrily waving a revolver.

A moment's horrified silence held us, the atmosphere bristling with unasked questions. There was something wrong somewhere. "Oh, God!" groaned Homer, digging for his handkerchief. "I think my nose is broken."

"What were you doing in that attic?" Chief Lindsey ground out the words.

"Yes," added a stern voice behind us and there was Cousin Beau at the head of the back stairs, still calm and dignified, but panting a little from his hasty climb. "Suppose you explain what you were doing in the attic." He fixed Homer with an eye as cold and hard as his voice.

And then I realized the implications of Cousin Beau's question. Why had Homer been in the attic?

Drawing in my breath, I leaned against the doorjamb, forgetting that Cousin Chattie was using me for the same purpose. She grabbed the air, like a skater whose feet have suddenly taken off in all directions at once and except for Pat's quick outflung arm, she would have landed in a complete sprawl on the floor.

"Water!" Cousin Chattie gasped with returning equilibrium. For once Cousin Beau paid no attention, his eyes still fixed on Homer.

"I'm waiting for an answer," the Chief told Homer implacably, passing a hand over his forehead where a knot was already beginning to form. "What were you doing in the attic when everybody else was in bed?"

"What was I doing in the attic?" Homer growled behind the handkerchief held to his nose, his eyes bulging. "I was after the murderer, that's why I was in the attic. How the hell did I know you were still here when I found somebody snooping around the place in the dead of the night?"

"You might explain why you were snooping around yourself," the Chief told him acidly.

"Why—why—" Surely Homer's eyes would pop out of his head. "Major Richmond, I ask you, when have your guests had to retire by curfew?"

At that moment the mellow-toned old clock in the lower hall struck twice. "Not exactly curfew," Cousin Beau re marked dryly.

Pat, who had just brought a glass of water to Cousin Chattie, handed Homer a wet towel which he took automatically. Staring at it a moment, he raised his arm and mopped his face.

"I wasn't sleepy," he told Cousin Beau. "I went to my room at the same time Josh turned in." Homer glanced at Josh and received a confirming nod. "But all this—well, everything that has happened had me keyed up. I decided I wanted another smoke and discov- ered I was out of cigarettes. The light in Josh's room was out, so I went back downstairs and found some cigarettes in the library. I sat on the porch awhile—"

"How long?" asked Chief Lindsey.

"How long?" Homer flared. "How should I know? I wasn't try- ing to establish an alibi." He gazed angrily at Chief Lindsey, then went on. "All I know is that I came back upstairs and—thought I heard something—I stood still and listened for a moment but didn't hear anything else. So I started to go on to bed. Then," he shot me a fleeting glance, "I remembered about Ann thinking she heard someone in the attic the other night. So I decided it might be a good place to investigate."

"Why didn't you say so sooner?" Chief Lindsey growled, still eyeing him suspiciously.

"How could I say anything when you landed on me like a ton of bricks?" Homer demanded indignantly.

"You needn't have resisted," the Chief told him.

"Needn't have resisted?" Words failed Homer for a moment as he stared at Chief Lindsey. "Well—well," he sputtered, "if you think I was going to let myself be quietly put out of the way—you've got several more thinks coming up. I thought it was the murderer I was mixed up with. I thought I had him, too, there at the last."

"One of us had to quit," the Chief pointed out grudgingly, "with everybody trying to break the door down."

"It's all your fault, Beau," Cousin Chattie accused. "You should have told us Chief Lindsey was spending the night. I suppose that's where you ran off to just now—that back bedroom downstairs. As if Chief Lindsey or anyone else could have slept through all this horrible noise."

Cousin Beau ignored the fact that Chief Lindsey was not likely to have slept through a bedlam he was helping to make. "I only hope," he announced heavily, "that, from now on, all you amateur detectives will keep hands off and let the Chief do his job. In the meantime, everybody had better get back to bed—" He turned his head sharply as sounds of an altercation broke out on the other side of the hall.

David Scott was trying again to force his way into Cynthia's room and was being repulsed by Mrs. Markham, who had come from her own room out into the hall and was standing in front of Cynthia's door, her arms outspread behind her against the white panels. Wearing a dressing gown of cool lavender silk crepe, white hair neatly tucked under a net, she looked fragile in spite of her plumpness. David Scott could have shoved her aside easily.

"I've told you she can't see you." Mrs. Markham's voice broke. "She—she isn't able to see anyone. The shock has been too much for her."

Cousin Beau raised an eyebrow and glanced at Chief Lindsey. Then he moved across the hall, Cousin Chattie tagging behind and insisting that everybody must be going crazy.

At the first sound of raised voices, the Chief had pricked up his ears and stood as though waiting to pounce. But as Cousin Beau approached Cynthia's door, David Scott turned and, looking neither to the right nor to the left, walked off down the hall toward his own room.

Taking Mrs. Markham by the arm, Cousin Beau gravely escorted her the few steps to her room. Cousin Chattie fluttering at her other side. He stood back for them to enter, then followed and closed the door. But it remained shut for only a minute or two.

"Yes," Cousin Beau assured Mrs. Markham, trying to make his tone light as he backed out again behind Cousin Chattie, "Homer caught the Chief of Police. Just a case of mistaken identity. Try to get some rest."

"Rest?"

We could hear Mrs. Markham's thin, indignant wail, and then the door closed again.

Mrs. Markham had not appeared at dinner but had had some food sent up on a tray. Even when all the hullabaloo in the hall was at its highest, she had ventured only a few timid steps from her own door. Apparently she had not recovered from whatever had happened to upset her in the afternoon when she asked me to come to her room. You couldn't just ascribe it to reaction from excitement. She was frightened.

"Better go to bed," Cousin Beau told us again, firmly steering Cousin Chattie toward their rooms at the front of the house.

"What I can't understand," said Homer, "is why anyone would want to go prowling around that attic. Nothing up there but junk."

"Maybe," said Chief Lindsey. "Maybe not, but it's a good place to stay away from for more than one reason."

"What do you mean, it's a good place to stay away from?" Homer demanded.

Apparently regretting that he had committed himself to that extent, Chief Lindsey refused to go any further. "What I said was just for your protection," he told us. "Stay out of the attic." Jaw set, he stalked off downstairs to his back bedroom.

Taking Josh by the pajama sleeve, I dragged him toward Cousin Beau's and Cousin Chattie's sitting room. "He's got to tell us," I said.

"Do you think you'd better?" Josh objected, lagging behind. But after one look at my determined face he gave up.

No one answered our knock. Thinking Cousin Beau had gone on to his bedroom, I opened the door and entered, Josh following. The door of Cousin Chattie's room was partly open, and she was saying hysterically:

"But I won't stay here. I don't want all my hair to fall out. I don't want anaplastic anemia and all those other horrible things. I—"

She stopped as she caught sight of Josh and me transfixed in the doorway. Following her glance, Cousin Beau turned and faced us.

"Well?" he asked grimly.

"Cousin Chattie, what is it?" I begged. "You tell us."

She opened her mouth and looked uncertainly at Cousin Beau. "I—think—" she quavered.

Cousin Beau shook his head wearily. "Ann," he told me, "you've got to go back to bed. You must take my word for all this. I can't tell you anything tonight, but—I think I can tomorrow."

He looked questioningly at Josh who nodded his head. "Yes, sir," he agreed. "After all, what difference can a few hours make?"

XV

COUSIN CHATTIE DIDN'T COME DOWN to breakfast Tuesday morning, and Cousin Beau said he had to go into Brunswick with Chief Lindsey but would be back in an hour or so. "Just have a little patience," he told me with a meaning look.

A few minutes later Mrs. Markham sent for me to come to her room. While she nervously smoothed the skirt of her black and white print dress, her glance wandered this way and that. "My dear," she said tremulously, "I don't like to ask Mrs. Richmond. She has so much to bother her already, and Viola says she isn't feeling well this morning. Perhaps you can tell me. Would it—" She hesitated a long time, then swallowed and went on: "Would it be possible for me to move to another room?" Her eyes, still scared, clung to mine.

"Why"—I tried not to look too startled—"I'm sure it can be arranged. Let me see— I'll move into the little room next to Josh in the old nursery and then you can have my room."

"Oh, no, no!" she protested. "I wouldn't dream of putting you to all that trouble. Let me take the little room."

"But you'd have to share a bath with Josh. Oh, I know what we'll do. We'll move Josh to the sleeping porch with Mr. Scott. Don't worry"—as she raised her hand in protest. "There's plenty of room. You see," I rattled on, trying to reassure her with the light touch, "that sleeping porch was built to take care of the overflow of Cousin Chattie's hospitality. She parks all the husbands there when she invites her reading club down from Atlanta and the ladies

146

double up in the bedrooms. Cousin Chattie says the reading club never reads anything, because with all the bridge clubs it's about the only chance they have to talk."

Mrs. Markham managed a smile. "Thank you, my dear."

"You haven't found this room noisy, except that one time last night, have you?"

"N-no"—dubiously. "It isn't that. It's just," she hesitated and went on not very convincingly, "well, I don't like to disturb Cy-Cynthia. The same bathroom, you know. She's so nervous. The horrible shock and everything." Mrs. Markham's eyes did not quite meet mine.

"What does the doctor say?" I asked.

"He thinks she should stay in bed, at least another day. And, of course, there are arrangements to be made about the funeral. So I thought, if just for tonight—" Her voice trailed off.

"I'll tell Viola to see about it," I assured her. "Wouldn't you like to come down and get some air?"

She shook her head. "I'll—I'll wait until Viola comes in."

Downstairs on the porch Pat and Josh were smoking as they idled over a second cup of coffee. Pat was wearing a crisp yellow gingham and all her sparkle. She didn't look a bit like the girl who was sure she'd seen—something—in the hall Sunday night.

"I think," Josh told me, "I'll run over to Dexter's shack and pick up my cigarette case while Cousin Beau's in town."

"Let's go along," I suggested to Pat. It was a beautiful day and any excuse to get away from the queer, strained atmosphere of Heron Point seemed a good one.

Aaron's fishing camp is one of the many secluded spots you never would guess are tucked away on the Island if you stick to the beaches at St. Simon's and Sea Island. "Surely," said Pat to Josh as we approached, "you didn't walk all the way from here to Heron Point Saturday night?"

"Served him right if he did," I said.

"I'm a little more resourceful than that," Josh grinned, lazily. "Borrowed Dexter's car and sent it back by Zack. He's resourceful too: had his wife, the ever-handy Viola, trail him in the station wagon."

We passed the camp, and a little farther along Josh turned off and nosed into an overgrown road which apparently led straight into the green heart of the jungle, for vines and branches scraped the sides of the car and slapped us in the face as we practically blazed a trail. Suddenly we were in a small clearing in which stood the most desolate-looking, one-room shack imaginable. Complete silence hung over all, and the only sign of habitation was a rather abused-looking coupé parked near the door.

"What a place for a hide-out!" Pat observed in her low, throaty voice.

"Dexter was pretty well shot and came down here for a rest, I understand," Josh told us. "You girls wait outside. I don't know what shape he's in, or whether he's here. Probably is, though—there's his car. Anyway, I'll only be a moment."

It was such a lonely place that Pat and I got out to look around, but we tactfully walked away from the house in the direction of what island Negroes call the "dreen"—one of a series of drainage canals which get pretty deep when the tide is in.

Pat, in the lead, stopped so suddenly I almost fell over her.

"Look!" she gasped, white as a sheet as she gazed down into the drain.

Moving closer, I saw—what she saw.

Instinctively we groped for each other and shrank back, our eyes glued to that frightful thing in the canal. The tide was out, and at this point an old footbridge had fallen in. Caught in the wreckage of the bridge and staring up at us with sightless eyes, was the partly exposed body of a man. His discolored and bloated face, floating gently with the slow lapping of the shallow water, left no doubt that he was dead, and had been for some time.

Only the upper part of his body was visible, his shirt slimy with the black muck of the drain; for his legs were caught under the broken timbers of the bridge. One arm was sprawled on the partly rotted wood, a gold seal ring shining brightly on a swollen finger. The other arm was pinned beneath him. But that dead face, staring up at us with the sightless eyes, froze us in our tracks.

Behind us we heard Josh say, "Nobody home, but I found the—
Well, for Pete's sake what's the matter with—" Then Josh saw it, too.

"My God, it's Dexter." After that first startled exclamation Josh
stared a long time into the shallow water. Then he said, huskily:
"Seems I didn't do him such a favor after all, when I brought him
home. He must have wandered out and fallen in. . . . But I'd better
make sure there isn't something we can do. You girls wait for me
in the car," he added, as he climbed down the steep side of the
drain.

Josh shook his head when he joined us a little later, using his
handkerchief to wipe the black muck from his hands. "I'd feel better about it if somebody from Aaron's could help me get him onto
the bed before we go," he said. "Wouldn't do, of course—the police
won't want anything touched until they get here."

It did seem heartless to leave the dead man there alone, but we
were all glad to leave. The heavy green foliage closed in around
the shack, blotting it out as completely as though it did not exist;
and I wished I could blot out as easily that other vision—that horrible face staring at me from the drain.

We stopped at the fishing camp and broke the news to Aaron.
It was safe to bet that Aaron and all his helpers would steer clear
of the place until the police arrived. We left him shaking his black
head and muttering dolefully that he hoped the law wasn't "goin'
to make no trouble" for him.

Chief Lindsey was still at headquarters and himself took the
telephone message about Dr. Dexter's death. Later he and Cousin
Beau returned to Heron Point, and it seemed to me that the Chief
showed undue interest in the case. He questioned Josh at length
about his acquaintance with the drowned man. He also attempted
to draw him out on the subject of Dr. Dexter and Sylvia. Strangest
of all, he kept hammering at the rest of us—not just Pat and me,
but the entire house party—in an effort to discover some connecting link with Dr. Dexter.

"Some man came here to call on Sylvia," Cousin Chattie said
vaguely, "but I can't remember his name." Cousin Beau was equally

indefinite. Homer readily admitted that he might have met Dr. Dexter at the beach with Sylvia. "There's always a crowd, you know."

"No doubt about it in your case, I guess," Chief Lindsey told David Scott with a meaning look. "Not when you were having him tailed on account of his—er—interest in your wife."

"Do you have to go into that?" David Scott winced. "After all, they are both dead."

"Yes," agreed the Chief, "they are both dead." Then he turned to me. "How about it, Miss Carroll? Could this Dexter be the man you think you saw at the door Saturday night?"

I shook my head. I was certain of that, at least. It was not Dr. Dexter who had rung the doorbell and vanished. It was not Dr. Dexter who had stared at me across that open grave in the garden.

"Sure?" Chief Lindsey insisted.

"Yes, I'm sure. That time in the garden—I had a good look. I'd know him if I saw him again." I shivered a little, hoping I wouldn't see him again.

Mrs. Markham, hearing through Viola echoes of the excitement, called me to her new quarters. She was trying to work a crossword puzzle, but put it aside and clasped her hands in her lap as she invited me to sit down. She looked lonely and a little forlorn. With her insatiable interest in life, her love of chatter, this solitary confinement was hard to understand. Downstairs, at least she would have company and might forget her jitters for a little while.

"I'm not surprised that this Dr. Dexter followed Sylvia south," she commented, when I had finished my recital. "Men usually fall hard for her. But she is never able to hold them. She demands too much. Not just diamond bracelets—but body and soul." Her blue eyes were bright with the intensity of her feeling. "She's just like her mother was before her—a human vampire—taking everything from a man, driving him to his ruin if he doesn't pull away in time. And when one of her," she hesitated before saying the next word, as though the modern interpretation was distasteful to her, "lovers does manage to get away, she hates him—tries to revenge herself in any way she can."

"But she's dead now," I reminded her.

Mrs. Markham's blue eyes had a startled expression. "Yes—yes, of course, but it is so difficult to remember. And the evil men do lives on, you know. I don't see how David stood it as long as he did."

"Then you are still sure he—" I stopped, reluctant to say, "killed her."

"I—I—" her voice died as she glanced self-consciously out of a window.

"But surely you don't think it could have been anyone else."

"I only meant to say that I shouldn't suspect anyone." She slowly brought her eyes to mine.

"I do wish you'd come downstairs," I told her. "It's a gorgeous day. Maybe you'd enjoy the garden."

She hesitated and then smiled resolutely. "Thank you, my dear. You're very sweet. Perhaps, a little later."

In the hall I found Cousin Beau and Chief Lindsey tramping down the stairs from the attic. They went into the big sleeping porch and finally came out again, then into my room, and from there into Pat's. It was all very mysterious, for Chief Lindsey appeared to be making tests with an instrument in a glass case which he held in front of him like a camera as he moved from room to room.

Eventually they came down to the first floor and followed the same strange procedure. Pearl left the kitchen with them, muttering darkly that she did not intend to be blown up by any infernal machine. Later they went outside and walked slowly here and there, Chief Lindsey still holding the queer instrument in front of him.

Anticipating that they would find their way to the mysterious grave, Pat and I took a walk in that direction; and when voices approached we carefully kept out of sight but not out of hearing.

"I'll show you what I mean," said Chief Lindsey, as they came at last to the grave. "I'm pretty sure it's still here."

"Ah," said Cousin Beau, "but why was it left here?"

"It was a plant." Pat and I exchanged a glance. So Sylvia's wild flowers really had meant something. Perhaps she was on the trail of the Lost Gordonia or whatever it was that Bartram discovered so long ago.

"Yes," the Chief went on. "Owens planted the thing to see if anyone would return for it. He meant to stick around and watch this hole. Or if the excavation had been disturbed, he could search the house again. Of course, when he got hit by that truck Saturday it threw a monkey wrench into his plans."

"Ah-h," breathed Cousin Beau, "it works!"

"Yes, watch the leaves." Those strange botanical terms again.

"They're moving." Cousin Beau drew in his breath. It was all too much for Pat and me.

"Well, well!" Cousin Beau ejaculated, the slight quivering of his nostrils indicating that he was not too pleased to see us. Chief Lindsey, however, did not look in the least surprised.

"What on earth is that funny flower-in-the-bottle arrangement?" I asked, unable to restrain my curiosity any longer.

"It's an electroscope," the Chief explained, holding the glass case out for inspection. Inside the glass was a rod on which was a cluster of gold leaves.

"But what's it for?"

"All in good time," said Cousin Beau, a little impatiently. "We're going back to the house now. I want you to get everybody together in the library."

"I'll try to make this as snappy as possible," Chief Lindsey told us when we were all gathered in the inquisition chamber. The telephone in the hall rang, and Woodrow entered.

"It's for you, Mr. Chief, sir. They said it was headquarters."

When Chief Lindsey came back, he was the hard-boiled shock trooper again. You knew it even before he opened his mouth to say a word. Plumping down in his chair, swinging around as he glared from one to another of us, he flung his hand grenade.

"Dexter wasn't drowned."

"But—but—" Cousin Chattie began.

"Dexter," said Chief Lindsey, "was stabbed in the back with something like an ice pick. Weapon's probably in the drain. They're going back to look for it now."

"Oh, no!" Cousin Chattie gasped. "Not—stabbed in the back—like Sylvia."

Chief Lindsey nodded. "Yes," he said quietly, "exactly like Mrs. Scott." His narrowed eyes rested on Josh for a long moment. "You were the last person known to have seen Dexter alive," he told Josh, his voice deadly calm. "You admit the servant who returned Dexter's car says he found no one in the cabin, but pushed the door open and left the car key on the table."

Josh returned his gaze steadily. "Dexter was alive when I saw him last. I worried about his cigarette—thought it might set the bed on fire—even considered going back to see about it."

"But," I cried, "Josh would have no reason—"

Cousin Beau shook his head at me and Lindsey glanced around irritably. "Dexter's death clears up a good many things," he said. "Makes the case against the murderer of Mrs. Scott all the stronger, for it's plain now that the two murders were done by the same person. Someone"—he looked again at Josh—"who was fond of stabbing in the back. Besides there were other—considerations. All we needed was the connecting link."

XVI

IT WAS LIKE A RECURRING NIGHTMARE. Josh in the library again with Chief Lindsey, and I myself suspended in a vacuum outside.

"Let's get some air, Ann," Pat suggested.

I looked at her blankly, then at Cousin Beau, who was clearing his throat to say something. But I did not wait to hear. "Why," I cried, "does Chief Lindsey think both murders were committed by the same person? Why should he think Josh had anything to do with it?"

Cousin Beau motioned toward the yellow room. "Suppose we go in and sit down," he said gravely. "There are a few things I haven't been at liberty to explain until now."

"And then"—Cousin Chattie's voice was badly off key—"we must get away from here. It's dangerous to stay."

David Scott did not follow the rest of us into the room. "Perhaps it is just as well," said Cousin Beau, when we were seated, "for there's no getting away from the fact that—all this started with Sylvia. As Lindsey has just told us, she and this Dr. Dexter had been having—an affair. Scott put a detective on their trail to get evidence for a divorce. Sylvia seems to have been willing enough to agree to the divorce, but only for a large cash settlement. Scott got plenty of evidence aside from the fact that Dexter had given Sylvia quite a few trinkets—"

"Diamond bracelets," Cousin Chattie translated. The old merry glint returned to her blue eyes, then she sobered as Cousin Beau went on.

"That's Scott's defense, of course," Cousin Beau agreed. "That there was no reason why he would kill his wife if he could divorce her without difficulty." He paused. "Well, let's get back to Dexter. It seems that he was head of a private hospital near New York inherited from his father. Some months ago he collected a sizable amount of insurance on some radium which was stolen from the hospital. The radium—a gram for which a philanthropist friend of his father paid a hundred thousand dollars when he presented it to the hospital—was used in the treatment of cancer and—er—allied diseases."

Cousin Chattie shivered. Cousin Beau patted her hand, and she leaned back in the yellow brocade wing chair, her fingers nervously picking at her handkerchief.

"Well," he went on, "for some reason the insurance company got suspicious and put a detective on the job to find out whether the radium was actually stolen. Don't know why they didn't do all this before they paid out their money"—he shrugged. "Anyway, they found that Dr. Dexter had been drinking a lot, and that both he and his hospital seemed to be on the skids."

Cousin Beau reached for a cigar, lighted it, and resumed. "Dexter had been pretty smart about the radium. The insurance company probably wouldn't have got very far with its investigation except for Dexter's technician. Only the technician and Dexter had access to the vault in which the radium was kept, and the technician was naturally anxious to keep himself in the clear.

"Dexter was first to report the alleged theft of the radium. A small tube of the stuff had been used in the treatment of an old lady suffering from skin cancer. The case did not react as expected and it was found that the radium tube was empty. Investigation disclosed that the complete supply of radium was missing. Only a few empty tubes were in the vault."

"But what's all this got to do with Josh?" I broke in impatiently.

Cousin Beau frowned through cigar smoke, and Homer said placatingly: "Nothing, of course, but let's let Major Richmond finish."

"Well," Cousin Beau took off again, "the insurance company, as I said, became suspicious for some reason and Dexter was watched—"

"But"—it was Homer who interrupted this time—"I don't see. What could Dexter do with the radium if he couldn't use it in his hospital?"

"Sell it," said Cousin Beau tersely. "Not easy to dispose of, I understand, but there are ways. I'm not an expert on the subject. My information comes from Owens, the insurance detective. He got bunged up in an automobile accident Saturday and has been in the hospital in Brunswick ever since. Otherwise, he would be on the job. Owens tells me that radium offered for sale must be accompanied by a United States Bureau of Standards certificate, but there are a few radium brokers in the country who buy up bankrupt stocks and resell at a little less than the market price. Such a broker might accept the radium 'as is' and himself send the stuff to Washington for a certificate to be issued in his own name."

"But could Dexter have risked selling it?" Homer asked.

"Well," Cousin Beau scratched his head, "that's where the plot thickens. Owens says they expected Dexter to try to dispose of the radium through some second person or maybe under an assumed name Naturally, they—er—scrutinized his associates, and this brought Sylvia into the picture. Through Dexter's technician they came into possession of a letter from Sylvia, mailed in Atlanta, telling Dexter she had received a package and was putting it where it would do the least damage. They believed this meant the radium. Well, when Sylvia came down here to the Island and a little later Dexter followed her—they were pretty sure."

When Cousin Beau said the word "package," my face grew hot and I gripped the sides of the chair to keep my hands from trembling. This must be the mysterious package discussed in Sylvia's telephone conversation. This was the package Dr. Dexter expected to dispose of through some second person or go-between. I didn't want to believe it. I knew it wasn't true. Yet why else would Sylvia have shown such concern about the package? Cousin Beau's next words did nothing to reassure me.

"We know," he told us, "that Sylvia had the radium in her possession here on the Island. We're pretty sure Dexter found out he was being followed." Cousin Beau paused and again I could see Dr. Dexter's isolated shack near the fishing camp. Pat had been right. It was a hide-out.

"Anyway," Cousin Beau continued, "Owens says Sylvia began to shift the radium from one place to another. Evidently she was acting as a fence for Dexter until he could dispose of the radium. Owens thinks she was to get a cut out of the proceeds."

He took a long pull at his cigar and glanced at Cousin Chattie. "As soon as Sylvia and Cynthia moved over here from the Cloister, Owens came to me and asked if he could keep a lookout. Sylvia's interest in wild flowers gave us a lead. The logical thing, of course, would be to bury the radium, for it was not only what Owens called hot as stolen property, but highly dangerous. He—"

"And Beau never told me a word about it until after the murder," Cousin Chattie broke in. "When you think of all the horrible things that can happen from overexposure to radium—cancer, anaplastic anemia, sterility, baldness—" She ran nervous fingers through her own gray-sprinkled, light brown hair as though expecting to find it thinned.

"Calm yourself, my dear," Cousin Beau told her. "Lindsey and I went over the house with the electroscope again this morning. If the radium were anywhere about, that is, near enough to cause serious damage, I'm sure we'd have found some trace of it. As to my not telling you, Owens swore me to secrecy. The radium was packed in a lead container which he said would provide immunity from exposure for at least twenty-four hours, and he expected to locate the stuff right away. Besides, you may remember you told me your guests were leaving Saturday. When I found that they were staying on—" He shifted his glance in my direction. "That's when I telephoned you, Ann."

"We thought you just didn't want to be bothered about the decorating," I said. "And that you disapproved of Josh's having anything to do with Sylvia. I'm—I'm—" My voice broke before I could say "sorry."

Cousin Beau, contrite, patted me on the shoulder. "You understand now why I couldn't explain," he said.

"But just the same, Beau," Cousin Chattie reproached, "I don't see why you had to let me worry about that grave and—the burglar. You could have told me something."

"Oh," breathed Pat, "so that accounts for the grave?"

Cousin Beau nodded. "Owens did all that digging. He knew Sylvia had been there before him, because his electroscope located one little tube of the radium. The stuff seems to have been in a dozen or so very small tubes of platinum and silver, and these were packed in glass wool inside a lead container; but the top fitted loosely, and it was possible for the tube to work out."

"But why," Homer asked, "did Owens dig that particular sort of—excavation—like a grave?"

Cousin Beau looked at him impatiently. "Owens had a devil of a time finding that one tube of radium," he said. "There wasn't much radioactivity from such a small amount of the stuff. The electroscope indicated that radium was within a few feet one way or the other, so Owens worked backward and forward and up and down within a—certain radius. Even after he found the one tube, he wanted to make sure there wasn't more. That hole just happened to look like a grave. Nobody ever really said it was one."

He went on a bit more amiably. "Well, Owens reburied the one tube of radium as a plant and waited around to see if Sylvia or Dexter or somebody else would return for it. Then he decided it hadn't been missed. So Friday he asked permission to search the house, and that was our so-called burglar. After all my trouble to get the servants off the place, Pearl had to come back unexpectedly. Owens, otherwise, wouldn't have been hurried, and nobody would have suspected the search."

"Of course," Cousin Beau explained, "Owens wanted to get his hands on the complete supply of radium before trying to make an arrest."

"It's the most fantastic thing I ever heard of," said Homer, eyes practically out on stems. "Sylvia Scott burying radium all over the garden. Then she gets scared because Dexter tells her he was being followed. So she digs it up and puts it somewhere else. And now she's dead and he's dead, and nobody knows where the radium is."

"Unless," Cousin Beau reminded us reluctantly, "some third person happens to know. Lindsey thinks that is who you heard in the attic Saturday night after the murder, Ann." He nodded at me. "Naturally, I told Lindsey Sunday morning all about the radium angle. He thought then it was Dexter who had come over here to look for the radium. His idea was that Sylvia had told Dexter she'd hidden it in that vase in the attic but neglected to tell him when she moved it again. Otherwise, why would her room have been turned upside down afterward?"

"How would Dr. Dexter have got in?" Cousin Chattie demanded.

"Lindsey doesn't think now that it was Dexter," he admitted slowly. "They think at police headquarters that Dexter was already dead. Lindsey went to his cabin Sunday, but found nobody home. He thought Dexter would be back as all his things were there. Seems he didn't notice the name on Josh's cigarette case, but took for granted it belonged to Dexter. When Dexter hadn't returned Monday, Lindsey was sure he had skipped with the radium. But he still couldn't understand how Dexter got in the house here at Heron Point Saturday night after Sylvia was killed—unless someone opened the door for him.

"But Lindsey insisted that we keep quiet about this angle of the case, hoping the go-between—if there was one—would give himself away by some overt act. Now that we know Dexter is dead, Lindsey feels certain there has to be a third person mixed up in it all. This person no doubt believed the tide would carry Dexter's body out to sea, and the obvious conclusion would be that Dexter had, as Lindsey first thought, skipped with the radium after murdering Sylvia. With both Dexter and Sylvia out of the way the murderer could hold the radium indefinitely. Lindsey thinks Dexter told this—person about being shadowed. Anyway, something threw a scare into him. Or perhaps he just decided he didn't want to cut the proceeds of the sale three ways."

"I still don't see why it couldn't be Mr. Scott," I insisted stubbornly.

Cousin Beau smiled with weary patience. "Lindsey doesn't think it likely Scott would hire a detective to watch his wife and Dexter if he himself were involved with them in the radium business. Besides, Scott is solvent, and the radium represents a relatively small amount."

"I wouldn't consider a hundred thousand dollars chicken feed," I said, "and with the insurance it would add up."

"There's where you're wrong," said Cousin Beau. "One hundred thousand was paid for the radium twenty or so years ago. Today the top price would be under thirty thousand—about twenty-seven thousand, I believe."

"What?" Homer asked incredulously, always interested in the financial angle. "Why, wildcat stocks don't often plunge like that."

"Don't know much about it myself," Cousin Beau told him. "Owens says Belgium used to control the world's supply. Then they found carnotite ore or something in Colorado. But it was the Great Bear Lake deposit—seems they started bringing it down from the subarctic by airplane—that permanently lowered the price."

"But why," Pat inquired, "would this Dr. Dexter want to collect the insurance if the radium was worth no more than thirty thousand? It wouldn't be worth the risk."

"Owens says he was broke," Cousin Beau explained. "Probably thought he could salvage something before the hospital went into bankruptcy."

"But why didn't he just sell the radium?"

"It was a gift to the hospital—maybe some strings tied to it. Anyway, as Ann says, with the sale and the insurance it would— add up. And—"

"Look," Cousin Chattie broke in distractedly. "The fact that Sylvia and Cynthia stayed on—doesn't that prove that the radium is still here, even if you haven't been able to find it?"

"Owens made a pretty thorough search," Cousin Beau tried to reassure her. "Even without the electroscope he'd have found the radium if it were still in the lead container, because this container weighs five or six pounds and wouldn't be so easy to hide. The radium itself is no more than a quarter of a teaspoonful of bluish salt. This, as I've told you, is in very small tubes of silver or platinum or—what's that other stuff?—iridium. Of course—" He hesitated.

"Go on," Cousin Chattie prodded.

"Well, I was just going to say if Sylvia took it out of the lead container—and maybe threw the container in the river—she could hide a tube here and there very easily. Even with the electroscope, it might take a good deal of hunting—just as it did in the garden."

Cousin Chattie rose up as though she had suddenly discovered herself sitting on a tack and moved from her cushioned wing chair to a satinwood shield-back Hepplewhite, which groaned under the impact. "I—I was thinking how things lodge under cushions," she explained self-consciously.

"I can set your mind at rest there," said Cousin Beau, rising heavily and going out into the hall. He came back with the queer-looking flower-in-a-bottle contrivance.

"What's that?" Cousin Chattie asked suspiciously as he advanced on the wing chair.

"Owens calls it a 'radium detective,'" Cousin Beau smiled grimly. "'Electroscope' is the technical name. Have to be careful not to touch this." He pointed to a metal rod at the top, most of which extended down into the glass with a cluster of gold leaves attached midway. "It's charged with static electricity, and the glass acts as insulation." As he talked Cousin Beau passed the electroscope over and around the wing chair. "When in the proximity of radium, these bits of gold leaf inside the glass begin to droop as the electricity is drained from the rod by radioactivity." Fascinated, we all watched breathlessly, but the gold leaves refused to droop.

"Owens says this thing is very valuable around a hospital," Cousin Beau remarked as he carefully placed the electroscope on a table. "In spite of every precaution, radium is sometimes discarded in a dressing. The dressing may be carried out with other waste—or get into the laundry when the sheets are changed. Of course, such cases more or less follow a groove. Sylvia—had more range."

Although I had been absorbed in Cousin Beau's story, every nerve in my body had been waiting for the slightest sound that would indicate the opening of the library door. And when it came at last, I jumped to my feet, ready to fly to Josh.

Chief Lindsey came out first, and his expression and Josh's flushed but determined face as he towered behind showed that no "confession" had been forthcoming.

The others had followed me into the hall, and the Chief stopped to glower at us. "Maybe, you are all in this," he ground out, eyes narrowed. "Anyway, I'm going to get to the bottom of it."

In the babble of protests that followed, Cousin Chattie finally won the floor. "The very idea!" she told him indignantly. "I practically never heard of Dr. Dexter until this morning. And I barely knew Sylvia Scott."

"You—barely knew her," Chief Lindsey goggled. "Then how did you happen to invite her to be your house guest? Surely—"

"Why—why—" Cousin Chattie choked. She looked helplessly at Cousin Beau. Another time it would have been worth a laugh. As if Cousin Chattie ever knew why she asked any particular guest!

"I believe," said. Cousin Beau hesitantly, "that Mrs. Scott rather sought the invitation. She seemed to be interested in wild flowers and asked if she could explore this part of the Island. That seems not to have been her real purpose. At the time I rather had my doubts."

"You had your doubts?" Chief Lindsey sputtered, as though it was all getting to be too much.

Cousin Beau cleared his throat and spoke with great dignity. "I mean that I thought her real interest was in—" He looked at Josh, then realized the implications of what he was about to say and left the sentence unfinished. "Naturally," he said, "I know now that she was really looking for a hide-out for the radium."

"Well," said the Chief, taking out his tobacco tin and filling his pipe, "there's a third party in this somewhere. Unless, of course, you can prove that Mrs. Scott and Dexter killed each other. And since Dexter didn't disappear with it, where's the radium?"

He stood and glared at us, then took one more shot at Josh. "How do I know you all weren't looking for it this morning?"

"But can't you see," Josh was evidently repeating something he'd already said more than once, "that this third person could be somebody none of us ever heard of?"

"It could be the man who rang the doorbell," I said desperately.

"How'd he get hold of the dagger?" Chief Lindsey asked coldly.

We were back at the beginning again.

XVII

"WHERE'S SCOTT?" GROWLED CHIEF LINDSEY, frowning as he glanced up and down the wide central hallway.

From overhead David Scott's own raised voice answered the question. "But, Cynthia, I must see you."

"Come on down, Scott," Chief Lindsey called out crossly.

A few moments later David Scott appeared on the stairs. Pulling at his dark hair, his eyes restive as those of a caged animal, he looked at Chief Lindsey as though greatly surprised to find him still on the premises.

As the library door closed behind them, Cousin Beau stalked across the hall to the coat closet, found his Panama hat and carefully turned down the inside band, running a finger all the way around the crown.

"What's all that about?" Cousin Chattie demanded.

"Just something that occurred to me," he said trying to sound offhand and looking anything else.

"Now listen, Beau Richmond," she told him. "I'm not up to any more mysteries."

Cousin Beau turned the band back, replaced the hat, and remarked, with a sidewise glance, "I don't know that you'll care for what I'm going to say, either. I just happened to remember reading a story somewhere in which somebody tried to murder somebody else by secreting radium in his victim's hatband."

"Oh, dear God!" gasped Cousin Chattie.

Cousin Beau took her by the arm and piloted her out to the porch, while the rest of us followed.

"Why should Sylvia want to murder you?" she asked, more or less collapsing in the chair he placed for her.

"I don't know," he replied. "It just occurred to me."

Cousin Chattie leaned back and shut her eyes.

"I warned you, you wouldn't like it," Cousin Beau went on, "but you made me tell you. It just occurred to me that if Sylvia thought detectives were on her trail, she might have disposed of the radium in the way she thought would do the most good. In other words, she would be diverting suspicion in various directions and playing no favorites in the little matter of—radium burns and other pleasant possibilities."

"It's the most diabolical thing I ever heard of," Cousin Chattie declared, her blue eyes wide.

"I don't think she loved any of us much," Cousin Beau pointed out. "But don't get excited. I was just thinking of the Borgias and how they would have enjoyed radium. Now, now," he hastened to add, "I didn't really say Sylvia did anything like that. Nobody knows what she did."

"Which makes it all perfectly lovely," Cousin Chattie agreed witheringly.

But the suggestion had its insidious effect.

"Looking for cigarettes?" Josh asked Homer, who smiled sheepishly.

"I was just wondering if I might find a tube of radium in my pocket," Homer confessed. "Not very pleasant, thinking of all the things one of those little tubes might do to you."

After having sounded that general alarm, Cousin Beau tried to soft-pedal things a bit, but he wasn't very convincing. "Radium," he told us, "is one of the greatest boons to mankind—properly applied, of course. If we can help to locate this batch and get it back to the hospital—"

"I'm much more interested in making sure that it isn't in the house," Cousin Chattie cut in. "After all, the patients can go to some other hospital. But think what may happen to us from radium burns." She shuddered. "And the horrible part is that none of us has the faintest notion where the radium is nor how long we may have been exposed to it."

"We'll go over the place foot by foot with the electroscope," said Homer resolutely, stepping into the drawing room and coming out with the "radium detective."

"Mind if I take a look at that gadget?" asked Josh.

Carefully Homer extended the instrument. "Watch out, don't touch the rod," he cautioned.

There was a crash and the tinkle of broken glass. One of them had fumbled. The ruined electroscope lay at our feet—useless, now.

Better not think about it, I told myself, as I helped pick up the pieces. It couldn't have been anything but an accident. Josh had always had butter fingers.

And the search went on, even without the electroscope. Nobody found anything, but I must say that we thought of a lot of places to look. Clothes were turned inside out and everything else, even the bedding, turned upside down. Poor Viola went about with a sour expression, putting things to rights for the second time in one day. She had never heard of radium, and I wished I had not.

In the middle of all the excitement, a banshee wail from the lower hall brought us all tumbling down the stairs again.

One look at Cousin Chattie in a near swoon against the powder-room door, and I knew what had happened. Chief Lindsey, who had erupted from the library, also appeared well aware of the cause of this sudden wild alarm. In her search for the radium, Cousin Chattie had brought out the dagger sheath and glove which I had hidden in the drawer of the dressing table.

"Its one of my old gardening gloves," Cousin Chattie told us hysterically, holding the unlovely object out with two fingers, her blue eyes pathetic in their frightened bewilderment. She drew back with a shudder as Cousin Beau picked up the dagger sheath carefully with his handkerchief, as though it might still bear fingerprints.

"I'll never invite anybody to this house or anywhere else again," she declared tearfully. "To think that a guest should so abuse my hospitality." She looked from one to another of us as though trying to decide who could be guilty of such a breach of etiquette.

Chief Lindsey's glance followed hers, his eyes full of speculation. For that incriminating evidence was out in the open at last. But whether he drew any sort of conclusion, I could not say. Everybody looked harassed enough to confess to almost anything by now. "Where do you usually keep your gloves?" Cousin Beau asked Cousin Chattie.

"Where they belong, of course," she snapped. "In the extra pantry in the kitchen where I keep all the containers for cut flowers. Usually the gloves are in the drawer with the garden shears."

"Always?" Cousin Beau asked.

"Now, don't you start trying to act like that—" Catching sight of Chief Lindsey, she broke off. "Naturally, I might lay them down somewhere if I were called to the telephone," she told Cousin Beau. "Sometimes I leave them on that table on the back porch."

"When did you have them last?"

"How can I remember? Sylvia used them a lot last week. How should I know what she did with them afterward? She probably left them wherever she happened to be."

The mate of the garden glove was not in the pantry drawer. It was on the table on the back porch, in the basket Cousin Chattie used when cutting flowers for the house. The garden shears were also in the basket. Anybody might have seen the gloves or could have picked up one of them.

Viola, the whites of her eyes shining against her dark skin, came forward to say that she had found one of Cousin Chattie's gloves in the upstairs hall Sunday morning and later put it in the basket on the back porch. "I couldn't find the mate nowheres. Course, I didn't look in that dressin' table drawer, 'cause why would it be there? This un I found was just outside your door, Miss Ann."

The Chief shut her off. "O.K. Here, you can put this one in the basket, too," he added casually. The sheath he took from Cousin Beau and dropped in his pocket.

"But—" Cousin Chattie protested.

"It's O.K.," he said again.

She started to sit down, but thought better of it. "I'm going to the Cloister," she told Cousin Beau desperately. "I—I won't stay here another moment."

At another time I might have smiled at the thought of Cousin Chattie walking out on one of her own ill assorted house parties. But not then—not with Chief Lindsey looking at Josh out of narrowed eyes as he motioned David Scott back into the library. I hated to think what he would make of that broken electroscope.

Josh himself appeared completely unaware of the scrutiny. "Look, Cousin Chat." He smiled with some of his old casual charm. "Why don't you imbibe a little air while the rest of us go on with this Easter egg hunt?"

"It's a good idea," Cousin Beau agreed with alacrity, taking her by the arm and heading for the door.

They were barely out of the house when Woodrow appeared, without his usual grin. "It's about lunch, Miss Ann. Mamma sho is sick."

So much had happened on this crowded Tuesday morning that I could hardly believe it was only lunchtime. Under all the circumstances I was not surprised that Pearl was sick. But the moment I saw her I realized that this was no ordinary spell of misery brought on by house pests. Limp and gaunt in her white uniform, she lay across her bed in the servants' house, her eyes full of fright.

When I spoke, she raised herself to a sitting position and two big tears rolled down her bronze cheeks. At first she would not talk, but kept twisting and untwisting those brown fingers that were so skillful in concocting dishes to keep Cousin Beau happy and Cousin Chattie overweight.

Suddenly she burst out: "Viola say you all tearin' up the place, and I got to tell you."

"Well, for heaven's sake, what is it?" I asked. "Something about the murder?"

She nodded her head, gazing around fearfully.

"Pearl, do you know who did it?"

Again she nodded. "Leastwise, I think I do, baby."

"Well, why didn't you tell Chief Lindsey when he talked to you?" I tried to keep my voice calm. "Who—who is it?"

"Oh, baby!" she cried. "Will they put me in jail if I tell?"

"Not unless you did it yourself."

Evidently I had said the wrong thing, for she began to wail and rock back and forth. I shook her shoulders and tried to calm her.

"It was that Viola got me into it," she finally confessed. "Oh, baby, when I see our boy just th'owin' hisself away on that no-'count—" She stopped, swallowed, and then went on. "Well, when she moves herself here in our house and spects to carry on right in the bosom of the fam'ly, I know I got to do somethin'."

"What did you do, Pearl?" I asked gently.

She looked at me slyly. "You know what them men been lookin' for?"

"The radium?"

"That what you call it? Well, they ain't lookin' in the right place."

She had said something like that before. "Pearl, where is it?" I asked firmly.

"Will the law git me if I tell, baby?"

"They'll probably thank you. Besides, Cousin Beau wouldn't let anything happen to you," I said, knowing she would have more faith in his protection than in the equity of the courts.

"I ain't know she really gonna die," Pearl began to wail again. "I jus' wanna scare her off and gone. Viola tell me she'll die." Pearl flung herself back on the bed, and it looked as though we had come to another impasse.

"All right, Pearl," I said. "They probably are going to take brother and me to jail, and it's all your fault."

"No, I tell him," she said, rising. "I show him."

"Good. Let's go. Where is the radium? In the house or outside?"

"'Tain't in the house," she answered, determined to die hard.

"All right. Woodrow, you go and get Cousin Beau and Chief Lindsey," I said.

Pearl went into the bathroom and washed her face and followed me down the steps, nervously smoothing the wrinkles in her starched white uniform. Cousin Beau and Chief Lindsey, both looking properly disagreeable, with Josh trailing behind, were just coming down the steps of the big house.

"What's going on?" the Chief inquired gruffly, giving Pearl a suspicious once-over.

Pearl looked doubtfully from me to Cousin Beau.

"She says she knows where the radium is," I told him, "and that she knows who killed Sylvia."

"My God!" ejaculated Cousin Beau.

"Oh, Mr. Beau!" Pearl whined. "I ain't mean no harm. I jus' wanna run off that bad woman. I ain't mean to get her killed."

"All right, all right," Cousin Beau said testily. "Let's have the radium, and then you can tell us about it."

"It's all your fault," Pearl spat vindictively at Viola, slinking down the steps.

"You wanted to git her gone," Viola answered, eyes snapping. "She gone, ain' she?"

"What is this?" Chief Lindsey inquired. "A run-around?"

"Pearl," Cousin Beau eyed her firmly, "where is that radium?"

Pearl began to whimper. "Under the doorstep," she told him. "Down in the basement."

So we all went trooping down to a spot that must have been directly under the back steps. "She always came in through the back when she drive her car around," Pearl explained. "Can't bury nothin' under back steps, 'cause they all shut up. Here 'tis." She pointed to the coal pile.

"You mean it's under all that coal," Chief Lindsey asked, with some dismay. I held my breath for fear he would decide to make a preliminary test with the electroscope.

"Just got in an extra supply the other day," Cousin Beau explained, "for the hot water. Well, Woodrow, I suppose it's up to you."

The unhurried rhythm of Woodrow's swinging shovel irritated Chief Lindsey beyond endurance. He grabbed another shovel and scattered coal wildly until perspiration dripped from his brow and soaked his khaki shirt. Then he had to slow down, while Woodrow kept on at an even, effortless pace, accompanied by a low whimpering from Pearl. When Josh offered to relieve him, the Chief handed over the shovel promptly and got out a handkerchief to mop his face.

None of us knew what the package of radium was supposed to look like. Mr. Owens had told Cousin Beau that it would be in a number of tiny metal tubes, and these should be in a lead container; but the tubes might have been removed from the container and the radium from the tubes, for all we knew.

When a small, paper-wrapped package was finally unearthed, the Chief swooped down on it. Tearing off the paper, Chief Lindsey brought to light a small, dirty cloth bag, loosely filled with something soft. "Well," he grunted, "I guess this is it. Maybe we'd better go upstairs where we can sit down. Come along," he motioned to Pearl.

Upstairs in the back hall, Chief Lindsey took a sheet of paper from a drawer of the old secretary, laid it flat on the desk, untied the cloth bag and emptied its contents onto the paper.

For a long moment we all stood and stared at what appeared to be a tablespoonful of gritty, gray-looking dirt. Chief Lindsey stirred the stuff with his stubby forefinger, and several dark hairs came to light.

"Radium, hell!" he growled. "What's all this, anyway?" Turning to Pearl, he barked, "What do you mean radium?"

Cringing backward, she muttered, "White folks call it 'radium.' Colored folks call it 'mojo.'"

"Might have expected something of the sort," said Cousin Beau dryly.

"Oh, Pearl!" I reproached, limply dropping into a chair.

Puzzled by our reaction and anxious to vindicate herself, Pearl was now all volubility. "Viola take me over to Harrington," she said. This was the Island settlement made up largely of the descendants of former slave residents. "And we go to see a old woman who make mojo bags. She say git some of that bad woman's hair and finger-nails and she mix with some graveyard dirt and make a mojo to cunjuh that bad woman. I ain' believe in it," she interpolated defensively, "but I try it.

"I put it under the doorstep that afternoon," she went on, "and I watch Miss Silly go up them steps so gay. She singin' a little song and then she look back over her shoulder and say, 'Hurry up, Cyn, we got to dress. Gonna be short of men tonight, so we got to put them two sweet young things in their places.' An' I say to myself: 'Uh huh, yo' sins gonna find you out. You leave my chillun alone. You gonna be cunjuhed clean away from here.' An' sho nuff"— Pearl's eyes were wide with horror—"it happen that same night."

"So that's how she was killed?" Chief Lindsey agreed with heavy sarcasm. "And here's the radium."

Pearl looked at him doubtfully.

"Mojo and radium are two different things," I explained to her.

"But," she argued, "y'all done been scared o' ra-radium. You say it bad to have 'round. Viola tell me—"

"Yes," I cut in, "that's right. But don't worry about the mojo. Mrs. Scott was killed with a dagger. The mojo had nothing to do with it. Chief Lindsey will tell you that."

"I ought to call the patrol wagon and run you in," the Chief growled at her. "When I think of shoveling all that coal—" He stamped back to the library to continue his questioning of David Scott.

"What's that you're muttering?" Cousin Beau called out as Woodrow followed Pearl toward the kitchen.

"Nothin', Mr. Beau, sir," Woodrow hastily assured him. "Nothin', sir."

"Out with it. You were saying something."

"It was just a verse," Woodrow stammered, with a shamefaced grin, "I was just sayin':

"Up the hill and down the level
Gran'ma's puppy treed the devil."

As Woodrow made himself scarce, Chief Lindsey came charging out of the library. "Where's Scott?"

"Probably gone to his room," said Cousin Beau with forced calm.

But David Scott was not on the sleeping porch. He was nowhere in the house or about the grounds. His car was still parked in the garage, but Chief Lindsey's car was gone.

While we had all been down in the basement unearthing the mojo, David Scott had escaped. The tollkeeper would not question Chief Lindsey's car.

XVIII

CHIEF LINDSEY WENT INTO A TAIL SPIN when he discovered David Scott's escape. It had been fairly plain all along that he had kept us cooped up there together hoping someone would make a break. He'd even said something to that effect: that it was a slip or a tip that solved most murder cases. But David Scott had taken the one way out that offered any hope of success—a break in Chief Lindsey's official car.

Just as he arrived at Heron Point for the second—or was it the third?—time that day the Chief had been called to the telephone and had left his car for Woodrow to move out of the driveway. It was not carelessness, as the Chief now contended, that Woodrow failed to take the keys to him afterward. Nobody ever had bothered about removing car keys at Heron Point where until recently even the doors of the house were left unlocked.

As Chief Lindsey barked into the telephone, you could almost see the dragnet spreading; telephone, telegraph, radio, city and county police, state troopers, the Coast Guard—all would be on the lookout. How could one lone human being hope to elude them?

And yet somehow I hoped David Scott would escape. His marriage to Sylvia must have become one long nightmare, driving him to distraction, driving him finally to murder.

Chief Lindsey's conversation with the tollkeeper at the causeway apparently was not very satisfactory. No toll is charged for outgoing cars. But all automobiles, except those with "Glynn County Police" lettered on the side, had been challenged since the

172

murder, and the occupants and license numbers checked with descriptions furnished by the police department. No doubt this had been a great nuisance to members of the summer colony and an even greater bother to the tollkeeper.

This morning the keeper seemed a bit uncertain as to the number of times Chief Lindsey's own car had crossed the causeway—going and coming. All he could say definitely was that none of the cars bearing the specified license numbers had passed. The Chief nearly choked on that.

He banged out of the house in a terrible temper and was just about to get off in David Scott's car when Homer flagged him down to ask if he might leave for Atlanta—now that the identity of the murderer was established. "I've got some important conferences—and engagements—for tomorrow," Homer explained.

Chief Lindsey glared at him, bore down on the accelerator; the car plunged and the motor choked. "Damnation!" The Chief ground his teeth and forced himself to concentrate on the business of getting started. As the motor roared and the car leaped forward, he yelled back, "Nobody's to leave until I get a line on Scott."

Homer looked after him in complete exasperation. But you could not really blame the Chief. He had had a bad morning. First the news of Dr. Dexter's death and the later bulletin that this was not a simple case of drowning, but murder. Then the search for the radium which had not been radium at all. Still, it was that crazy business of the mojo bag that had produced the reaction he had been waiting for—a crack-up or a break for freedom.

"I've got a good mind to go anyway," Homer muttered, as the car disappeared down the avenue of moss-hung live oaks.

"I don't think the party for Lord and Lady Heyward would be worth it," I teased. "After all, the Chief might think you were trying to escape too."

Homer forced a smile. "Hadn't thought of that," he admitted grudgingly. "But this whole business is insane. Why haven't they arrested somebody before now? Then the rest of us could go on about our business. Naturally, things need looking after at the office. I only came down here for the weekend."

In all the excitement Cousin Chattie apparently had forgotten her design for doing over my life while I did over Heron Point. It was just as well, I thought, as Homer and I walked back into the house. Too much had been happening for me to be concerned about such relatively unimportant matters as Homer's intentions regarding Pat. He was probably making progress, I decided, remembering that Pat had asked me some carefully casual questions about his financial status. I suppose a rich girl always has the fear that people are interested mainly in her possessions. I smiled wryly at this upset of Mother's plans. She had wanted me to marry Homer and Josh to marry Pat, and instead those two were probably going to marry each other. The home team wasn't doing so well.

As Homer and I passed the open kitchen door, I heard raised voices. "I'll be sharp as a tack when I step out in 'em." Waving Homer on, I paused. That voice sounded strangely familiar, yet unfamiliar, too.

"You better not let Miss Chattie know nothin' 'bout it. She done told you 'bout beggin' things offen her comp'ny." That was Pearl, stern and forbidding.

"But Miss Cyn give 'em to me of her own free will. I am' ask her for nothin'."

Glancing in, I saw Viola, with a cat-that-ate-the-canary expression on her sooty black face, and a pair of plastic sandals with high red heels in her hand. As I entered, she thrust the shoes behind her. "I's just down here to get Miss Cyn's lunch tray," she told me guilelessly. With the natural imitativeness of her race, she had been putting on vocal airs for Pearl. That was why I had not recognized her voice.

Today was Tuesday, and Sylvia had been killed Saturday night. It seemed to me that Cynthia should have rallied to some extent by now. With David Scott no longer in the house, she might even venture from her room. But after all, if Viola didn't mind carrying trays, why should I bother? Apparently Cynthia was making it worth her while, though I doubted that Viola could wear the sandals with any comfort.

I decided to look in on Mrs. Markham. Shut off in her locked room, there in the nursery wing, she probably knew nothing of David Scott's escape.

"I'm so glad," she exclaimed fervently, when I told her, "because he didn't kill Sylvia—"

"What?" I gasped. "Then who did?"

Mrs. Markham had gone quite white under her soft rose-petal pinkness, and her eyes had that scared-rabbit expression again. As I stood there in the open door, she cast a wild look beyond me into the narrow passage, her hands fluttering to her bosom. "I— I— How would I know?" she quavered. Forcing her eyes to meet mine, she pointed tremblingly toward the passage.

I turned and looked behind me. "There's no one there," I said, shaking my head.

"I—thought I heard someone," she whispered.

It was strange, but I had had the same idea, and had half expected to see Viola coming along with a tray.

"Mrs. Markham," I ventured, "is there something I can do? Are you worried about anything?"

She seemed to hesitate, then she swallowed and shook her head. "No, thank you, my dear." Her eyes strayed around the room and came to rest on the newspaper with the still unfinished crossword puzzle. "Perhaps," she smiled uncertainly, "you could help me with this?"

If there was anything I didn't want to become involved in at the moment, it was a crossword puzzle, especially a puzzle that someone else had begun. But I had asked for it. Hoping to announce myself as baffled as Mrs. Markham, I picked up the newspaper. As I lowered my eyes to the black and white squares and Mrs. Markham's spidery handwriting, she cast another uneasy glance toward the passage, rose and closed the door.

The main difficulty with the puzzle seemed to be that in the space for a five-letter word meaning domestic animal, Mrs. Markham had written "tiger." Suppressing a smile, I still could not help remembering Cousin Chattie's experience Saturday night just after the murder when she turned on the lights in the blue room. She had sworn she saw the moving shadow of some huge animal. Had Mrs. Markham seen something of the sort, too?

We compromised on "horse" as the five-letter domestic animal to replace "tiger," and once again I tried to persuade Mrs. Markham to come downstairs. "Pearl will be sure to give us a good lunch," I said lightly, "to make up for all that funny business about the mojo."

"Viola is bringing me a tray," she smiled evasively. "Perhaps I'll come down later in the afternoon and we can go for a walk."

Just as I expected, Pearl had put herself out in preparing lunch. There was a hot shrimp pie, cold baked country ham, and a marvelous green salad with tarragon and just the tiniest suggestion of garlic in the dressing. And ready to be dipped into powdered sugar were chilled fat red strawberries, their green stems still intact. We might have enjoyed it more if we could have freed ourselves of the notion that we were sitting on a couple of tubes of radium.

Cousin Beau had not allowed us to discuss the murder at table, but now the lid was off. I had told them already about the peculiar change that had come over Mrs. Markham so soon after her arrival. Now I tried to bring up the subject again, for I could not rid my mind of the pathetic picture of a frightened old lady trying to lock herself away from something she would not name. But everybody was absorbed by the sensational escape of David Scott.

"What I can't understand," said Cousin Chattie, "is how Mr. Scott could have murdered this Dr. Dexter. After all, Dr. Dexter was alive Saturday afternoon, and how would Mr. Scott have known the way to his cabin?"

"Why couldn't he have gone there with Sylvia?" Homer asked. "They disappeared for quite a time from the dance."

It was pretty generally agreed that this would have been possible. "She could have taken him to Dexter's shack with the idea that Dexter might talk Scott out of using that evidence for a divorce," Josh suggested. "Say the two men got into an argument and it ends in a fight. Dexter is killed. Later Scott realizes he has to kill Sylvia because he knows she will blackmail him the rest of his life."

"But were there any signs of a struggle?" Cousin Beau asked.

Josh looked thoughtful. "No," he agreed, "I remember thinking when we found Dexter that he'd probably wandered out and fallen into the drain."

"Sylvia and her husband could have taken him for a walk," Cousin Chattie suggested.

Cousin Beau nodded his white head. "Very probably," he agreed.

It was not pleasant to think where that walk had led.

Everybody scattered after lunch. Cousin Chattie said that, radium or no radium, she just had to have a nap, and she didn't believe Sylvia could have hidden the stuff in her room, anyway. "But," she contradicted herself, "I'll never rest a moment until it is found."

I must have dozed on the side porch overlooking the river, for I came to with a jerk at the sound of some sort of altercation near the boat landing.

"But it's gone," a man's voice was protesting loudly. "I tied up down here to deliver them fresh crabs for Miz Richmond, and when I come back it was gone."

"But why should you think they took it?" Homer was asking reasonably.

By this time I was halfway to the pier myself. The center of the disturbance seemed to be sunburned, overall-clad Mr. Hawkins, who sometimes peddled fish to the summer colonists. At the moment he looked as though he thought Homer must be deaf, dumb, or blind, and probably all three. Standing around with open mouths were Woodrow, Pearl, Zack, and Viola.

"They was a-settin' here on this boat landin' when I come up," Mr. Hawkins told the assembled company indignantly, "and when I come back they was gone, and so was my boat."

"Who was gone?" I asked breathlessly.

"That young couple." Then recognizing me, he pulled off his battered straw hat, and relief struggled with ire on his sunburned countenance. "It was yo' brother Josh, Miss Ann, that's who it was. Spoke just as nice as you please when I come up. And that pretty girl with the blue eyes, she smiled. And then they go play a trick like this." Words failed him for a moment. He reached into his pocket, drew out a plug of tobacco, and bit off a chew. "What I say is"—the tobacco interfered somewhat, but he made himself clear—"somebody's got to lend me a boat. And Woodrow says the boat-house is locked and the police won't let nobody have the key."

"There's some mistake," I told Mr. Hawkins. "Josh wouldn't do a thing like that."

"Unless—" said Homer.

Everybody knew what he meant. Even Mr. Hawkins's flat-bottomed fishing boat, with its kicker motor, could make the mainland by way of the tidal rivers that laced the inland passage.

The fact that none of this made sense could not prevent my suffering a cold chill right there in the hot June sunshine. But if Josh were trying to escape, why drag Pat along? Left behind, she might spread the alarm, of course. But, at most, Mr. Hawkins would have been back within a few minutes, so Josh could not have hoped for much leeway.

Could it be—this was the wildest speculation yet—that Pat was trying to escape and Josh was helping her? Maybe they had hoped Mr. Hawkins would think the boat had floated away.

It was too much for me to figure out.

You could think you knew somebody—knew him well enough to be certain what he would do in any given set of circumstances. Then one day a door slams in your face. And that can be your own private torture. Josh and I had always been close, but he had never voluntarily mentioned Mrs. Scott to me. I had thought that was bad—but had hoped to ride out the storm. The tide had carried us far since then—far out of sight of land.

Homer's voice cut through my numbness. "We can't notify the police. One just doesn't do that sort of thing—not to one's friends. And if we don't, the police will be on our own necks."

"Look!" I said to Mr. Hawkins desperately. "I'll see that you get your boat back. If you don't, Cousin Beau will buy you a new one. Woodrow can take you home in the station wagon."

"Well," he agreed reluctantly, spitting tobacco juice into the river. "But I need that boat. Guess I could borrow one for a spell, though."

"Of course you can," I agreed feverishly. "Anyway, Josh and Pat have probably just gone for a little—little spin and will be back soon. We'll send the boat around by Zack."

Josh knew the Island and its small neighbors so well that he might hope to get somewhere, in spite of the Coast Guard, I had to admit to myself. He and Pat could hide on Little St. Simon's until dark and then put out again.

But after that—after he reached the mainland, didn't he know all the roads would be watched?

A tall blond, sun-tanned young man with blue eyes. Bareheaded and wearing white shirt and slacks. A girl in a yellow plaid gingham frock, her red-brown hair tied back with a yellow ribbon. This was the description that would go out over the wires. Probably neither of them had a penny at the moment. Josh must be going crazy. And I was only half a jump behind.

David Scott and Josh and Pat—all gone. What would Chief Lindsey say? Maybe the Chief wouldn't come back any time soon.

I turned, and there he was, standing almost close enough to touch, short and square and inexorable as the last judgment. How much he had heard, I could only guess.

He had heard enough to piece things together, and now he was ready to mow down anything or anybody who stood in his way as he raced toward the house to telephone the Coast Guard and police headquarters. Then he was back again, barking orders to the group of frightened servants. Woodrow, still in his white coat, was fumbling at the lock of the boathouse, and I realized that Cousin Beau's speedboat, the *Miss Chattie*, was to be pressed into service for the chase. With Woodrow at the wheel and the Chief grimly reaching back to make sure his revolver was in place, they nosed out and were off, cutting the water clean, white spray rising high in their wake as the boat gathered more and more speed.

Mr. Hawkins looked at me doubtfully, as though he felt somehow responsible for it all. "I sure hope your brother don't get in no trouble," he said.

It was not long really, though it seemed a long time. Cousin Beau and Cousin Chattie, roused from their naps by all the commotion, came downstairs and had to be told. After that we sat without saying much. Waiting. Waiting for the telephone to ring. Waiting for whatever was to happen. Trying not to think what that might be.

Then, faint at first, we heard the sound of a motor. Cousin Chattie put her hand to her throat as though she found it difficult to breathe. Then we were on our feet, for the *Miss Chattie* was rounding the Point. Secured by its painter, the empty fishing boat bobbed behind.

Through a sudden blur, I saw that they were all in the *Miss Chattie*. Josh, Pat, the Chief, Woodrow, and—I could not believe my eyes. It could not be David Scott.

David Scott had left Heron Point in Chief Lindsey's automobile. How could he be coming back in the *Miss Chattie?*

"Better wait here," Cousin Beau called, as I raced toward the pier.

Out of all the excited exclamations and explanations one fact emerged clearly. I could not understand it at first—how Josh had happened to ground Mr. Hawkins' fishing boat in the marshes. Josh, who had shot march hens ever since he could hold a gun. Josh, who was just as much at home in the celebrated marshes of Glynn as Br'er Rabbit in the brier patch.

"It was something of a surprise to me, too," Pat admitted a little later with a twisted smile. We were in her room, and a bath was running. Pat's yellow gingham was streaked with brine, and her usually sleek hair was all windblown.

"You see," she told me, as she skinned out of the bedraggled frock, "Josh and I were sitting there at the pier when the fish man came and tied up his boat and went around to the kitchen with whatever he had to sell. It didn't seem nearly long enough for him to be back when we heard someone running toward us. And there was David Scott, looking like a perfect wild man and waving a gun at us.

"Well," Pat was now efficiently cold-creaming her face, "he ordered us into the boat. The idea being, of course, that Josh would take him to the mainland. We tried to reason with him, but you can't reason with a tornado, not when it's waving a gun in your face. Then Josh gave me a funny sort of look and said we might as well accept Mr. Scott's kind invitation and be off to the races."

Pat smiled as she removed the cream with tissues. "It wasn't funny then," she assured me. "It seems Mr. Scott got lost when he tried to get away in the Chief's car and never found the causeway. You know how helter-skelter he is. He came back, apparently ready to give up. Then he saw the fish man and had the bright idea of thumbing a ride—by force—to the mainland. But there were Josh and myself at the pier, and he had to revise his plans.

"Of course, neither Mr. Scott nor I had the faintest notion of the proper direction," Pat pointed out. "Mr. Scott told Josh not to try any funny business and refused to put up his gun. It was fairly grim. We went on and on, the sun broiling down; and then"—Pat looked at me under the fringe of her long lashes—"we got stuck in the marshes. I realized immediately it was what Josh had in mind all the time, and I think Mr. Scott suspected too. Anyway, he was pretty excited there for a while.

"They say crazy people are always convincing," Pat flung back as she disappeared into the bathroom. The rest of it, borne on the familiar fragrance of specially blended bath salts, came out as she splashed in the tub. "I almost believed Mr. Scott myself when he said he was only trying to get away in order to check through his wife's papers with the idea that there might be something to show who this go-between is—the person who was to sell the radium, you know. It's just the sort of cockeyed thing he would do. He said he knew the Chief would never let him go."

At that moment the Chief was busy on the long-distance telephone. "We'll do this checking for you," he had told David Scott dryly.

It seemed very strange to the rest of us that he did not arrest David Scott, but only said something vague about expecting to break the case within a few hours—and that meanwhile we might as well hang together.

"Or hang separately," Josh added under his breath, winking at me.

XIX

THERE COULD BE ONLY ONE REASON why Chief Lindsey did not arrest David Scott. In spite of all the evidence, the Chief apparently was not certain of the man's guilt. Or he had evidence pointing in another direction.

What was in the Chief's mind, I could not guess. But, as it appeared to me, someone had committed a murder which was so near a perfect crime that no one clue pointed with certainty in any given direction.

There was Josh's letter to Sylvia. Maybe you could send a man to the electric chair for that. I wouldn't know. Reuben Allen probably was smart enough to win an acquittal, regardless of evidence. But after such a trial a lot of people would always believe the defendant guilty. And what would this do to Josh—to his gay lightheartedness, his sensitive pride, and his innate honesty and decency?

David Scott had motive, of course. But according to Cousin Chattie he was standing at her side just before the murder took place. And there were affidavits attesting Sylvia's misconduct which would enable him to combat her demands for a cash settlement when he filed suit for divorce.

If you keep churning your mind up and down, things come to the top that you might never think of otherwise—scraps, apparently unrelated to anything else. But I was desperate and grasping at straws.

What came to the top of my mind was really literal enough, but the possibilities were too fantastic to contemplate.

A pair of shoes.

Sunday night on my return from that trip to the cemetery with Rufus Blair, I had gone to Cynthia's room to try to convince myself it was not she I had seen in the churchyard. I recalled my quick look into her closet and something which had made little impression at the time. A shoe tipped sidewise against its mate on the floor. A plastic sandal, exactly like glass, except for its high red heel and strap.

The first time I had seen those glass sandals with their red heels was Saturday evening. Sylvia had worn them with a white chiffon gown printed with red poppies. I might not have noticed especially except for that near strip tease when Sylvia displayed her suntan in the drawing room before dinner. The strip tease had been too graphic for me to be mistaken about which twin was wearing which pair of shoes at the time. And because my decorator's training made me more than ordinarily conscious of details in color combinations, I had noticed that Cynthia, the other twin, was wearing all-red sandals with her white lace dress and a red rose in her dark hair.

Later, when Pat and I put Cynthia to bed after the murder, she had been wearing plastic sandals with red heels. I had unstrapped them myself and put them in the closet.

Either the twins had exchanged shoes before going to the dance or they had exchanged dresses.

And now Cynthia had given those plastic sandals with the red heels to Viola.

I sat there in my room for a long time, stunned by the potentialities of those glass slippers with their wicked red heels. It could not be, of course. If the wrong twin had been killed, the surviving twin would be the first to reveal that fact.

Unless—unless Sylvia herself had killed Cynthia.

The implications of that seemed beyond all reason, much too horrible to consider seriously.

And if such a thing had happened—why?

Well, suppose Cynthia knew something Sylvia wanted suppressed? Something that stood in the way of the cash settlement Sylvia was trying to squeeze out of David Scott.

Perhaps Cynthia had discovered something about the radium.

Or perhaps Sylvia's jealous resentment alone would have been enough. That remark her husband had made to Cynthia at the piano Saturday evening: "You should have been named Sylvia."

The words of the old song came back, hauntingly. "Who is Silvia?" Who, indeed?

One thing was certain. Sylvia had easy access to the dagger.

I still did not see how it was possible. The murder had taken place among a group of people. There was no opportunity to change costumes afterward. But there was plenty of time while the twins kept us all waiting on the porch after dinner before we went to the dance. Some variation in the size of Cynthia's and Sylvia's feet made it impossible for them to change shoes when they changed frocks.

But how could Sylvia persuade her twin to lend herself to the masquerade?

As a joke, perhaps? Mrs. Markham said they had had a lot of fun, fooling their dates, before they were married. Even at the wedding, it had been a subject of comment.

Why, I told myself, excitedly, it all hung together: those shoes, everything. The morning after the murder, when I had taken Cynthia (or Sylvia) her coffee, she had been standing in Sylvia's room with a pair of play shoes in her hand. Obviously this was because the shoes in Cynthia's closet were not of the correct size.

It was the Cinderella story turned backward. The envious sisters had whacked off a toe or a heel, trying to wear the glass slipper Cinderella lost as she ran away from the ball at midnight. But the blood had betrayed them.

> There's blood on her shoe,
> Not the right bride for you—

The doves or the pigeons had cried out some such warning to the prince. Now there was no visible blood on any shoe, but David Scott's wife was posing as the sister she had always envied.

It must be that. Otherwise, why should she refuse to see David Scott now that the other twin was no longer present to assist in a masquerade which was easy enough to put over after cocktails? Cold-sober, David Scott might not be so easy to fool.

And Mrs. Markham. This would explain why she had changed so suddenly. When she first arrived, she had seen her granddaughter only briefly in a darkened room. I remembered the words of her greeting: "Oh, Cynthia, darling, suppose it had been you!"

What was it she had said to me on the way home from the airport? That there was never any difficulty in deciding which twin was which if you knew them very well. And she had shown no grief at Sylvia's death.

But when she had called me to her room shortly before the inquest, there were unmistakable traces of tears on her rose-petal skin, and her eyes had been rimmed with red. Shock—grief—fear. No wonder she was upset. Fear would keep her from betraying Sylvia. Fear of what would happen to Sylvia? Or fear of what would happen to herself?

No wonder—after a night of it—Mrs. Markham asked to change her room. If Sylvia had killed her own twin sister, she would not hesitate to put her grandmother out of the way in order to avoid a threat to her safety. Nor would Sylvia hesitate to put anyone else out of the way who appeared as a menace. Sylvia could have killed Dr. Dexter. She could have slipped away while the rest of us were dressing for dinner Saturday night. No doubt David Scott had told her in that angry encounter on the front porch that he was prepared to fight her exorbitant demands for money. As a result she had decided to cash in on the radium, probably believing it to be worth its original hundred thousand.

Incidentally, Sylvia would now come into possession of her sister's money and would be her grandmother's sole heir. Mrs. Markham had said Sylvia was extremely mercenary, extremely vindictive. Here was the perfect motive: the perfect revenge on the sister she envied—on her husband who loved that sister—on all those who would be suspected of the murder.

When Cousin Beau had said Sylvia would have enjoyed broadcasting the radium in order to divert suspicion while exposing us all to the dangers of uncontrolled emanations, he gave a life-sized picture of her character. But even this did not quite prepare me for what I now believed to be the solution of the murder.

If there were only some way to check on the identity of the twins! Mrs. Markham would be afraid to commit herself. But I might extract the information without her knowledge. I could try, anyway.

Mrs. Markham did not answer my knock. I turned the knob, and the door opened. The room was empty. So was the bath. Apparently, she had kept her promise about going downstairs after lunch. But I could not find her on the lower floor or the porch. Remembering she had said something about taking a walk, I started out to look for her in the garden. With one foot on the porch step, I stopped, for I had thought of what seemed an even better plan.

The thing to do was to make sure if the dead woman was wearing all-red sandals. This would be proof enough that she was Cynthia instead of Sylvia.

But how to go about getting such information and where? In Brunswick at the mortician's? Or would the clothes of the murdered woman be "held in evidence" by the police, along with the dagger and Josh's note and my handkerchief?

I didn't like using the telephone at Heron Point because of all the extensions. Anyway, Chief Lindsey was holding the line open for long distance. And none of us was allowed to leave the Island.

Then I thought of Rufus Blair. He could get the information I wanted. If it took sleuthing, if it took persuading, he would get it. I'd hop right over to the Cloister and ask him to take on the job. But first I would check out with Cousin Chattie and Woodrow, just in case Chief Lindsey should happen to inquire as to my whereabouts. I didn't want any dragnet spread for me.

I was halfway to the Cloister before I remembered that Rufus Blair had called and left his number while Josh and Pat and I were away on that fateful trip to Aaron's fishing camp. In the ensuing excitement I had forgotten to return the call. Suppose Rufus had telephoned to say goodbye. He might not even be at the hotel.

At the desk, thank Heaven, they thought Mr. Blair was playing tennis. I said I would wait in the garden while they sent for him, and sitting stiffly in a chair that was meant for reclining, I watched a frog trying to climb out of the lily pool. He would get just so far on the concrete edge and then slip back again. It seemed to me that this was exactly the progress of our murder investigation. Unable to bear it any longer, I went to the frog's assistance and gave him a shove to dry land with the open toe of my white sandal. The ungrateful wretch precipitately jumped right back into the middle of the pool, splashing my green linen tennis dress, just as Rufus Blair appeared.

"It's a nice picture," he grinned, "but there's something wrong with the lady's expression."

"That's why I'm paging Sherlock Holmes," I told him, all at once feeling very self-conscious and wondering how on earth to begin. And as I stood looking up into his questioning dark eyes, my hand in his, something strange happened to me. One moment I was conscious of the tinkle of teacups and light laughter from the cloistered veranda. Of a girl and a man swinging tennis rackets as they strolled past. Of the frog still splashing in his lily pool. Of a red-winged blackbird swooping low over Rufus Blair's dark head bent toward mine. Then suddenly I was so acutely aware of Rufus himself that everything else became unreal, like something in a dream.

We stood there, marooned on a small island of intimacy. With flushing cheeks I withdrew my hand, and Rufus Blair asked huskily, "Is anything wrong? I mean is anything else wrong?"

"You'll think I'm c-crazy," I said, "but I've had a brain storm. And—well, there's something I want to ask you to do for me. Could you take time to drive around a little in my car?"

"Of course," he said.

We went out and got into the car. With Rufus at the wheel, we swung away from Sea Island, across the causeway to St. Simon's, and took the turn for Frederica.

He did not argue with me when I told him my fantastic theory about the twins and the shoes, only asked a question now and then, his face growing more and more serious.

"It's crazy enough to be true," he agreed, "but—"

"But what?"

"I was just wondering—how anyone could be such a monster?"

We had reached Christ Church and he parked the car under one of the great trees across the road from the entrance. Like an official greeter, a big black cat with a white spot between the eyes came stalking out of the cemetery, crossed the road slowly, and fixed us with an unblinking stare.

"Scat!" I said, clapping my hands.

Rufus laughed aloud. "It's just a cat," he said. "What have you got against the poor animal?"

"It's not just a cat," I smiled back at him. "It's a graveyard ghoul. That's the reason we couldn't find Sylvia the other night. She's changed into this cat. That's why she laughed. Don't you see how she's looking at us now—laughing up her sleeve?"

As the cat continued to return his gaze without batting an eye, the grin left Rufus Blair's face. "Darned if she doesn't look that way," he admitted. Deliberately he got out of the car and, with a great deal of scatting and hand clapping, chased the cat away.

"I'm beginning to come around to your way of thinking," he said, as he climbed back.

"About the cat?"

"About Sylvia Scott. I think we did see her the other night. After all, she could have taken that back road to Heron Point and got in without being seen."

"It isn't much more than a bridle path," I said, wondering how Rufus himself knew about the road. "Anyway, Viola says she didn't leave her room."

Suddenly I knew what had happened. Those vocal airs of Viola's in the kitchen. I remembered Homer's embarrassment the time he invited the new maid at home to go with him to a movie, mistaking her telephone voice for mine. All the new school of colored maids sound exactly like the lady of the house when they answer the telephone. That must be it. Sylvia had posted Viola in her room while she went to the cemetery Sunday night. It was Viola who had talked to Pat while Sylvia slipped out of sight until the coast was clear.

"But why would Sylvia be coming here to the cemetery?" I asked Rufus.

"You wouldn't have any idea?" He grinned at me, and his dark eyes were very bright.

"Tell me," I begged impatiently.

"The radium, of course. Nobody would ever think of looking for it in the cemetery."

"Of course," I cried, flinging open the car door in my excitement, ready to start the search then and there.

"Wait," he said, reaching across and closing the door again. "It looks like a small cemetery, but there's a lot of territory to cover. I think we should have an electroscope."

"But I told you—it's broken."

"Maybe I can get the fixings while I'm in Brunswick, after I find out about the shoes. It's just a simple little problem in physics. Let's see, a bottle and some gold leaf and—well, leave it to me. By the way, I don't think I'd say anything about all this until we're sure. Somebody might try to cover up."

"All right," I agreed dubiously. "But call me the very first minute you can. We'll meet here."

When I got back to Heron Point after dropping Rufus at the Cloister, where he was to transfer to his own car, I found the place in a new uproar.

Mrs. Markham had disappeared.

"Disappeared or dead." Woodrow rolled his eyes as he broke the news. "Miss Ann, this place sho is givin' me the jitters." He regarded me anxiously, then went on again. "Reckon that man took her off?"

"What man?"

"That man that rung the doorbell. Listen, Miss Ann. When I was goin' over to St. Simon's this afternoon to git some things we forgot to order this morning," Woodrow paused impressively, "I saw him."

"How do you know who it was?" I asked, trying to keep my tone matter-of-fact and casual.

"Well, he looked just like you said he did. Course, I weren't close to him. You know where the old pasture is, off to the left of the road? Well, Miss Ann, I was drivin' along in the station wagon, mindin' my own business, and I just happened to look over that way. And there he was comin' toward me, all in black and twice as tall as he ought to be. Then, while I was lookin', he sees me and he sort of fades into the bushes, and I put my foot down on the gas and I got away from there."

"You're crazy," I said. "What do you mean, twice as tall as he ought to be?"

"Well, maybe not," Woodrow conceded reluctantly, "but them long legs sho could get him places in a hurry."

"And then Mrs. Markham disappeared?"

"She was gone when I come back. Maybe she was gone before. Viola carried her up a cup of tea but couldn't find her nowhere. She never took no hat nor no pocketbook. Don't look to me like she went willin'."

Maybe she had already gone when I myself looked for her earlier in the afternoon. Her hat and purse and her gloves were all in the bedroom. And she belonged to an era when no lady ventured beyond her front door without gloves. Woodrow was right. She hadn't gone willingly.

"She was horribly afraid of something," I told Chief Lindsey.

"You mean you think something might have happened; that she didn't just wander off and forget to come back?"

"I don't know," I admitted miserably. "Did you ask Sy— Mrs. Harrison? Did you—look in the attic?"

"Yes," he agreed soberly, "and there was blood in the attic. But it was dry, and we think it's only a souvenir of your boy friend's little hitch at detecting the other night. You didn't take the old lady away with you when you drove off this afternoon, I suppose?"

"Woodrow saw me drive away. I couldn't very well have concealed her, unless I'd put her in the trunk."

From the look that came into the Chief's eyes, I knew he was going to search that trunk, perhaps the trunks of all the cars. "I hear your man in black has turned up again," he said on the way out. "You didn't see him this time, did you?" His eyes were half mocking, half serious.

I shook my head, repressing a shudder.

XX

THE WORD WENT OUT, and again the dragnet was spread—for Mrs. Markham. A search of the Island was organized. We combed the neighborhood around Heron Point. There was talk of dragging the river.

But when, wearily, we sat down to dinner at last, there was still no news. Mrs. Markham might have vanished into thin air.

I had come home from that talk with Rufus with my head in a whirl. And now this.

Could Sylvia have killed her grandmother too? If so, what had she done with the body? It would have been easy to push the old lady into the river. But how could Sylvia and her grandmother have left the house without being seen? This would have been easy too, I realized. The pier was visible from Cynthia's room. Sylvia—I was morally certain it was Sylvia who occupied that room—would have heard the commotion following the flight of Mr. Hawkins's fishing boat. She would have seen us all clustered there, excited and uncertain. She could have persuaded Mrs. Markham to take a walk with her toward the wild garden. Or—more likely—she could have followed Mrs. Markham without Mrs. Markham's knowledge. Out of sight of the group at the pier, she could have toppled her grandmother into the water.

Of course, Sylvia had to make certain about the lock on the screen door in order to get back into the house without being seen. I must ask Woodrow about that as soon as dinner was over. Maybe he would know if a door had been left unlocked.

When Rufus called—if he said the shoes were red—I would ask him to come to Heron Point, and we would tell Chief Lindsey what we believed to be the solution of the mystery.

All my wild fancies about Sylvia dead, inspired by her appearance in the cemetery Sunday night—and that mocking laugh—were as nothing compared to the horrible reality.

Perhaps there had been some immediate necessity for killing her sister. But she never could have done so except for the hate nurtured in her heart all these years—years in which Cynthia had tried to shield her from the consequences of her own fiendish temperament and utter lack of moral scruples. And finally Cynthia had died as a result of all this. She had died, but she was to live on as a dreadful caricature of herself in Sylvia's body. Rufus Blair was right, Sylvia was a monster.

Did Sylvia really expect to carry on the deception permanently? Could she, now that she would have everything that belonged to Cynthia—now that there would be no Cynthia to be jealous of—could Sylvia play the role of Cynthia?

With her very life dependent upon it, I decided that she could. If this new Cynthia did not seem quite herself—or if she wearied of continuous effort—she could always plead that she was suffering the after-effect of shock.

We got through dinner somehow.

"Ann," Cousin Chattie reproved, "Chief Lindsey has spoken to you twice."

"Oh," I apologized, "I'm sorry. I was just thinking. So much has happened, you know."

Chief Lindsey's sharp eyes were fixed on me speculatively. "We were talking about a little experiment that might be interesting," he said. "About that—person you saw on the stairs the other night. I've a theory that if you saw the same person under the same circumstances, you would recognize him, even though you were not sure of his identity."

Everybody at the table was looking at me. I laid down my fork because I could no longer hold it steady. "I don't understand," I said.

"Suppose," the Chief told me, "we set the stage and reenact the scene. You—"

"Oh, no!" I cried. "I—I couldn't." Of course, it must have been Sylvia in the attic—changing the hiding place of the radium. But I had to know about the shoes. Suppose Rufus and I were wrong. Suppose—

"Nothing to get excited about," he went on calmly. "Everybody goes up to the attic. You are in the upstairs hall—"

"But the lightning," I objected. "There was a flash of lightning. You can't stage that."

"No problem at all," he assured me. "As each person comes down the attic steps and stops at just the point where he could peek around the wall, we'll switch on the light for a second. It will be O.K. And if the scene looks familiar, you can give me the tip-off. Or perhaps it would be better to wait until everybody is down and tell me privately."

"Oh, no," I said desperately, "I couldn't possibly. Suppose—"

"There's a possibility," he pointed out, looking up and down the table, then bringing his glance back to mine, "that it was no one in this group. You'd like to establish that fact, wouldn't you?"

He waited for my answer, eyes narrowed. Everyone was waiting. "Yes, of course," I whispered, "but—"

"All right," he cut me off. "Suppose it was someone you know. He's on a spot. He's going to be pretty desperate before we are through. He'll kill again, if necessary. Maybe he has already. Maybe that's what's happened to poor old lady Markham. And maybe she won't be the last."

"Oh," I moaned, "I don't know what to do."

"Think it over," he said, sprawling back in his chair, as dessert was brought in.

Coffee was served on the terrace without benefit of my presence. I did not want to stray even that far from the telephone. Three times its shrill insistence flicked my nerves as I sat waiting in the big cool hall; but Woodrow was always ahead of me, and the call for some-one else. And Woodrow, when questioned, could not remember that any screen door had been left unlocked during the afternoon.

The first of that series of telephone calls was for Chief Lindsey, after which he rang up headquarters and asked that a policeman be sent to Heron Point to relieve him. Then he and Cousin Beau went off somewhere in the Chief's car, probably to continue the search for Mrs. Markham.

I was just about to give up on Rufus when the telephone rang for a fourth time. A moment later, elaborately mysterious, Woodrow beckoned me into the dining room.

"But why didn't you call me?" I reproached when he told me Rufus Blair had left a message.

"He was in a hurry, Miss Ann. He wants you to meet him at nine o'clock at the farm back of Mrs. Parrish."

"What? At the farm back of the Parrish place? But—"

No use to argue with Woodrow. If that was what Rufus had said, that was what he had said. But why? What had he discovered? A glance at my wristwatch told me that it was already twenty minutes of nine. And I had to go almost from one end of the Island to the other, between ten and twelve miles.

"Listen, Woodrow," I said, hurriedly, "start Mr. Josh's car and drive it out beyond the entrance. Leave the engine running. I don't want anybody to know I've gone."

Woodrow looked worried. He hesitated, frowned, then blurted out: "But, Miss Ann, that's a long way. Shouldn't I go with you?"

"You know you can't get away without a lot of explanation," I said impatiently. "I tell you I don't want anybody to know I've gone. Oh, for Heaven's sake"—as Woodrow still looked dubious and it occurred to me that he might think this a romantic rendezvous— "we think we've found a clue. Mr. Rufus is trying to help us. Now, keep it quiet."

Woodrow was right. It was a long drive, and in all my visits to Heron Point I had never before taken it alone at night. The breeze, stirring the leaves, filled the wood with whisperings, which seemed to approach, pause and recede, then approach again and pause indecisively, as though marshaling for some eerie onslaught. The floating gray moss, caught in the faint glimmer of the headlights, was like some ghostly nebula which might assume definite form at any moment. What was the matter with the headlights, anyway? Perhaps there was fog. At any rate, I must drive slowly and cautiously for fear of going off the narrow road into the thick undergrowth.

Breathing a sigh of relief, I stepped on the gas as the lights at last picked up the pavement on Couper Road. But I remembered that I must not step too hard, for Josh had said something about the brakes—that they needed adjusting or relining or something. Off to the right, around that curve on Frederica Road, was Christ Church and the cemetery. How had Rufus Blair discovered that the radium was somewhere else?

Back of the Parrish place. That would be the old Thomas Cater farm, abandoned long ago and now part of the property surrounding the winter home of Mrs. Maxfield Parrish, which would be deserted at this season. As a cache for the radium, the Cater farm was perfect. It would be safe from honest people and prowlers as well, for island Negroes gave the farm a wide berth.

Thomas Cater, so the story goes, had been murdered by an overseer who coveted his wife. Accordingly he was buried standing up and is said to walk about his farm at night. No need to ask how Sylvia had happened upon this perfect hiding place, for the Parrish property also includes the site of the historic Battle of Bloody Marsh, always pointed out to visitors.

As I turned into the driveway, I slowed down, for the faint tracery of the old plantation road was somewhere to the left of the garden pool, around which two headless children are said to dance on moonlight nights. They would not be out on a dark night like this, but it occurred to me that if ghosts really do come back, a convention might assemble here at any time. I shivered a little, seeing in imagination the specters of those Spanish soldiers who fled in wild retreat into the nearby marshes, there to be hopelessly cut down by British fire—losing their lives and eventually the continent of North America.

Yes, this was the old plantation road, leading to the Cater farm. I must pick my way now. There was a narrow unrailed bridge somewhere across a tidewater creek—I must watch for that.

And then it happened.

Headlights that seemed to materialize out of nowhere, the great blasting of the horn of a car that swooped down upon me like a dive bomber. Blinded and deafened, I could only react automatically, swerving sharply to the right and slamming on my brakes. But those brakes were not meant for slamming.

What would have happened at even average speed, I do not know. But, driving slowly, I was now both helpless victim and horrified spectator. I realized I must have swerved just before reaching the bridge, for the car took its leap fairly deliberately. Had the creek, with its steep vertical banks been wider, the car might even have landed on the bottom right side up instead of crashing sidewise into the opposite bank, shuddering, settling finally halfway over on its side in the water.

Slipping and sliding with the car, I still gripped the steering wheel. Otherwise, I might not have been pinned beneath it with water half covering my body. I lay for a moment, afraid to move, afraid I would discover broken bones. But except for the steering wheel and my cramped position, I seemed to be intact. I felt as though I had been picked up and bounced against a brick wall and part of the wall had fallen back on top of me.

The lights were out and the engine was silent, but I cut off the ignition as an extra precaution. Squirming experimentally in my unnatural position, I discovered that I was fastened as securely as though I were a part of the car. I could reach the handle of the door, but the door was stuck.

Rufus, of course, would be on the job of rescue in a moment. What I could not understand was why he had driven out of the Cater farm as though pursued by all the demons of the lower regions. He could not fail to know my car had been crowded off the bridge into the creek.

"Rufus!" I called. "Here I am. Rufus!"

There was no sound of any kind, except the *jug-a-rum, jug-a-rum* of the frogs and the lapping of the water against the car. Someone had remarked at dinner that the tide would be high at ten o'clock. I knew that, in this creek or drainage canal, the water might easily rise as high as seven feet by that time. Much too high to think about comfortably.

"Rufus!" I called again, trying to keep my voice under control.

Then I heard footsteps approaching. They came on and stopped at what must have been the edge of the bank just above me. "Rufus, I'm down here," I cried. "I can't get out. I'm stuck under the steering wheel." Nobody answered. The quiet was as complete as though the whole earth had suddenly become soundproof. Even the frogs were silent, as though listening.

But I had heard someone. It could not have been a dog or other stray animal. Those were human footsteps.

"Help, help!" I cried again, but with less conviction.

Still there was no answer. Desperately I began to squirm to try to release myself. But the pulling and twisting were too painful. It was as though there was a fire in my side, a fire that shot sparks all over my body, sparks that became stars in front of my eyes. I sank back helplessly into the water.

It took me a long time to realize that whoever had crowded my car off the road, whoever had come back and stood above me, did not intend to offer help.

This was so incredible that I began to doubt I had even heard those footsteps, began to believe I had been fooled by wishful thinking. Or perhaps the island Negroes were right and I really had heard the phantom footsteps of Thomas Cater.

It took me a longer time to realize that I had been the victim of a plot, that somebody had wrecked my car deliberately. Like a forgotten picture of memory, I could see the plantation road which I had approached so cautiously. Just beyond the bridge was a curve to the right and a slight incline that led behind a dense wall of shrubbery. Someone waiting in a car, behind the shrubbery with lights out, could have timed his attack with the accuracy of an artillery barrage.

And he had come back to make sure there was no miscarriage of his plans. To make sure, if I were still alive, that I could not escape the incoming tide. Tears rolled down my cheeks to join the deeper flow rising about me.

But who? And why?

I knew why, of course. That cockeyed plan proposed by Chief Lindsey to reenact the scene in the upstairs hall. Could Sylvia have heard through Viola? Or did Sylvia have an outside accomplice?

Again I struggled wildly to free myself, holding my breath, trying to make myself even smaller in order to wriggle sidewise. But the car seemed to close like walls about me, restricting my movements on all sides, even as the wheel held me down. Waves of nausea swept over me and for a moment I thought I was going to faint.

I screamed then, again and again, hoping that someone passing along the main road might hear me. Now and then I could hear the quick swish of a car as it sped along that lonely stretch of highway, but if anyone heard my screams, there was no sign of it.

The horn. Why had I not thought of the horn? But it was dead. Dead as the lights. Dead as I was going to be.

Perhaps there are a lot of things you are supposed to think about when your hours are numbered. But I did not have an hour, and I could only think what a fool I had been. I had realized somebody suspected me of knowing too much. That person, faced with the possibility of immediate identification, would not hesitate to take whatever steps his or her safety demanded. Chief Lindsey had told me that. But I had been so sure that the call was from Rufus.

It seemed to me that the tide was rising faster, making little gurgling sounds as it penetrated various parts of the car. Time and tide wait for no man, and nothing mattered to me now but time and tide. Less than an hour. An hour that moved in minutes, and in water creeping higher. Water that would fill my nose, my mouth, my ears.

I had learned to swim under water pretty well. That would prolong things. But I must try not to struggle too much when that last dark moment came. Only, of course, I knew that I would.

Loneliness engulfed me, deep as the rising tide. To die like this—

But it was hard to believe that this was the end. Hard to believe in death while the blood still flowed warm in my veins, implicit with all the bright promise of what I had dreamed my life was to be. Hard to believe in death, even with the water salt in my mouth.

XXI

FOOTSTEPS. FOOTSTEPS COMING BACK. Was I delirious? I had not heard the approach of a car. I did not know that anyone was near. I only knew that I could not hold out much longer in my cramped position, trying to keep my head above water in that wrecked car.

Perhaps they were only phantom footsteps.

"Help!" I cried, not too hopefully. "Help!"

"Ann!" Rufus called in reply. "Ann, where are you?"

"Here—here in the creek."

The beam of a flashlight found me. "My God!" he said. And then he was climbing and slipping down the steep bank into the water.

"Oh, Rufus!" I cried, and my head dropped back. But the salt water revived me quickly enough. "Get me out," I begged, "It's the steering wheel."

"Yes," he said quietly. "I see. Are you hurt?"

"It hurts when I move. Oh, Rufus, get me out."

Moving the flashlight here and there, he said: "I think it will have to be the hacksaw. Thank God, there are tools in my car."

"But don't leave me," I cried. "I've been here forever, and the tide— Don't you see? It's coming in."

"I won't leave you," he assured me gently. "My car's just over there. I'll be back in a jiffy, and—I'll whistle all the time I'm gone, so you'll know I'm not far away."

"Hurry! Oh, do hurry!"

That whistle was a little thin on the night air, and the tune—if it could be called a tune—was not one I recognized. But it was a comforting sound just the same, and Rufus was back more quickly than I had thought he could be, climbing down, bracing himself against the side of the car in order to keep his shoulders above water.

"That thing doesn't look like much of a saw to me," I said, as he gave me the flashlight to hold.

"This?" he made a great show of cheerfulness. "Why, this is what prisoners use to carve their way out of jail. It's a very handy gadget." His voice sobered as the hacksaw grated against the metal of the steering wheel, splashing water in all directions. "Can you stand the—jarring? I'll be as easy as I can."

"Don't bother, about that," I urged. His remark about jail breaking. It could only be a wisecrack, I told myself, clenching my teeth against the vibration of the steering wheel. "How long will it take?"

"Not long. Ten minutes or so," he answered, inhaling deeply, arm pumping back and forth.

"Cousin Chattie says you are a man of mystery," I babbled. "But I don't care. You are always in the right place at the right time."

"A little late this time," he chuckled, "but not too late."

"How did you know where to come?"

"Well, I had promised to telephone. Remember? Gosh, this thing makes an awful sound—"

"Don't mind that. Go on."

"Well, I had the devil's own time finding gold leaf in Brunswick. It was late when I started, you know, and later when I got back to the hotel. But I fixed up the electroscope and called Heron Point. Woodrow promptly went into a fit, because he said you'd gone to meet me. Finally he calmed down enough to tell me where to look for you, and I hurried here as fast as I could. But," he added ruefully, "not fast enough to see who tried to wreck you."

"Tried?" I said bitterly. "Seems to me it was a pretty good job."

"And pretty smart, too. Nobody would ever believe it was anything but an accident."

"Somebody was certainly taking a long chance. Suppose our cars had come together?"

"Somebody had to take a long chance. And by the way—" He paused but kept doggedly on with the saw.

"What is it?"

"Those shoes—they were red."

"Oh," I gurgled as my head plopped back. Up again like a jack-in-the-box, I sputtered through salt water: "I can't believe it." And that was the truth. To suspect somebody is one thing. To have proof is another. Sylvia, the super-monster, alive and posing as the twin she had murdered.

It was then that the blade of the hacksaw broke. "Damn!" Rufus muttered under his breath, adding quickly: "It's all right. Don't worry."

Hastily removing the longer piece of metal from its framework, he grasped the blade with his bare hands. It bent and twisted as he worked. "But we're coming along," he assured me cheerfully.

We did not get on very fast, but I was no longer worried about the tide: there was something about Rufus Blair—a touch of daring, perhaps—that inspired confidence in his ability to do things. And then at last he was saying, "Careful, there's a rough edge," and holding the severed steering wheel in his hand. And I was trying to speak but finding my voice all out of control.

"Easy does it," he said gently. "I think you'd better put your arm around my neck."

"I may choke you," I gulped.

Incredibly I was out of that deathtrap. We were in Rufus' car. We were standing at the lighted entrance of Dr. Hame's combined office and residence, both of us dripping black muck and sea water. But the doctor did not bat an eye when he opened the door.

"Just bruises," he told me, after an examination. "You may have a cracked rib or two, but I don't think so. We'll take an X-ray tomorrow, if necessary."

Then, with a grin, he prescribed a shower for each of us and brought out some of his own slacks and shirts. "Just saving myself work. Don't want to have to treat you for summer colds."

Rufus and I looked even funnier when we were dressed again, for the doctor's clothes swallowed me and were small for Rufus; but they were dry and clean. "I have a hunch I should take you over to Brunswick to a hospital," Rufus said, his bandaged hand white against the steering wheel as we drove back to Heron Point. "You could telephone Mrs. Richmond and tell her you were there on account of X-rays or something."

"But why?"

"Well, after all, somebody tried to murder you tonight."

"Cousin Chattie would be all upset. Besides, you'd have to hide me in the luggage compartment in order to get past the tollkeeper. And, anyway, I have a key to my door, thanks to you.

"I'd like to check with Woodrow as to where everybody was at nine o'clock tonight," he said grimly.

But Woodrow told a strange tale when we reached Heron Point.

"Everybody been gone," he said, rolling his eyes either at our costumes or at the news he had to tell. "Everybody gits telephone calls and slip away like they don't want nobody to see 'em."

"Wait a moment," Rufus told him. "What do you mean, everybody? Did Mrs. Harrison go out?"

"Naw, sir. Leastwise, I ain't seen her. Ain't none of the ladies went out. 'Ceptin' Miss Ann. Just the gen'lemen."

"Has anybody asked for me?" I questioned.

Woodrow grinned, his white teeth gleaming in the dark of the back porch. "Yes'm, they sho is. And if we'd been back in Atlanta, they'd had out the fire department lookin' for you."

"Gosh," I said, "I should have phoned from the doctor's office, but I didn't know there would be all this hullabaloo."

"They sho wuz," Woodrow assured us with relish. "Miss Chattie, she ring and ask where you at. First I say, you gone out, and she say that's funny and to bring some ice water. When I come back, she ask more questions, and I have to tell her you gone to meet Mr. Rufus. Then we find out all the gen'lemen gone, and she say she bet somebody is up to somethin'."

Woodrow paused for breath, then took off again. "I tell Miss Chattie I hear Chief Lindsey phone to Brunswick 'fore he leave to tell 'em to send another policeman here to take his place. An' Miss Chattie, she say, 'Yes, and where is that policeman?' 'cause ain' nobody seen him and things has come to a pretty pass. She tells me to roust Zack out o' bed, and me and Zack git the butcher knife and the ice pick and we do what Miss Chattie calls sentry duty in the hall."

"But why did all the men leave?" I wondered.

"They all git tips about how somebody can tell 'em where Mrs. Markham is at and it may be too late if they, don't hurry," Woodrow announced importantly. "That's why they all leave. And then, bimeby, they all come back—"

"Did they find out anything?"

"No'm, they sho ain'. They all been to different places and nobody nowhere to tell 'em nothin' about Mrs. Markham. Mr. Josh say them telephone calls was fakes. He gits home first, and when he hears you ain' here he's fit to be tied—"

"Oh, dear!" I said.

"Well, I tell him Mr. Rufus is gone after you." Woodrow's tone couldn't have been more complacent if he'd said the Marines had landed. "But Mr. Josh, he's fixin' to start out hisself when Mr. Homer comes in. So he tells Mr. Homer, and Mr. Homer says Chief Lindsey done got you murdered, sayin' he wants you should reco'nize somebody in the attic. So then they both light out, lickety-split, to the Parrish place. They ain' been gone long when Mr. Beau and Chief Lindsey come back. Mr. Beau, he's puffin' and blowin' and plumb disgusted, and everybody starts tellin' the news. And Miss Chattie, she's cryin' and says Chief Lindsey's a fine policeman, gittin' you murdered. And Chief Lindsey he sho does git red in the face. He busts out of the house and says for everybody to stay here, and he jumps in his car and goes rearin' off. And Mr. Beau and Miss Pat they takes Miss Chattie up to bed."

"Lindsey was a damned fool to suggest any such plan and then let you out of his sight," Rufus said with unexpected heat.

"But here I am," I answered shakily, "thanks to you."

"Let's don't forget Woodrow," he said hastily, as though embarrassed at any show of gratitude. "And by the way, about the cemetery—" He turned to Woodrow. "There's a package in my car for Miss Ann. I wish you would put it in a safe place and keep an eye on it."

"It's the electroscope," he explained as Woodrow disappeared down the steps.

"Well," I said, and paused, once again overcome by self-consciousness and that acute awareness of Rufus Blair standing there so near me on the dark porch.

I had a queer conviction that this was one of those moments in time that stand alone; that I could take or leave it; but that perhaps I should never feel quite like this about anyone again.

The thing to do, of course, was to laugh it off. Not to say in that strained, unnatural voice, "Well, thanks for saving my life." Not to look up into dark eyes. Not to reach out to touch somebody because suddenly it was the thing you wished most to do in the world.

There was a dreadful moment when I hung as though suspended in space, uncertain what he might do. He might even laugh. He was such an unpredictable person. Yes, I should have laughed first. Only now I could not laugh, because of those battered ribs we had both forgotten. Afterward, standing back from that crushing embrace, I said incoherently, "I didn't mean—I only meant—"

"I understand," he said stiffly, adding—of all things—"I'm sorry."

Before I could open my mouth again he was gone, striding off into the night. And that moment I had snatched was gone too, shattered into a thousand bits.

"What must I do with this, Miss Ann?" Woodrow asked, coming up the steps.

"What?" I asked vaguely. "Oh, I don't know. Put it somewhere. Anywhere. I don't care."

"Mr. Rufus say to keep a eye on it," he said doubtfully. "Listen, Miss Ann, I'll hide it behind one of them big pots in the kitchen. Ain' nobody gonna see it there, 'cept maybe Mamma, and she won't bother it."

Because they offered a short cut, I climbed the back stairs to the second floor. As usual, the upper hall was dimly lit, and the back stairs completely in shadow.

Just as I reached the top step, I heard the creak of a door and paused. For it was Cynthia's door—or Sylvia's, as I now believed.

Cautiously a head emerged. Then with the coast clear, the door opened a little wider and a man slipped quietly out, closing the

door softly behind him. He stopped a moment to listen, his head
on one side. Then, soundlessly as a moving shadow, he vanished
into the deeper darkness of the sleeping porch.

I should have challenged him. But I could not. The man who
had disappeared into the darkness was Josh.

It had all seemed fairly simple—Sylvia, the murderess—and the
radium in the cemetery. Now I was completely at sea again. Why
had Josh gone to Sylvia's room? Why had she received him when
she made so much fuss about keeping everybody out?

Stumbling down the hall to Cousin Chattie's room, I tapped on
the door and pushed it open. Pat was there, bathing Cousin
Chattie's brow with lavender water, and Cousin Beau was sitting
at the foot of the bed, looking so haggard and worn he should have
been in bed himself.

This was the scene that met my eyes, and for a moment everything remained the same as in a tableau. Or perhaps it was only
that my eyes retained the impression, while the scene itself was
breaking up, becoming vocal, becoming animated question marks
and exclamation points—all hurling themselves at me in mass attack, but falling short somehow, losing themselves in a blur through
which the lights of the room winked like stars and streaked like
comets.

"Watch out," Cousin Beau's voice, sharp with warning as he
sprang to his feet, cut through the fog, and involuntarily I straightened up. Fatigue and excitement and the thought of facing a barrage of questions had come near being too much for me.

The comfort of the chaise longue was like arms supporting me,
and the lavender water was cool and refreshing as Pat transferred
her ministrations. Woodrow appeared magically with sherry, and
Cousin Beau was saying: "The Chief never meant to make you go
through that crack-brained plan to reenact things in the upstairs
hall. His idea was that the suggestion would scare somebody into
making a break or exposing himself in some way. Of course,
Lindsey didn't anticipate anything like this. And Mrs. Markham
complicated things. Naturally, he couldn't afford to ignore that call.
The old lady may still be alive, you know. Anyway"—his tone took

on a note of reproof—"Lindsey had nothing to do with your rushing off without telling anybody."

"But Woodrow knew. And Rufus had said he'd phone. He had an idea we might find the radium." Haltingly, between sips of sherry, I told them what had happened. It was wild enough without including the Sylvia-Cynthia angle. Anyway, there was nothing we could do about that until Chief Lindsey got back. Why had Josh gone to Sylvia's room? I wondered again. I could ask him, but would he tell me?

"You don't know a thing about this Rufus Blair," Cousin Chattie's voice broke in fretfully, "except that he's always hanging around."

I knew that he was twenty-six years old and had dark eyes that seemed perpetually amused at life. I knew that he could be tender, too, and unexpectedly touchy. And I'd hoped he was hanging around because— But this was no time to be thinking about such things. No time to admit to yourself that you'd fallen in love at last— all out and forever—with somebody you'd probably never see again.

There was a quick tap on the door, and Josh came in, relief lighting up his blue eyes as a hasty once-over assured him I was all in one piece. "Yes, sir, Lindsey's still at the Parrish place," he answered Cousin Beau's question, lankily subsiding on a footstool near Pat. "He sent Homer and me back. Accused us of obliterating tire tracks and acted as though he thought we might be doing it on purpose." Then, turning to me, "What's the big idea, barging off like this?"

"Don't forget," Pat reminded him, "that everybody went barging off on fake calls, even the high and mighty Chief Lindsey."

Josh grinned sheepishly, and Cousin Chattie took the center of the stage: "I was terrified. All these murders. And poor Mrs. Markham gone. Then all the men lured away. I was sure we were to be kidnapped or murdered, or that something else terrible was to happen here."

"No," Cousin Beau said, regarding me gravely, "the idea seems to have been that something was to happen at the Parrish place—

to Ann. Either somebody on the outside wanted to protect himself by throwing blanket suspicion this way by calling us all out or—"

"Go on," Cousin Chattie prodded.

"Or someone here didn't want to be conspicuous by his absence."

The doctor came a few minutes later, and Cousin Chattie snorted indignantly when he told her that all she needed was a sedative and quiet.

"I've as much chance of being quiet here as in a boiler factory," she declared.

As if to bear out her words, Woodrow banged on the door and almost fell into the room. His teeth were chattering and his eyes rolling. "It's—g-gone," he stuttered. "I—I—can't find it no-nowhere."

"Get hold of yourself," Cousin Beau ordered. "What's gone?"

"The butcher knife," Woodrow gulped. "Miss Chattie tell us she need pertection, and the gunroom's locked, and so Zack and me git the ice pick and the butcher knife. And now the knife's gone." Woodrow cast an apprehensive glance back into the hall as though he expected someone to be lurking in the shadows with the knife.

Cousin Beau rose heavily to his feet. "All right," he motioned Woodrow out. "Let's look into this."

"I'll come too," Josh volunteered.

Cousin Chattie's head lolled back on the pillows. "It's bad enough," she moaned, "to have a murder in the cemetery. If we've got to have another here in the house—"

The doctor filled two glasses with water. "Take this," he told her, holding out a small yellow capsule, "and here's one for you, Miss Carroll. You should have been in bed long ago," he admonished as I swallowed it. "Well, that will put you to sleep."

"But—" I objected, remembering all I had to tell Chief Lindsey.

Pat and the doctor smiled, and Pat took me by the arm. "Not exactly a close fit," the doctor designated the costume he'd lent me earlier. It was the first time anyone had noticed that costume since I reached Heron Point.

Pat tucked me in and I was just drifting off when she dropped by again to tell me they had not found the butcher knife. "I thought you'd better lock your door." Not greatly concerned about anything by that time, I decided I might as well take her advice.

So grand of the doctor to ring the curtain down like that, I thought, as I climbed back into bed. To shut out all the problems that pressed so close.

But they were not shut out entirely, for in my troubled dreams, I was searching the cemetery with the electroscope—following the gold leaves and discovering suddenly that I had followed them into a dark forest and was lost. It was a forest done by Dali, with trees that became grotesque threatening figures in a mad ballet. Trees dancing about me on every side, leering and jeering and cutting off every avenue of escape even if I could have guessed my way out again.

XXII

IN SPITE OF THE SEDATIVE, I waked early next morning. My head ached, and I had a bad taste in my mouth and felt knocked about generally. On top of everything else I had an odd feeling of urgency. There was something I must do—but I could not quite remember what it was.

I must have a talk with Chief Lindsey, of course. He'd laughed when I told him of the ghostly figure Rufus and I had seen at the cemetery Monday evening—and that horrible mocking laugh. He'd laughed when Pat told him she had seen someone she thought was Cynthia in the upstairs hall that same evening—someone who had melted away right before her eyes. He'd called it mass hysteria. What would he say when it was proved to him that we had really seen Sylvia? Not Cynthia—but Sylvia. And that she had gone to the cemetery to hide the radium.

That was it. That was what I must do. I must find the radium.

Rufus Blair had made an electroscope for me, and I had rather taken for granted we would track down the radium together. How could I guess he would go stalking off without giving me a chance to explain that I had only intended to say I hadn't meant to be cheap? Oh, dear, it all seemed too involved even now! How could anybody ever know what anyone else meant? But after the unexpected violence of that kiss I'd had to say something, for I had so plainly brought it all on myself. Why did he have to blurt out his ridiculous "Excuse me," almost as though he was not in the habit of kissing girls. "I understand," he'd said, and had not understood

209

at all. Stop it, I told myself. Take an aspirin. You'll never see him again. What does it matter?

I took the aspirin. Maybe, after all, it was just a headache and getting all bruised up that made me feel so awful.

My wristwatch on the bedside table said five-thirty. Such a long time until the household would be astir. And I could not go back to sleep. Not with this inner compulsion to hurry.

I lay there for a long time, and it was only five thirty-five when I looked at my watch again. The radium was at the bottom of everything that had happened. Rufus and I had guessed its hiding place, but someone might move it again. Sylvia might even plant it on— Josh. She had wanted to harm him. She herself had given the police that note he'd written her. If the radium could be handed over to the police at once—

Quietly, I slipped out of the big bed and into the bathroom. Cold water felt wonderful. I dressed hurriedly, thinking as I took a crisp apple-green chambray playsuit from its hanger that green would be less noticeable against the other green of the cemetery and that tennis sneakers would get me out of the house quietly.

As I brushed my hair and tied it back with a green ribbon, the mirror might have been Pearl, reproaching me. "Look sort of peaked this morning, baby." And what was it Cousin Chattie had said? "Don't forget, blondes fade early." Lipstick helped my morale a little.

The next thing to do was to find the electroscope. Woodrow had mumbled something about pots and pans. Almost holding my breath, I crept down the back stairs to the lower hall and into the big, airy kitchen.

There were so many pots and pans. I must be careful not to drop one while making my search. Cautiously, I removed a huge aluminum boiler from its hook, certain that this must be the one Woodrow had picked. But it was empty. So were half a dozen others of varying sizes.

Suppose somebody had already taken the electroscope. The person who appropriated the butcher knife, perhaps. That knife had disappeared as the dagger had disappeared—only no one had noticed about the dagger.

Here was the electroscope at last, and it was just my luck to knock a small pan to the floor. All ears and apprehension, I stood frozen in my tracks, but apparently the big house still slept. The only sound that broke the early morning stillness was the chatter of birds outside. The only sign of movement was the flutter of red and white checked gingham curtains swaying in the breeze. But still I waited—waited while the tiny hands of my watch moved from six-ten to six-fifteen.

Satisfied at last that I was safe, I slipped out onto the porch, only to have Gin and Bitters greet me with joyous yaps, certain they were to be released for a frolic. Hushing them as best I could, I filched the bicycle Cousin Chattie is always going to use for reducing and was on my way.

Out of sight of the house I breathed more freely. This old back road, now mainly used as a bridle path, was a short cut. Rufus was right—Sylvia could have followed it when she went to the cemetery to bury the radium. She could have turned her car around before getting out so that it would be headed back toward Heron Point and concealed from the road.

It must have been something of a shock to Sylvia when Rufus Blair and I appeared on the scene. She could have identified us easily enough by the headlights as we got out of the car. No doubt she had lingered outside the cemetery to make sure we were not after the radium. She could not be certain, of course, that the detective had not given out some information about it. She could laugh that we had thought her a ghost.

But later, perhaps, she was not so sure. That visit I had made to her room upset her. So she came to my room Monday evening to see how the land lay. And perhaps to take steps, if they were necessary. Suppose I had accused her—there in my bedroom—not of being Sylvia, of course—but of having some connection with the radium.

Pedaling vigorously, I mulled over all these things. The morning was fresh and clear about me, and in my mind things were also becoming clear. I could see now why detectives always considered motive so important. Sylvia had got rid of two people who cluttered her life, and she would be rich as a result, independent of any action her husband might take.

Yes, I had the motive, and in a little while now I would have the radium. Inhaling long draughts of the fresh morning air, I felt a sudden exhilaration. It would be fun to let Woodrow present the radium to Chief Lindsey on a silver tray, along with his morning coffee, there on the side porch.

I would peep around the corner. And already I could see the way Chief Lindsey's head would jerk back on his short square neck, the startled expression in his eyes as he squinted at the tray.

"Will you have it with or without cream?" I would ask,

I parked the bicycle back of the church. No need to leave it out where it might attract attention. Glancing behind me before I turned, I had the strange impression that the trunk of one of the trees on the far side of the road moved slightly, or that someone standing behind it had moved. But, as I stood and watched, the great tree remained stationary and I smiled, telling myself that I had been remembering my dream of the night before when the trees had danced about me, leering and jeering in a mad ballet.

This morning the cemetery was nothing like that dream. With the sunlight filtering through veils of gray moss and the arched green branches of great live oaks, it was difficult to associate this cloistered serenity with the violence that had occurred here only a few evenings before.

Yet, as I moved among the weather-worn slabs—holding the improvised electroscope in front of me as I had seen Chief Lindsey do at Heron Point—it seemed to me that here on these slabs, in the quaint legends which were the fashion of a more leisurely time, were reflected all the impact of passion, all the turbulence and tragedy which are life, no matter when or where it is lived.

Perhaps the blood flowed a little hotter here where the old South lay buried, I thought, as I read the inscription on a broken marble pediment. But what was that mark on the marble? A cross, made with something that looked like lipstick—deep, purplish red.

I read the inscription again: "Who fell a victim of his generous courage on the third day of December 1838, aged 32 years." I remembered how dashed I had felt when Cousin Beau told me it was really not a lady's honor which was involved. One gentleman had spit in another gentleman's eye, or something of the sort, as the result of a boundary-line dispute. And so they had settled with coffee and pistols at dawn.

If there was any hidden meaning in that inscription, I could not figure it out. And the gold leaves of the electroscope were completely unresponsive.

Watching the leaves closely, I moved on. Surely here under one of these flat slabs, resting on low built-up walls, would be the perfect hiding place. The radium would be safe here. And it could not harm the dead.

Trying to raise one of the slabs, I found it unexpectedly heavy. Perhaps the slab had been cemented down. Some of them were loose but even these were quite heavy. Sylvia would have looked for a small grave. Well, infant mortality had been high enough.

Then I discovered another red cross, and I was ready to swear it was made with lipstick such as the twins used. I read the inscription:

Beloved wife of . . .
Sleep on, my love, in thy cold bed,
Never to be disquieted;
Stay for me there, I will not fail
To meet thee in that hollow vale;
And think not much of my delay—
I am already on the way.

Maybe, there was something there, something that offered a clue to Sylvia's hiding place for the radium. I pondered over it a long time, but all I got was an eloquent tribute to masculine fickleness, for the husband's grave was nowhere about.

Here was another of those cryptic crosses:

JOHN LORD COUPER
Died August 24, 1862 at Gordonsville, Va.

An artist by profession, a poet in na-
ture, bright and gentle-hearted, he
shared manfully as sergeant major of
the sixtieth Georgia regiment in the
hardships and perils of the common
cause and sacrificed a life full of
promise.

Even in my preoccupation with the search for hidden mean-
ings, that phrase, "bright and gentle-hearted," made me think of
Josh and what life and wars can do to people. But a sudden rustling in the shrubbery beyond the church brought me back to earth.
Turning quickly, I saw no one. And though I stood listening I heard
nothing further, except when the raucous cawing of a crow broke
the silence. The rustling could have been caused by a dog or perhaps that cemetery cat. I preferred to think it was a dog.

Apparently there were no more crosses. Probably they did not
mean anything, anyway, for the electroscope stubbornly refused
to register any signs of radioactivity. And then in the lot to which
members of the King family had been brought, one by one, in final
slow procession from King's Retreat plantation, I picked up another cross. Here was perhaps the most sequestered spot in the
cemetery, and not even the bright morning sunshine intruded upon
its privacy. But Sylvia had been here, or I missed my guess.

As I stood holding the electroscope in front of me, I heard again
a faint rustling in the shrubbery somewhere about. All at once the
cemetery took on an eerie quality, and I felt a little chill as though
some cross current of air eddied at the back of my neck. Hastily I
looked around. There was nothing to see.

Forcing myself to calmness, I read an inscription:

ANNA MATILDA PAGE KING
A faithful Christian, as daughter,
wife and mother, as a mistress to her
people, a woman loving and gra-
cious, upright, tender and true.

A complete life story, it seemed to me—even though it offered no clue to a possible cache for radium. And she had died just in time—1859—just before the fateful sixties and the War between the States.

Then my pulse quickened. For on a grave that Anna Matilda had not lived to see—the last resting place of her son, Captain Henry Lord Page King, who died on a Virginia battlefield fighting vainly to preserve the world she knew—I found freshly disturbed earth.

The gold leaves remained indifferent, but perhaps there was some flaw in Rufus Blair's hastily improvised electro scope. How silly of me to have come off without a trowel! Excited grubbing with my fingers convinced me at last that this was indeed a blind alley—the underground tunnel of a mole.

I came out of the King lot, subdued and more than a little discouraged. My head was beginning to ache again; I was conscious of various bruises, and I wondered if I would find the radium, after all. Closing the iron gate behind me, I remembered dejectedly that, whatever happened, it all came down to this. Remembered too that men now chase little white golf balls over the broad green acres on which the white boils of the celebrated Sea Island cotton once flourished at King's Retreat plantation.

But Anna Matilda Page King had had a full life, whereas they could put it all in one bleak word, "spinster," on the tombstone of Ann Page Carroll.

Doggedly, I plodded on with the electroscope, first in one direction and then another, now thoroughly convinced that the red crosses meant nothing at all. Perhaps they had been left by some schoolgirl collector of epitaphs who meant to return later with pencil and paper. Of course, it was possible they had been used for identification by Sylvia, who had marked a given slab and broadcast other crosses in order to confuse the issue, just in case anyone should happen to guess.

Then, as I stood on an absolutely open space, wondering which way to turn, the gold leaves began slowly to droop. It was uncanny. They were actually moving.

While my pulse raced madly, I held myself down to a slow pace, eyes glued on the leaves. I stopped in my tracks when the leaves themselves stood still. I knew I had veered from the trail and, once on the right track again, I must follow closely lest radioactivity exhaust the electricity in the rod of the electroscope before I reached the radium itself. I couldn't dig up the cemetery as Detective Owens had dug up Cousin Chattie's wild garden. Anyway, I was sure Sylvia had hidden the radium under a stone slab. Turning to the left, I saw that the leaves had begun to droop again.

Suddenly I had a feeling that someone was watching me and felt again that chill current of air eddying at the back of my neck. But I could not take my eyes from the gold leaves. If I missed the direction now, the rod would have to be recharged before the electroscope would function again.

Anyway, I was all keyed up, ready to imagine things. Did Sylvia dream I suspected her masquerade, I wondered? That attempt to put me out of the way last night—that must have been because someone feared to be identified on the attic steps. But Rufus Blair and I had both seen Sylvia in the cemetery Monday evening—and now that the news was out about the radium—she might realize we would suspect she had hidden it there.

I must hurry. I must get away from here as soon as possible.

Here—this must be the one. This small grave of an infant, forlorn as only a forgotten grave can be, with the loose slab on its low crumbling base. Yes, it was marked with a cross, too. Sylvia had marked the others to prevent this one from being conspicuous.

The gold leaves hung limp against the rod on which they were clustered.

In just a minute now I would have the radium. The mystery would be solved. For surely, confronted by this evidence, Sylvia would not have a foot to stand on no matter what shoes she wore.

Kneeling, I set Rufus Blair's electroscope on the ground and grasped the slab with both hands.

The stone was not heavy, and I was able to lift it easily. Underneath was the boxlike lead container described by Chief Lindsey.

I had found the radium.

Just as I reached for it, some slight sound, some instinct of caution, warned me to look around. But it was too late. Something hit me on the head and the black-out was complete.

XXIII

OPENING MY EYES TO THE DISMAL DISCOVERY that the radium was gone, I had a groggy glimpse of Woodrow, returning from a nearby hydrant with a hatful of water. Not greatly surprised to see him, I was still a little curious as to how he managed to be so omniscient and omnipresent.

Then the water hit me full in the face.

"I got up early to look after my set hooks on the river," he explained as he helped me into the station wagon. "But first I go in the kitchen to git myself a little snack. Mr. Rufus say keep a eye on that electro-what-you-call-it, so I take a look. And it ain' there. I study a minute and decide maybe the best thing is to slip upstairs and tell you 'bout it, Miss Ann—"

Well, Woodrow had tapped at my door and, receiving no answer, had stuck his head in cautiously and discovered that I was gone as well as the electroscope. So he had added two and two and got his usual five. And as a result I was back in my own bed, still wearing my green play suit, and the doctor was grumbling about never having any time for his regular patients. "Possible concussion," he told me, "Don't stir out of bed. I'll be back this afternoon."

"Chief Lindsey's foaming at the mouth," Cousin Chattie told me as she followed the doctor out. "And here's Viola with your breakfast."

From the mixture of upraised masculine voices just outside, it was obvious that Chief Lindsey was trying to shake Josh and Homer off his coat tails.

"You can see her later," he told them firmly.

218

"But," Homer insisted, "I won't be back until tomorrow, you know, and I'd like to be getting off. This is Wednesday, and one of those appointments I told you about is for this afternoon."

That would be the Grahams' cocktail party for their English visitors. So Homer had succeeded in getting leave to fill those all-important social engagements. "You can wait a little while," the Chief repeated. "I won't be long."

"Kiss Lord and Lady Heyward for me, Homer," I called out facetiously.

"Gosh, Ann!" Homer shouldered his way inside the room. "I'm glad you are all right."

His face had a strained look that smoothed out a little as I smiled at him, immediately sorry for my unnecessary flippancy. After all, perhaps I was equally snobbish in a different way.

Lindsey shooed him out then and grimly closed the door, while I burned my tongue and throat trying to fortify myself by swallowing half a cup of coffee at one gulp.

"No use to ask why you went off without telling anybody," he growled, plumping down in a chair by the bed. "People think they are too smart to need any help. So what? So you get cracked over the head and the radium's gone."

"I suppose I'm lucky I didn't get carved up with Pearl's butcher knife," I admitted miserably.

"Oh, that! The maid found it under Scott's pillow. He swears somebody planted it there." Chief Lindsey switched abruptly. "Any idea who hit you?"

I shook my head, wincing a little. "I thought I heard somebody shortly before I found the radium, but decided I was mistaken."

"Guess that was Blair. Anyway, he's gone—"

"You don't mean—" My cup rattled the saucer as I set it down. So that was why Chief Lindsey was letting Homer go to Atlanta. He thought Rufus Blair was guilty.

"Talked with him last night after I left the Cater farm." The Chief glowered at me. "He didn't sound exactly on the up-and-up then. And this morning he's checked out and nobody knows where he's headed for."

I pushed the breakfast tray aside. What little appetite I had was gone.

"Well, he may put it over," Chief Lindsey admitted grudgingly, "but we've got everything covered. Chances are he's going to step right out of his car into the arms of a policeman."

"But"—I managed to find my voice at last—"how could he have killed anybody in the cemetery Saturday night if he was driving the car—to produce the ghost?"

"May not have been driving. Everybody just took it for granted he drove. But he's always around when things happen. You can bet on it he was there at the cemetery this morning."

"But if he knew where the radium was hidden, why wouldn't he just take it?"

"Maybe he didn't know. Maybe he was using you as a cat's-paw. How did you happen to look in the cemetery?"

Chief Lindsey was waiting for my answer, and I came out of the fog and remembered there were a lot of things I had meant to tell him. "I'm sure you're wrong about Rufus Blair," I said, "because—"

As he listened, his expression—at first condescending, as though he thought that crack over the head might have affected my mind—became noncommittal, then speculative, almost eager. Evidently nothing could surprise him, for he registered no shock at the horrible thought that one sister had killed another.

My own convictions were strengthened, rather than weakened, as he asked an occasional question: about the shoes worn by Sylvia before dinner Saturday evening and the supposed-to-be Cynthia after dinner; about the ghost in the cemetery who looked like one of the twins. He nodded his head, and his narrowed eyes were points of steel as I told how Rufus Blair and I decided later she went there to bury the radium.

"Maybe she did the killing," he conceded reluctantly, "and Blair's just the middleman. Or, maybe, you can explain why he sold out like he did this morning?"

Since I could not bear to think about it, much less try to explain it, I ignored the challenge. Surely Rufus' little flare-up last night could have inspired no such summary departure. "Of course,"

I said, "it would be better if we had some incontestable proof of Sylvia's identity. I'd counted on Mrs. Markham—"

"What about that fingernail?" he asked quickly. "The one the photographer found out there in that so-called grave. How long does it take for a fingernail to grow back?"

"Of course," I agreed excitedly, "the fingernail would prove it. She could have used an artificial nail to cover up. You can get them at the dime store. I hadn't noticed her nails because—well, at first I naturally thought she was Cynthia. An artificial nail would be easy to detect if you paid special attention."

"Well," he said, "now—"

There was some sort of commotion in the hall outside. The door was unceremoniously thrown open, and there stood Mrs. Markham, pale but composed as a lady on her way to the guillotine, and looming behind her were Josh and Cousin Beau. She was still wearing her black and white silk print and her head was bare, but every white hair was beautifully in place.

"I—" Mrs. Markham began, then her lips moved without words.

"She says she must see you, Chief," Cousin Beau told him.

Chief Lindsey, already on his feet, his face one big red question mark, escorted her to a chair by the bed, first nodding at the two men in the hall and closing the door in their faces.

"Are you all right?" Mrs. Markham asked me with anxious eyes.

"All right," I assured her, for she was obviously very upset.

"Where've you been?" Chief Lindsey could contain himself no longer. "We've turned the Island upside down, looking for you."

"I—was with a friend," she told him, evasively. "Wait." She held up a small, plump, blue-veined hand that shook a little. "I'll tell you all about it. I didn't mean to come back, because—" Again her voice died.

"Suppose you start at the beginning," the Chief advised her gently. "Would you like—some aspirin or anything?"

She shook her head. "I—I was afraid—for my life," she whispered. "But I realized Ann was in danger, and I had to come back to—warn her." Mrs. Markham smiled tremulously at me. "You've been very sweet to an old lady, my dear."

"What's this danger you want to warn Miss Carroll about?" The Chief's voice was faintly indulgent as though he might be talking to a child afraid of the dark.

Mrs. Markham looked at him doubtfully and clasped her hands in her lap. But there was something in her eyes that must have made Chief Lindsey feel a little immature for a moment at least.

"I've nearly lost my mind," she told us, her voice barely above a whisper. "I knew what I should do, but—I'm not sure I can do it, even yet. Can't you—can't you let Ann go home—go away, go anywhere, so long as she can leave this terrible place?" Her eyes pleaded with Chief Lindsey.

"What is it you have to tell?" he asked. "It's possible we know, already."

"Is it about Sylvia?" I broke in.

Mrs. Markham shrank back in her chair, glancing furtively this way and that. "So—you—do know?" she breathed. "It's why I left. You see, I recognized her. Not immediately, because the room was dark and my eyes are not what they once were."

"You knew she was Mrs. Scott?" the Chief prodded. "Then why didn't you say so?"

Mrs. Markham looked miserable. "Because Sylvia convinced me she was in danger from—the murderer and, if we kept quiet, the police would track him down."

"What's this?" Chief Lindsey's face mirrored his inner befuddlement.

"She told me that she and Cynthia changed clothes Saturday evening before going to the dance—because Sylvia wanted to fool her husband into some—indiscretion. You see, David had told Sylvia there would be no big cash settlement for her because he had evidence to prove that she—" Mrs. Markham spread her trembling hands, paused, and forced herself to continue. "Sylvia knew David Scott loved Cynthia, and she thought if she could pose as Cynthia and get him to—make love to her, she could use it against him—

"Of course, Sylvia didn't tell Cynthia that. She said David was cross with her, and asked Cynthia to pour oil on the troubled waters. That's the way she was able to persuade Cynthia to lend herself to the masquerade. David was drinking, and it was night. Otherwise, of course, he would have guessed."

"But why didn't you come to me as soon as you found out about all this?" Chief Lindsey demanded again.

"I was afraid." Mrs. Markham looked at him pleadingly, and you could not doubt her. "Sylvia swore to me that she did not kill her sister. She said that at first she believed David committed the murder, and that she was frightened to death for fear he might discover he had killed the wrong twin and try to do away with Sylvia herself. So she refused to see him and stayed locked in her room, hoping"—she straightened up and gave the Chief a faintly reproving glance—"that the police would get everything straightened out. Of course, Sylvia said she could not be positive it was David, because—well, there were others who did not feel kindly toward her. And she—she told you everything she knew that might throw light on the situation. About the note from Ann's brother—about the quarrel with Ann and Pat."

"But you yourself didn't believe her?" Chief Lindsey probed.

"I didn't know what to believe," Mrs. Markham confessed slowly. "At first, I did believe that it happened as Sylvia told me. Then I thought about it and it just didn't seem possible. Sylvia really hated her sister. And don't you see? This would get rid of her—give Sylvia everything that was Cynthia's. Then I realized Sylvia suspected I did not quite believe her. I was frightened. After all," she looked at the Chief appealingly, "it is not safe to know too much."

"You were afraid she might—put you out of the way?" he asked, his eyes fixed on the little old lady huddled in her chair, hands gripped tight in her lap.

Mrs. Markham shuddered. "Yes," she whispered. "And I—wanted to warn Ann, but I left—rather hurriedly. Viola told me Ann saw someone in the cemetery who looked like one of the twins and—well, I knew then that Sylvia must be guilty. She was undoubtedly trying to hide the radium, and she would know Ann would suspect—something. The fact that nobody took Ann's story seriously would make no difference to Sylvia, because there was always the possibility Ann knew about the radium and would find it. And Sylvia couldn't just keep moving the radium from place to place. Someone else might see her."

"Then," I said, "it must have been Viola in Sylvia's room Sunday night pretending she was Sylvia, while Sylvia was just getting back from the cemetery. You see," I explained in answer to Mrs. Markham's perplexed frown, "Pat thought she saw Cynthia in the upstairs hall, but when she spoke to her, whoever it was just faded away. Pat walked over and knocked on Cynthia's door and somebody answered from inside. She thought it was Cynthia, but it must have been Viola."

"Oh, no," Mrs. Markham shook her white head, "it—it must have been Sylvia. She could throw her voice—ventriloquism, you know. It's one of the things she picked up from those queer friends of her mother's when she was quite small. Sylvia's mother was an actress," Mrs. Markham explained to the Chief, "but she went downhill and finally could get only vaudeville engagements. Sylvia even learned a little hypnotism. She frightened me with it sometimes. Oh, don't you see why I couldn't stay?"

"Sylvia tried to frighten me with her hypnotic talents when she came to my room Monday night," I remembered. "Well, anyway, I'm glad it wasn't Viola who talked to Pat from inside Cynthia's— Sylvia's room. Still, Viola probably helped Sylvia get in and out of the house without being seen."

"Then you think," Chief Lindsey asked Mrs. Markham, "that it was Mrs. Scott who knocked Miss Carroll out this morning in the cemetery?"

"This morning?" she echoed blankly.

He gave a quick summary of what had happened, but Mrs. Markham only shook her head.

"I don't know what happened. Perhaps someone was in this with Sylvia" She glanced at me apologetically. "I was afraid it was your brother, but surely he wouldn't—"

"Bash his sister over the head?" Chief Lindsey finished.

"Well, whoever it was," she hurried on, "I'm afraid Sylvia was really to blame. I'm sure she ruined this Dr. Dexter, just as she tried to ruin David with her unreasonable demands. She probably thought up the plan to sell the radium. And if Dr. Dexter was to be disgraced, and Sylvia herself involved in a scandal, I don't think she would hesitate to take the way out that seemed most expedient. She is a terrible person."

Mrs. Markham shuddered, and the Chief brought her a glass of water from the bathroom. The glass clattered against her teeth; but she managed to swallow a little, and sat back and closed her eyes.

"God forgive me," she whispered. Then she opened her eyes and gazed up at Chief Lindsey, "Sometimes," she quavered, "I don't think it was David who was unbalanced but Sylvia. Maybe that is the real solution."

"What I don't understand," the Chief told her, trying to be stern, "is how you could disappear so completely."

She smiled wearily. "I'm so sorry. I—well, I was frightened and nervous." She glanced at me. "Yesterday afternoon while all the excitement was going on—about your brother and the boat, I went out to get a little air. I didn't like being in the house alone with Sylvia. I'd just reached the porch when who should I see but Colonel Markham's old friend, Professor Winslow of Philadelphia, coming up the steps to call on Major Richmond.

"He's a very fine gentleman," she explained, "really a sort of family connection. A little eccentric—that is, he's a botanist, always going off to try to track down some queer plant or other. This time it's the lost—now what was it he said?" She paused, distressed anew.

"Gordonia," I supplemented. "Cousin Chattie says every now and then botanists go on a rampage, looking for the lost Gordonia in this section."

"Yes," she nodded. "He—"

"Mrs. Markham," Chief Lindsey interrupted, "did you know we dragged the river for you?"

"Oh," she gasped, "I'm so sorry. But Professor Winslow insisted on turning his trailer over to me while he went to a hotel. He saw how upset I was, and thought if I got away for even one night I might feel better. I didn't tell him I never wanted to come back. And I was so nervous I didn't think of causing anyone trouble. With the house in such a state, I hardly expected to be missed. Anyway"— shivering—"I had to get away. Can't you understand? But in the night I kept thinking about Ann, and I—"

She was interrupted by a high, thin scream from the hall. "Oh, Lordy, oh, Lordy!" Viola's shrieks cut the air. "He's done killed her. Miss Cyn's done dead."

For a split second of frozen listening, Chief Lindsey's gaze remained fixed on Mrs. Markham. Then he was flinging himself across the room, reaching for his revolver, shouting back at us, "Stay where you are."

Viola, in hysterics, was still crying: "He's done killed her. Miss Cyn's done dead."

I didn't believe it, of course, as I stumbled after Chief Lindsey.

And now we were in the room which Sylvia—posing as Cynthia— had occupied since the murder of her sister Saturday night. And there Sylvia lay, her beautiful dark head twisted sidewise on the pillows, eyes staring grotesquely from their sockets.

Chief Lindsey went through all the usual motions, trying to find some spark of life. "Strangled." He almost strangled himself on the one word.

There were the marks on her throat.

It was all wrong. It could not be true. Sylvia was the murderess. But there she lay, lips sealed in death. If we had misjudged her, she could never tell us now.

XXIV

The thing that Sylvia feared had happened. She had been murdered in her bed. She had kept her door locked against everyone. Everyone except Josh, I remembered with an anguished cry as Chief Lindsey catapulted down the stairs.

Leaning over the rail of the stairwell, I caught a glimpse of David Scott in the hall below, dark hair on end, eyes wild, headed toward the back porch, brandishing a revolver.

"Drop that gun," Chief Lindsey shouted.

But he might as well have tried to shout down a hurricane. When I reached the lower hall, both he and David Scott had disappeared through the door to the back porch, and now Pearl's shrill screams rose high. But David Scott could be heard above everything else. Evidently someone was trying to restrain him forcibly, for he was yelling like the madman he was, "Stand back, you fool, stand back."

"Drop that gun," the Chief shouted again.

And then I recognized Josh's voice. "For God's sake," he begged hoarsely, "don't shoot."

My knees were folding, and I grabbed the back of a chair. For the space of a choking heartbeat, everything was quiet, and I dragged myself forward again. Then, incongruously, there was the sound of a motor starting.

And then I was at the door, but somebody jerked me roughly back inside, just as a shot was fired. "Do you want to be killed?" Cousin Beau growled in my ear.

227

Close on the first shot came a second report. The acrid smell of powder was in my nostrils; my eardrums were ringing and in my heart was a terrible certainty as I twisted my arm from Cousin Beau's restraining grasp.

I knew only too well what had happened: David Scott had killed Josh. Chief Lindsey had fired too late. Otherwise, there would have been only one shot.

But I had to see.

"Come back!" Cousin Beau grabbed at my arm again.

He was close at my heels when I came to a sudden halt on the porch, where David Scott, still raving, twisted in Lindsey's grasp as handcuffs were slipped about his wrists.

"My God!" Cousin Beau gulped thickly. "That lunatic thought Homer was trying to escape. Just listen to him."

But Josh was my one concern. He was standing by Homer's car, his eyes full of excitement, his hair bright in the morning sunshine. Apparently both shots had gone wild.

"Come on back in the house," the Chief ordered, out of breath from his struggle with David Scott. "Why were you selling out like that?" he shot at Homer, who was cutting off the motor as he climbed out of the car.

Homer stood speechless for a moment. "Selling out?" he sputtered. "You'd have sold out too if that maniac had come at you with a gun. I was all packed and just waiting the word from you. I'll be late getting to Atlanta as it is. Seems to me I've been the goat in this whole thing. Why don't you put him in a strait-jacket?" He eyed Scott truculently.

"Never mind about that," the Chief told him. "Nobody's going to leave here when we've just had another murder."

"Another murder?" Homer's eyes bulged, his mouth fell open, and his well-tailored shoulders sagged. I knew he was mentally kissing the Graham cocktail party goodbye.

"W-what?" Cousin Beau gasped. "Who?"

"Who?" David Scott gibbered foolishly. "Who?"

"Into the library, everybody," Chief Lindsey ordered, diving for the telephone closet. As we passed we could hear him issuing more orders to headquarters. "Yes, the other twin. Strangled. . . . Right away? . . . Sure, send the doctor. But she's dead."

Then he was standing short and square in the library door, shoulders hunched forward, eyes narrowed, exactly like a football tackle ready to charge. "Where's that colored girl?" he snapped, twisting about for a glance over his shoulder. "Here, you!" He beckoned to someone outside, then stalked into the room and took his accustomed seat at the desk, swinging around to count heads. Yes, we were all there, even Mrs. Markham, all waiting in a stunned silence.

Viola edged her way into the room. Her sooty black skin had a grayish pallor, and her eyes were walled in her head. "I—I ain't done nothin'," she mumbled.

"Who was the last person you saw in—that room?" the Chief bellowed.

Viola jumped, looking around wildly as though for some means of escape.

"It's all right, Viola," Cousin Beau told her quietly. "Just answer Chief Lindsey's question."

Viola raised a shaking black hand. "Him," she wigwagged at David Scott. "He—give me ten dollars to leave the connectin' bathroom door unlocked and go downstairs. He say he just wanna talk to Miss Cyn. Then when I come back—she's lyin' there, dead."

"What about this, Scott?" the Chief asked sternly.

"We all knew she didn't want to see him," Homer said. "You—" Scott lunged at Homer with his manacled hands. The Chief shoved him back into his chair, and he sat there, glaring at Homer, breathing in great panting gasps. "But—" he began.

"Calm down," the Chief told him. "You can have your say right now. Start at the beginning."

"The beginning? But I tell you—"

"Take it easy." Obviously the Chief was trying to maneuver a full confession while he was about it.

"All right." David Scott sat back again, but he still moved his bound hands restlessly. "This morning, I did bribe the maid to unlock the bath connecting the rooms which had been occupied by Sylvia and Cynthia.

"I—I had to see her," he went on, trying to speak with calmness. "I'd been in the room only once before, just after that alarm when Sylvia's room was turned upside down Saturday night. There wasn't much light then, but this time—well, I recognized—my wife. It—was a great shock. I'd thought she was dead—"

"Oh, dear Heaven!" gasped Cousin Chattie. Looking around the room, I saw David Scott's shock reflected on more than one face. Josh was sitting bolt upright, blue eyes riveted on the speaker. I could have sworn all this was news to him.

Some of what David Scott told the Chief, we had heard already from Mrs. Markham: that Sylvia had been afraid he would kill her if he discovered the wrong twin had been done away with by mistake; that she'd been frightened after Rufus and I saw her in the cemetery; that she'd also begun to fear her grandmother suspected her; that she had not known the radium was stolen, but only that Dr. Dexter wished to avoid publicity.

Then his voice rose excitedly. "I had the right idea about this all the time," he told Chief Lindsey. "I knew, if I could have a look at my wife's papers, I would find the name of the middleman in all this. All your long-distance telephoning was no good because Sylvia was still alive and had the papers here." Shifting in his chair, he struggled to draw something from his coat pocket.

Chief Lindsey rose deliberately, fished a paper from the pocket, and unfolded it.

"There's your murderer," David Scott cried.

The Chief inspected the paper carefully, not to be taken in by a madman's ravings, however reasonable they might seem to be. "Looks like a list of stocks and bonds," he said slowly. Then his head jerked back and he gave David Scott a long, appraising look.

"Yes," David Scott's voice was surprisingly calm. "There's your murderer's name in black and white. He'd been playing the market for Sylvia That was collateral she put up. He lost it all. And Dexter's radium insurance money, too. You see, Dexter had some foolish idea he wanted to return the money to the insurance company. That's why he killed Dexter, and why he tried to kill Sylvia

Saturday night." David Scott sat forward, straining at his hand-cuffs, then settled back again and went on.

"He wanted all the proceeds from the radium, you see. Dexter had told him the stuff was in the attic. Nobody knew Sylvia had moved it again. Saturday night Sylvia told him Dexter had got the wind up because he hadn't been able to get his money back. Sylvia demanded an immediate return of her own securities. To throw her off, he promised everything she asked, knowing he couldn't produce. That's why Sylvia didn't suspect him after her sister was killed. But this morning, when I convinced her I had not tried to kill her, had not killed anyone, and we talked things over, it was clear enough to both of us. He had plenty of motive if he was to stay out of the penitentiary for misappropriation of funds. He'd have got by with it, too, except for that little case of mistaken identity."

"You say," the Chief's voice was casual, "that it was a shock to you to find your wife still alive?"

David Scott gave him a look of cold contempt. "Do you think Sylvia would have given me a gun if she'd been afraid of me? Dexter had lent it to her for protection. She gave it to me and I went out to find her sister's murderer—to stop him if he tried to escape. I—couldn't find him at first, and then"—he slumped back in his chair—"it was too late, as far as Sylvia was concerned."

We had all been listening in a sort of trance, and poor old Mrs. Markham was not the only one who jumped when Chief Lindsey swung around and threw a question at her. "This morning, when you came in, Mrs. Markham, I suppose you told everyone about this twin mix-up: that it was really Cynthia who was killed at the cemetery?"

Mrs. Markham's chin quivered, and she shook her head.

"I told no one. But you already knew."

The Chief faced David Scott again. "You told no one?"

"No, I— Oh, my God!" His face flushed slowly, and he muttered, "So that's the way it was. At the door," he told Chief Lindsey, "as I was leaving, I said something to Sylvia, called her by name. Said she might as well come out of hiding since it wasn't necessary to try to fool me any longer. He must have heard. That's it." The words tumbled over one another now. "He didn't know he was too late; that we'd figured it all out; that Sylvia had already talked."

"But you saw no one in the hall?" the Chief asked.

David Scott shook his head. Then he was on his feet, unable to restrain himself any longer. "Why don't you ask him?" he shouted, waving both manacled hands at Homer.

"What about it, Norton?" the Chief barked.

"It sounds very neat, if you ask me," said Homer, his face a study. "Maybe nobody but a homicidal maniac would figure it out that way, but—neat just the same. Of course, I handled investments for Sylvia—Mrs. Scott. I'd looked after an account for her sister, and Mrs. Harrison recommended me to Sylvia. Sylvia, in turn, recommended me to Dexter, and he asked me to handle some money for him." He cleared his throat. "Also the radium. It was a little irregular, but I didn't know the stuff was stolen. Dexter said he didn't want any publicity because it had been a gift to his hospital." Homer's eyes met Chief Lindsey's squarely.

"Why didn't you say something about this before?" the Chief snapped.

"And stick my neck out?" Homer smiled ironically. "No, thank you. I'd have been a pretty fool to admit any knowledge of the radium after the murder. Besides, I've never really seen the stuff. Josh, now"—he glanced around the group of intent faces—"he brought the radium down from Atlanta for Sylvia. At least that's what she told me. You haven't heard him broadcasting that, have you?"

Chief Lindsey swung around toward Josh, Josh cast a puzzled glance at Homer. Then his eyes met Pat's. Something passed between them, but it was over my head. Now he faced the Chief and said: "Sylvia neglected to confide in me as to the contents of the package I brought down to her week end before last. She merely mailed me a latchkey and asked me to pick up this parcel in a storeroom over her sister's garage. Later of course, I rather suspected— but I've always been led to believe that the law concerns itself with certainties. Last night, I persuaded Cynthia, as I thought she was, to see me for a few minutes. I thought she might know something. Ann had been lured away and—"

"Ask Norton to produce my wife's securities," David Scott shouted. "He can't do it. That will prove he's guilty."

"What about it, Norton?" the Chief demanded harshly. "Can you authorize your Atlanta office to refund Mrs. Scott's collateral? Now's the time to speak."

"You've got no right to take that lunatic's word for any of this," Homer told him furiously. "Everybody knows I wasn't even certain I could come down to the Island this Saturday night on account of trouble with my plane, much less plan a couple of murders. He's crazy. He's made all this up to try to save his own skin. He—"

There was a loud rap at the door. Then it was flung wide, and there stood a tall, rangy, gray-haired man in a shabby, loosely hanging black suit. His piercing gaze focused on one after another of the silent group. I'd have known those eyes anywhere. They had frightened me Saturday evening before dinner when he rang the doorbell and disappeared, and again on Sunday when he peered at me across that so-called grave in the garden. They frightened me now, and before I knew it I was shrieking, "There he is!"

"Professor Winslow!" Mrs. Markham cried at the same moment.

"I— I tried to make him wait," Woodrow stuttered behind the tall, spare figure in the doorway; "but he say he done wait too long now."

The man in black paid no more attention to Mrs. Markham and me than to Woodrow. "Major Richmond?" His searching gaze rested on Cousin Beau, who had come dazedly to his feet and now moved forward. "My name is Winslow. I have a letter of introduction. I—er—owe you an apology. As Roberts, no doubt, wrote you, I came down here to look for the *Franklinia Alatamaha*, sometimes called the lost Gordonia. I should have called earlier, but I am a timid person. I did not like to—"

Chief Lindsey had been stunned into speechlessness; but now he demanded with heavy sarcasm, "Can't we postpone this little tea party until—"

Professor Winslow silenced him with a look. Timid he might be; but, once he got started, there was no stopping him. "Kindly do not interrupt," he told Chief Lindsey frigidly. "As I was saying, Major Richmond, I did not like to trouble you unnecessarily. Saturday afternoon, I came out for a little preliminary survey of the— terrain. I was just going back to my car when I met a car approaching your home, and I stepped aside. Someone called out, but, as I say, I am of a very retiring nature—"

"Will somebody tell me what this is all about before I go crazy?" Chief Lindsey raised his eyes to the ceiling.

Professor Winslow continued as though there had been no interruption. "Later I came back to explain, but after ringing the bell, I realized you had guests. Next day, I heard of the murder and felt that I should not add to your troubles; but my time was limited, and I felt there could be no objection to my research. But this morning—" He turned and faced Chief Lindsey.

"All right," growled the Chief. "What about this morning? Seems to me it's time you got to the point."

"This morning," said Professor Winslow quietly, "I realized it was not just a question of my personal feelings or even of the young lady's welfare, but a case in which the criminal should be apprehended and prevented from further wrongdoing. I—did not wish to become involved. I tried to forget it. But my conscience would not let me rest."

"The place is running over with lunatics," Homer muttered. "I'll be crazy myself in a minute."

Professor Winslow fixed Homer with that disconcerting stare. Then, suddenly pointing his finger, he became a terrible figure of wrath. "I saw him when he hit her on the head this morning," he said in a voice of thunder.

There was more: something about doing a little research in the neighborhood of the cemetery; about how he'd given chase but Homer had got away; and that Woodrow had appeared and he'd seen I was all right.

I only half heard, because a lot of things were happening at once. Chief Lindsey, on his feet, was all tangled up with David Scott, who was demanding the removal of his handcuffs. And Homer, in one quick bound, was outside the library door, locking it behind him—locking us in.

The Chief lunged for the door as though he would tear it from its hinges. Then he paused, listening, for outside there was a great bumping and bouncing, accompanied by grunts and some profanity. Then Pearl was unlocking the door. Homer had backed out almost into Woodrow, and he had no more than locked the door when Woodrow tackled him and with Pearl's assistance got him into the coat closet.

"Good work," the Chief approved as we followed him into the hall. "But he couldn't have got far," he told us, pulling out a police whistle and putting it to his lips. "After last night I wasn't taking any chances. I've had two men out beyond the driveway all morning, and two more at the airport to search him and his bags. Looked a little fishy all the time—the business in Atlanta and a plane on the Island.

"Hadn't been able to find out much about his financial affairs," the Chief admitted, "but I did find he'd studied to be a surgeon and given it up to take over the family business when his dad died. I guess that's why he had such a good aim with that dagger and ice pick. And this morning, when he got the other twin—well, I knew he was pretty strong from that bout we had in the attic the other night. Thought then he was after the radium, but couldn't get any proof."

The Chief allowed himself something approaching a smile as two husky patrolmen loomed in the doorway. Holding up a hand, he went on: "That was the trouble all the time. You all looked like nice people. Nobody looked like a murderer. Couldn't do anything but give you plenty of rope, hoping somebody would hang himself."

We did not stay to question the wisdom of his course, for none of us wanted to see Homer taken away. I couldn't even believe he was guilty until they found the radium in his bag. Couldn't believe he'd been willing to kill me.

"You'll have to remember how desperate he was," Josh said. "No one but a man with his back to the wall would have tried all those fake telephone calls and that business at the Cater farm. It's his being broke that's hard for me to understand."

"Told you he must be having some sort of financial trouble," Pat reminded Josh. Then she turned to me. "I told Josh that was why Homer was trying to marry me. It was all too sudden and, anyway, he was practically your property, Ann."

"Good heavens!" I said. "So that's why you asked me all those questions about his financial situation. I thought—"

Pat and Josh exchanged a smile that made me realize a lot had been going on I hadn't known about.

"I suppose," I said drearily, "I was always just a member of an old family to Homer, someone to make his position solid. That's why I never once suspected him. He had such a passion for the correct thing—for social prestige."

"That's probably why he started using his clients' money when he got in the hole," said Josh. "Money and position meant every-thing to him. So he kept plunging, hoping to recoup. Finally—it was murder or the penitentiary."

XXV

AND NOW THEY WERE ALL GONE. All except Professor Winslow, who had been persuaded to park his trailer in the backyard and occupy a guest room while Cousin Beau joined him in the search for the lost Gordonia.

In a fresh gray seersucker suit, Professor Winslow was not nearly so formidable as in the loosely hanging black alpaca which he wore for practical considerations while engaged in botanical research. But Woodrow, refilling the wineglasses at dinner, continued to eye him skittishly.

"I still can't see how Homer killed all those people," Cousin Chattie shuddered.

"Lindsey got a sort of—confession from him," said Cousin Beau. "Seems the proceeds from the radium would have been just about enough to tide him over. All that business about trouble with his plane was meant to plant the idea in everybody's mind that he was the least likely person to be involved inasmuch as he might not have arrived until Sunday morning. Remember he hired a car at the airport Saturday afternoon instead of phoning Woodrow? Well, that's when he drove to Dexter's cabin. When he got there he heard voices and backed into the bushes until Josh left."

"Then"—Cousin Beau raised his eyebrows and his wineglass— "he'd brought a gun, but the other way seemed better. Apparently, he'd meant all the time to entice Dexter out to the drain, hoping the body would be carried to sea and Sylvia would think Dexter fled with the radium.

"As we know, Sylvia took Homer into the library just before dinner Saturday night. That's when she told him Dexter had warned her to get her money back. Homer assured her everything was all right—she'd have her money the following Monday without fail. They returned to the yellow room, and there was all that talk about the dagger. After dinner Homer slipped the dagger in his pocket, and there at the cemetery he had his perfect chance. What nobody ever knew, what only Cynthia herself could have told us, was that he was standing there beside her all the time, his hand on her arm. Of course he thought she was Sylvia. He had only to step backward—"

"But what was the point in trying to scare me with that dagger sheath and glove?" I asked. "After all, if I'd recognized anybody—"

"He thought he put them in the linen room. It's just beyond, you know. He'd taken the gloves to use for his search of the attic and Sylvia's room. Then, when the alarm was raised, he rushed back to his own room and hid the gloves. Later, when Josh went downstairs for coffee, Homer moved them, adding the dagger sheath.

"Wednesday morning," Cousin Beau went on, "Homer was in the upstairs hall when Scott came out of Sylvia's room. Imagine his horror when he realized he'd killed the wrong twin. Not knowing Sylvia had told Scott about the radium and other transactions, Homer—slipped in and out of her room by way of the bath."

"I suppose you'll be telling me next it was Homer I saw in the blue room," Cousin Chattie challenged.

Cousin Beau nodded. "After the murder in the cemetery, Homer went to telephone, you know. Then he rushed out here, thinking he would get hold of the radium at once. But you ladies came home sooner than expected. He dashed into the blue room, knowing it was seldom used. Then you turned on the lights. He dropped behind a chair—and went out on all fours. You saw his shadow, my dear. That dash to Heron Point was the real explanation of Homer's breakdown with the car. He let the air out of that tire himself."

"But the doors," I reminded. "I thought that they were all locked."

"Against anybody on the outside, yes," agreed Cousin Beau. "But there is an extra set of keys hanging in plain view in the back hall. It was what you might call an inside job."

Except that you were likely to stumble on Cousin Beau and Professor Winslow in all sorts of unlikely places, Heron Point settled down to its usual drowsy serenity. Now and then a car of sightseers drove in, ignoring the "Private Road" sign where the long avenue of live oaks began. "Have to put up a gate," Cousin Beau grumbled.

Cousin Chattie had thought at first she could not bear to remain; but, of course, there was Professor Winslow. "You can't leave when you have guests," she pointed out, as though there had ever been a time when she did not have guests at Heron Point.

"Well, if you aren't going to close the house," I suggested tentatively, "we could go ahead with the redecorating."

Cousin Chattie's expression changed at least six times before she finally got down to a real answer. "Perhaps that would be the best way to lay all the ghosts," she agreed finally. "And I'll invite the reading club to come down. There'll be so much to talk about. After all," she reassured herself, "it was Sylvia who was the—evil influence; not the place itself. Heron Point's the same as always."

It was the same, yet not the same.

Something about it all, the velvet softness of the night, the shimmer of stars in the river's depths, the blended perfume of magnolias and gardenias, made me think of those lines Cousin Chattie fondly believed she had inspired, because they were written when the poet was a guest—a prized extra man—at Heron Point:

> Beauty can fill the shy with light,
> But not the empty heart when night has strung a
>   million stars above,
> She cannot fill the lamp of love . . .

Hearing a step behind me, I turned, startled. It would be a long time before I could hear unexpected noises with equanimity. "Telephone, Miss Ann," said Woodrow.

"Hold the line for Jacksonville," the operator told me, and my heart lurched with a sudden wild thrill of hope. But it was Chief Lindsey's familiar voice that came to me over the wire. Were we never to hear the last of him?

"Listen, Ann," he said. So I was Ann, now.

"Yes," I replied feebly.

"Say, I just wanted you to know we found Blair. Yes, Blair. He's an air cadet at the naval training school down here. What I wanted to tell you was that when all this business came up about the radium, the insurance company got in touch with him. You see, it was his dad who gave the radium to that hospital, and there were some strings tied to it. So, being so near and everything, Blair decided to come up and make a little investigation himself. He says Owens, the insurance detective, knew all about him. Of course the radium will go to another hospital now. . . . What's that? . . . Oh, well, I'm coming to that. You see, Blair had checked out at the hotel at Sea Island Wednesday morning and was on his way to Heron Point to see you when the military police got him. He was back in uniform—guess he wanted to impress you—and three days A.W.O.L.; so he's in the guardhouse with a shiner. But he says you ought to see the two M.P.'s. I gathered you'd be hearing from him, and I just wanted you to know he's a right guy."

For a long time after the line was dead I sat there with the receiver to my ear. Who would have thought it? Chief Lindsey, the old romantic!

COACHWHIP PUBLICATIONS

ALSO AVAILABLE

MEDORA
FIELD

WHO KILLED
AUNT MAGGIE?

ISBN 978-1-61646-274-1

COACHWHIP PUBLICATIONS

COACHWHIPBOOKS.COM

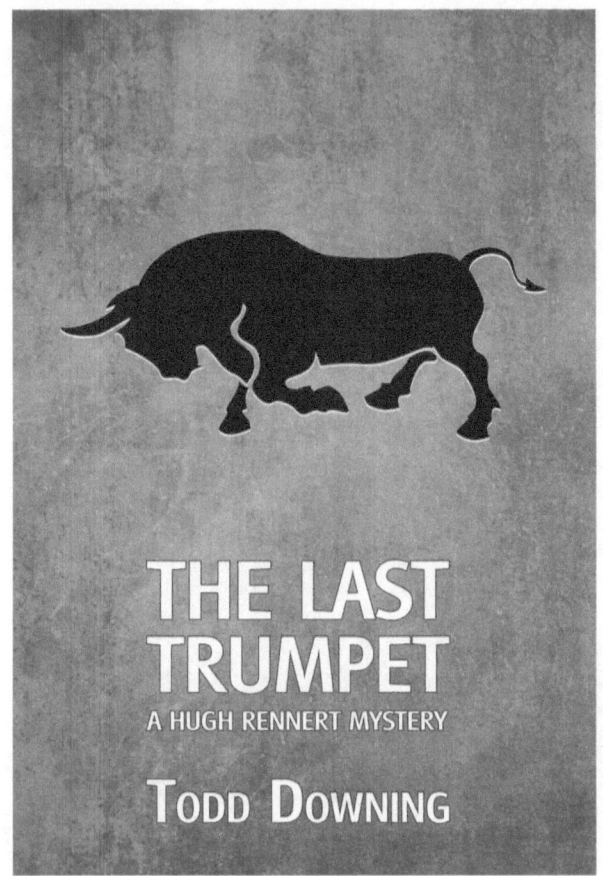

THE LAST
TRUMPET
A HUGH RENNERT MYSTERY

TODD DOWNING

ISBN 978-1-61646-152-2

THE QUINNY HITE
MYSTERIES

CHINESE RED · HERE LIES THE BODY

RICHARD BURKE

ISBN 978-1-61646-247-5

COACHWHIP PUBLICATIONS

COACHWHIPBOOKS.COM

MURDER OF
THE HONEST BROKER

WILLOUGHBY SHARP

ISBN 978-1-61646-211-6

COACHWHIP PUBLICATIONS

ALSO AVAILABLE

THERE IS
NO RETURN
THE ADELAIDE ADAMS MYSTERIES
ANITA BLACKMON

ISBN 978-1-61646-223-9

COACHWHIP PUBLICATIONS

COACHWHIPBOOKS.COM

ISBN 978-1-61646-232-1

MURDER
ON THE
FACE OF IT

Emma Lou Fetta

ISBN 978-1-61646-233-8

COACHWHIP PUBLICATIONS

COACHWHIPBOOKS.COM

THE STRAWSTACK
MURDER CASE
KIRKE
MECHEM

ISBN 978-1-61646-179-9

COACHWHIP PUBLICATIONS

COACHWHIPBOOKS.COM

THE
MYSTERY
OF THE
FOLDED
PAPER

HULBERT
FOOTNER

ISBN 978-1-61646-255-8

ORCHIDS
TO MURDER

HULBERT
FOOTNER

ISBN 978-1-61646-262-8

www.ingramcontent.com/pod-product-compliance
Lightning Source LLC
Chambersburg PA
CBHW020636260626
47157CB00008B/2772